NEVER MIND YAAR

K.MATHUR

SOUTHPAC PUBLISHERS

Copyright © by K.Mathur 2010

Published in New Zealand

Southpac Publishers Ltd., Wellington, New Zealand

ISBN 978-0-473-17479-8

Grateful thanks to William Pfaff, his agent and publisher for their permission to quote from Mr. Pfaff's book, The Wrath of Nations

Cover art and jacket design © A.Mathur 2010

Photo of the Banyan tree on the cover by Andrew Schmidt of www.theshotwellcollection.com.

Pencil sketch of the 3 girls by Krish Sahoo

Krish.sahoo@gmail.com; http://krishlogs.blogspot.com

Contents

Acknowledgments / Dedications

To my beloved and loving parents. Wish you could've been here.

To Dada - wish we could've shared this moment. And to Dadi with deep affection.

To my husband. I cannot thank you enough for your unstinting help and support. I wouldn't be who I am and *Never Mind Yaar* would not exist if it weren't for you. Also, the cover is wonderful.

To our kids. Life is special because you are in it.

To my extended family and friends with affection

To Krish for a lovely sketch of the girls.

Special thanks to my editor, Graeme Lay of Write Right, NZ.

To all who patiently read through the first drafts and gave me invaluable feedback. Ashok, Marion, Alan, Barbara H, Barbara T, Sarah; Also the Gyroscope genius and Ahsa, the inventor of wood and sood.

Thank you all.

"The crucial truth is that man as such does not grow better. He is free. He remains the beast/angel Pascal called him, a chaos, contradiction, prodigy. He progresses only by recognizing his nature, his misery together with his sublime possibility."

William Pfaff in "The Wrath of Nations"

CHAPTER I

-Through Benevolent Old Eyes -

Dr. Naakwaa of Gyan Shakti College couldn't help smiling to himself as he looked at the sea of eager, animated young faces. They all seemed to speak at once, or so it seemed to an old man like himself, their ceaseless chatter outdone only by sudden bursts of loud laughter.

Even as they talked and laughed in their own groups, he saw their eyes covertly watching the others. An air of breathless expectancy hung about them, as if something momentous would sweep them up on a wing and fly them away to an unknown destination. Without exception, they all clamoured to go, even the ones standing at the periphery, hesitant and slightly lost though they appeared to be.

Without any warning a wild screech hit his eardrums. He turned, mildly reproachful, to look at the youngster responsible. Even as he tried coming to terms with the sheer pitch and volume of that awful, grating sound, a sudden whoop of joy caught his attention. Sheer relief written all over her face, a young lady dashed across the room, grinning and waving to someone she recognised in the roomful of strangers. The sudden flurry of action startled those nearby. Whatever they were doing suspended mid stream, they turned to watch the five meter dash and a very joyous reunion. Sweeping somebody completely off her feet, the young woman refused to put her down. Uncaring of curious onlookers, the two laughed, one a little helplessly, suspended as she was in mid air, and the other, in blissful abandonment.

Suddenly noticing Dr. Naakwa in the doorway, they stilled. And following the direction of their eyes, so did everyone else.

This was the new batch of '99. They were the brightest in Mumbai, the crème de la crème. Dr. Naakwaa had every reason to feel satisfied. Like every other college affiliated to the University of Mumbai - good or bad, near or far – the college had to turn away more students than they enrolled each year. There just weren't enough seats. Gyan Shakti's reputation ensured they had the pick of the herd. Their seats were blocked for the toppers, those who earned maximum marks in school ...unless they were blocked for the progeny of families with connexions like the erstwhile politicians of Mumbai, their minions, doctors, judges, actors, producers and of course, the underworld.

The college was on the outskirts of Mumbai. Started in the early sixties by a philanthropist who named it Gyan Shakti – Gyan for knowledge and Shakti for strength - it boasted wide open spaces, plenty of resources and the very best faculty Mumbai could provide. The fees were hefty but parents, many of them middle-income, paid up happily. It was their sincere belief that an education was the only inheritance they could give their children. An education at Gyan Shakti was even better. The ones who gained admission through the clout of their parents' influence or money eventually passed too, knowing it gave them an advantage simply to say they'd studied at GS.

That reputation could have suffered a minor setback today. When Dr. Naakwa had reached the college early that morning Jayaram was in a flap. The list of new students and their respective classrooms had gone missing. It had simply disappeared. As they hunted around for the precious printout, he wondered what good it was to anyone except themselves. This had to be someone's utterly juvenile sense of humour. Unless whoever did this was trying to get at the clerk. It was too much of a co-incidence that even the backup from the front office had disappeared. Admittedly, Jayaram was insufferable with the students and deserved everything they gave back. But he wished they wouldn't play their pranks at the expense of the college.

Well, there was only one thing to do. Dr. Naakwaa marched through the corridors that were as yet quite deserted, to the computer room. Then, to add to his woes, the electricity chose that very moment to black them out as it did from time to time. He cursed his luck. How was he to get a copy of the list? It could take the Electricity Board minutes, or even hours, to locate and repair the fault.

A hundred and fifty gleaming new machines, 128 MB of RAM, 1 GB of hard disk, Windows '98 – the latest operating system, 17" monitors, internet connection for the faculty ……….. All this technology brought to its knees in one fell stroke by the MSEB, (the Maharashtra State Electricity Board), he fumed, aware with a feeling of total helplessness that there was nothing he could do. Well, I had better do something pretty damn quick, he thought with a mounting sense of panic.

I know, he decided in desperation, we'll use the originals. No, he shook his head, dismissing the idea almost immediately. Jayaram wouldn't thank me for having to sift through six hundred handwritten forms. At least

3

they are in alpha order, he argued as nothing else came to mind. I must convince Bhathena, Reddy and other members of the Board of Trustees to get us a generator of our own, he thought crossly, getting set to hurry back to his office for the originals when with a flicker the lights came on. *Jai*-Sri-Ram, the heartfelt words of thanks burst from him. *Jai*-ya-ram, you are in luck, he thought, feeling quite chipper on the one hand and aware with slight self-disgust on the other, that he allowed his mood to be dictated to by the vagaries of the MSEB, Rushing to get his precious printout, he prayed there wouldn't be yet another blackout. He knew from experience a second, slightly longer one might soon follow. Within no time, feeling decidedly upbeat, he hurried with as much dignity as possible to hand over the new list to Jayaram waiting impatiently at the entrance.

On his way back, he saw that the corridors weren't quite so deserted anymore. An ever increasing trickle of students had begun to fill them. Much relieved to have averted that slight calamity, he was more receptive to the 'good mornings' and 'hello sir-s' that came his way.

He headed for the stairs, anticipating the pleasure of meeting up with some of the other faculty who ritually gathered in old Billimoria's room at the beginning of each term.

– Jayaram –

Billimoria's office overlooked the gate. He and a couple of the faculty were already at the window, highly amused as they stood watching the clerk at the entrance. With the familiarity of old colleagues, they smiled Dr. Naakwaa a quick greeting and shuffled to make room before turning their attention back to the gate. Not

4

wanting to miss out on the action, Dr. Naakwaa hurried across to join them.

Good old Jayaram. He had been with the college since its inception, almost thirty years ago. Thin, neat and small, with an ego inversely proportioned to his stature, he was their very efficient, one man admin department.

Jayaram disliked students, tolerating their very presence at the college with grim determination. He found their exuberance loud and brash, unless they were quiet, when he labelled them dumb. As expected, he was being perfectly disagreeable with the new comers. Seated on a hard chair just outside the gate, he watched crossly as a queue of sorts approached him.

To get a better view of what was transpiring at his desk, each student moved slightly to the left of the one ahead. After a point, having reached the furthest distance from which they could see his desk clearly, the sideways line of students did an about 'U'. Soon they were standing two deep in front of his desk. As the second row slowly started snaking out rightward, Jayaram glared with irritation.

"Line, line," he yelled in his thin, reedy voice. The youngsters shuffled obligingly, almost aligning themselves behind each other. He ignored the young lady standing at the head of the queue for as long as possible, assuming an expression of grave import as he kept her waiting. He fussed with his list, sipped water from a glass and glanced at his watch. Running out of things to do, he finally deigned to look at the young woman, barking out in Hindi, "Which line?"

"What?" said the poor, baffled thing, darting a quick look at the line behind her and wondering if she ought to be in another one.

"*Arré*[1] Arts, Science or Commerce?" he said, enjoying himself hugely as he glowered at her. The four professors, safely out of sight behind the reflective glass, couldn't help laughing. The luckless sixteen-year-old mumbled, "Commerce". Jayaram, unable to resist a final well-aimed jibe, raised a bushy eyebrow high above the rim of his thick spectacles and wondered out loud how she would go through five years of college if she couldn't understand a simple question like his. Having scored his victory, he pretended to lose interest. Glancing at the young man behind her, his next victim, he cleared the formalities with the young woman and dismissed her.

The hopelessly disintegrated queue took one step forward en masse.

And so it was for much of the next half-hour as Jayaram, eyebrows high, barked at the youth in his thin, high pitched voice. The new students ignored his mocking tones and disdainful superiority. They understood how fleeting his moment of power was. Chalta hai yaar, they seemed to say without speaking a word, never mind bro. If the man wanted to extract full mileage from his moment by being rude and obnoxious, why let it rankle? After all they were at the threshold of their careers and he would soon have to go back to being Jayaram, the clerk.

Within no time, at his insulting best, the impossible yet indispensible clerk had efficiently despatched six hundred new comers to their rightful classrooms. The faculty on the first floor breathed a sigh of relief.

---

1 Arré – Tchh, for heaven's sake

- A Chance Meeting –

With her name duly ticked off in the correct register and armed with Jayaram's handout, the young woman walked into the majestic old building behind the clerk. Just before disappearing inside, she heard him yell out in a voice that bristled with importance, "Line, line."

Climbing the staircase with a host of others she stepped off the third floor landing into a long, wide corridor. It ran the length of the building and disappeared round the corner. She had often seen crowds of teenagers standing around these very corridors with the express purpose, or so it seemed to her, of enjoying themselves. That's when she had longed to be on the inside. And now she was! She took a deep, exhilarated breath.

A river of students had begun filling the corridor. As she stood there hesitating, she saw one or two look at her curiously as they were swept past on its tide. At little intervals tributaries of faces departed from the main stream and disappeared into classrooms through a row of doors. Realising she was blocking their path, she reluctantly joined the flow.

…305, -6, -7, room 308. This was it. The moment she had waited so long for. Inexplicably her feet slowed. Heartbeat quickening, she walked towards her new classroom, eyes mesmerised by that innocuous looking door.

As she slipped in quietly, many heads turned to look at the young woman. For a moment, she panicked. Students milled around her, secure in their own little groups, chatting away with old friends. She hesitated. Noticing a few students standing by themselves against the wall, she went and joined them.

"Louella!"

The young woman couldn't believe she'd heard her name. Unmistakably, she heard it again, even louder this time. Her head snapped up, eyes frantically searching the crowd from where it came. A familiar figure came hurtling towards her and with a whoop of joy, tried to lift her off the floor. Head spinning, the young woman stared with disbelieving eyes.

"Binny," she squeaked, smiling as she helplessly tried to get the young woman to put her down. This was incredible luck. "What are you doing here?"

"Contributing to the noise and general confusion?" speculated a grinning Binny, looking around. With a quick glance round the class and feeling utterly carefree once more, Louella laughed, ecstatic to see her old school friend. She didn't feel so alone any more.

With a series of flickers, the fluorescent lights that had blacked out twice already, came on. The fans started whirring gently. The two young ladies turned to each other. There was such a lot to say. Suddenly noticing Dr. Naakwa framed in the doorway, their voices trailed away. Their catching up would have to wait.

The noise in Room 308 dropped to a murmur. Dr. Naakwaa waited a moment longer for complete silence before stepping into the room. Putting a couple of books and the class register down on the familiar, long, wooden desk he took a moment to admire the high gleam to which it had been polished over the holidays. With a hint of vexed amusement, he remembered Jayu chalking "New Entrants" all over one early that morning. Why couldn't he have printed a bold sign in a large, colourful font on one of the computers? But no, Dr. Naakwaa thought, our bull-headed clerk has done it this way for the past thirty years and he'll continue doing so for the next thirty.

Composing his face to look suitably grave, the professor turned to face the new entrants of First Year B.Com, Gyan-Shakti College, Mumbai University and motioned for them to sit. Everyone made a mad scramble for a seat of their choice. After waiting for them to settle, he gently cleared his throat. The murmur of voices died away. He began to speak to them in his low, practiced voice knowing it carried clearly in the silence to the students in the very last row. "Good morning. My name is Dr. Naakwa. I am the head of our Commerce department. Welcome to Gyan-Shakti."

As he uttered those words, he saw the flush of excitement on some of their faces. This was truly a momentous occasion for many of the youngsters. "You have a busy five years ahead," he said, almost unconsciously studying those fresh young faces. "If you'll learn anything," he said half seriously, knowing his words would make no real impact until they were well into the year, "it will be the truth of the old adage …..Success is 95% perspiration and 5% inspiration."

Many faces broke into smiles at the familiar cliché. He saw at least one pair of eyes go steely with determination; another face assumed an expression of indifference – yawn, boring. A couple of boys at the back exchanged quick grins - they obviously had plans of their own. The two young ladies who'd met up so blissfully turned and started whispering to each other.

- Immediate Payoffs –

Louella was more concerned with the immediate pay-offs. She turned to Binny, "I cannot believe we can sit where we please," she whispered.

"Wear what we want," agreed Binny fervently. "I did so hate wearing that old blue and white uniform - that - that frock! It made me feel about four."

"...and those 'naughty boy' shoes - heavens, what a name!"

Louella looked at her friend's sneakers and then both looked at Louella's impossibly high platforms. They chuckled, revelling in their new found freedom. Both half listened to Dr. Naakwa. "I look forward to getting to know each and every one of you individually. I must admit that with each passing year, the sheer numbers are making it difficult. To me, it would be a sad year when you become just faces and ..." A slight swell of sound, which Dr. Naakwa suspected was nothing to do with his introductory speech, ensued from his students. A smooth skinned, dusky beauty had appeared at the door. Giving Dr. Naakwa an apologetic smile, she said, "Sorry I'm late sir," and rushed in towards the nearest available seat which happened to be next to Louella and Binny. The two friends moved in a little to make room for her.

"...ID card numbers," continued Dr. Naakwa, pretending there had been no interruption but ruefully aware that although his students had their heads politely turned towards him they had stopped listening. Binny, Louella and the rest of the class were covertly studying the newcomer. They couldn't help noticing how attractive she was. Her big brown eyes and long lashes perfectly complemented a smooth, dusky complexion. She saw the two girls studying her. "Hi," she whispered to both, her small, even, white teeth showing through her friendly smile, "I'm Shalini."

Dr. Naakwa deciding there had been enough distraction for one day raised his voice a notch. Shalini and the rest hastily turned their attention back to the professor. His voice assuming the assured rapidity of practice and his demeanour defying anyone to speak while he was talking, he plunged into his lecture. For the next hour, except for the scribble of ball point pens or pencils, there was complete silence. The three girls were completely absorbed. The lecture was so intense and detailed they barely had time to assimilate the facts. If they were distracted, even for an instant, they completely lost track. But the onslaught of information didn't stop. It was soon followed by another, as challenging as the previous one, by a Professor Billimoria, who grilled them on the intricacies of international trade. Lou looked at Binny in despair. Binny sighed. Was there to be no respite from studies? Apparently not – not even on the first day of college.

A single, loud clang from an old brass bell cut through their concentration, making them jump. As it reverberated through their beings they realised with relief that it meant the end of the lecture. For a moment the three girls simply sat there looking dazed. Finally turning to Binny, Lou softly said, "Let's get out of here, or my head will burst." Turning to Shali she queried, "Coming?"

- The Lay of the Land –

The trio decided they would explore a bit. The corridor seemed the best place to start. Rounding a pillar and pleased to find themselves in a relatively secluded spot, they walked across to the chest high wall of the balcony. Arms lightly on the balustrade, Lou leaned right out, turning her head left, then right. "Wow," she said making the others follow suit. The balcony overlooked the noisy, traffic-infested road on the one hand and the clean wide sweep of the college grounds on the other. A field with short, cropped grass dominated the landscape. In an overcrowded city of concrete structures, a noisy mangle of machines stirring up swirls of dust and a huge mass of humanity crowding every inch of the footpath and spilling over on to the roads, the nearly vacant field was an arresting sight. It just lay there, a wide, silent expanse of green ringed by lush tropical trees.

A high wall marked the entire boundary of the college. To discourage the unwelcome visitor, it had shards of glass protruding from the top. They'd seen the wall, stark and uncompromising on the outside, with nothing to soften the effect except the conical tips of a row of ashoka trees peering over the top. On the inside, the ashokas stood a yard apart, like a row of tall, thin soldiers guarding and decorating the bleak, high wall. Some were bent at the top, as if drooping with exhaustion. But most looked erect and graceful, dressed as they were in slim leafy skirts that flared out at the ankle.

The wall encircled the college, disappearing around either side of the building in which they stood. Lou mentally followed its course to the front of the building and to those front gates whence she'd entered and where Jayaram had so enjoyed humiliating the students.

"Wasn't that clerk at the entrance stupid this morning," she said, hoping the other two were way down the queue when he was trifling with her. "Line, line," said

Binny wielding an imaginary gavel. "Oh that funny little man at the entrance," said Shalini, an eyebrow raised. Having forgotten her id, she'd had to rush back home to fetch it. Arriving barely on time, she'd felt the brunt of Jayaram's sarcasm too. "He kept me waiting a good five minutes," she said, almost in disbelief, making Lou and Binny laugh. "I am *some*body," she added in an uncouth voice, "You can tell from the way I treat you nobodies." Waggling her fingers dismissively as she spoke, she looked down her nose at the other two. Binny and Lou laughed again. The three were in complete agreement. The clerk was a prize idiot. Falling silent they turned to watch groups of students walking across a long, narrow path alongside the field. They all seemed to be headed towards a single storied building on the far side. They could clearly see a single room of generous proportions that opened out onto a sizeable terrace through wide-open French doors. It was encircled by a chest-high balcony like the one they were leaning against and overlooked a patch of swept brown earth that lay enclosed within the arms of a low, uneven hedge. There were tables and chairs everywhere. "Ah," exclaimed Lou, "the canteen!" They watched as half a dozen young boys, barely eight or ten, cotton shirts tucked into khaki shorts and a duster slung over their shoulders, cheerfully wove in-between tables, taking orders. One of them approached a largish group on the terrace. Even from where they stood, the three girls could sense the easy camaraderie between those students. With much light hearted banter they gave their orders to the young lad, who, grinning widely and head nodding rapidly from side to side, took the order and disappeared inside through the French doors. Lou turned to the other two. "I'm hungry," she said. "I'm starving," concurred Binny and Shalini nodded in full agreement. Quickly walking down they almost got lost in a labyrinth of corridors before blundering out through the back of the building. "Phew," said Binny, grinning as they emerged, "I thought we'd never find our way out of there." Hurrying towards the canteen with a crowd of others who seemed to have the exact same aim, they entered through a gap in the hedge. Every table in the garden seemed to be taken. "Let's try our luck on the terrace," said Lou. They made their way up a couple of steps, immediately spotting a single vacant table. Anxious to book it before someone else did Binny tripped over a dozen feet and bumped into occupied tables. "Sorry," apologised Lou on her behalf, grinning. "Sorry," mumbled Binny, slightly red in the face. "That was embarrassing," she said, finally sitting down with relief. "You almost crippled those people but captured your *killa* (fort)," joked Lou, making her giggle. As they sat waiting, they took in the crowd and the surroundings. A youngster soon appeared and took their order. As he went away Binny, remembering the acute concentration of the past two hours, leaned her head back with relief. "Weren't those lectures intense?" she said. "I never expected such mind boggling detail on the very first day," agreed Lou. "I imagined we'd only touch on topics today and delve deeper from tomorrow."

"Tomorrow," exclaimed Binny, "I thought it would be more like a week." Lou laughed. After a moment she asked, "What was that organisation Prof. Billimoria was on about? CUTS?" Proceeding hesitantly to answer the question herself, she began, "Consumer …Unity and…"

"Don't you dare, Lou," Binny cut her short abruptly. "Concentrating so hard during the lectures almost gave me a headache and I don't want another one coming on."

As they chatted, Shalini looked around with interest. Happy in Binny and Lou's company, she let her eyes sweep idly over the occupants of other tables. Suddenly she found herself looking right into the eyes of a stranger. For a moment their eyes locked. Unable to turn away she felt her heartbeat quicken. With almost a superhuman effort, she forced herself to look away, trying hard to ignore the uncontrolled drumbeat her heart was performing all over her chest. "How embarrassing to be caught staring," she told herself, eager to acknowledge embarrassment - that comparatively innocuous emotion, rather than the uncontrolled turmoil of her annoying heart. Before he turned away she was acutely aware that he was as embarrassed as she. Where have I seen him before? she wondered in an effort to bring coherence to her disarrayed thoughts. Then it came to her. He was in their class. She cast a nervous glance at her new friends to see if they'd noticed anything unusual.

Binny was looking around too, her mind busy with her own thoughts. "Thanks, Homi," she whispered, sure her dad could hear. She believed his spirit guided and protected the family from wherever he was. She felt his presence even now.

Lou couldn't have felt more content. She simply sat there soaking in the vast, silent, tropical lushness of her surroundings which somehow managed to overshadow the noisy chatter in the canteen. A dozen old banyan trees stood sturdy and tall in a shady copse beside the canteen. Huge coils of hanging roots wrapped themselves round the trunks, giving the trees an unimaginable girth. Yet others reached straight down from branches to firmly embed themselves into the ground. Lou idly watched one, thick as a rope that ended abruptly in a tassel of flimsy roots a few inches from the ground. To her the fragile, exposed ends looked uncannily like the long, bony fingers of a powerless old hand straining to grasp the earth. As she watched, a slight breeze blew on them, teasing them apart and upward with ease. They feebly tried to resist but the wilful breeze made them float on its fancy a moment longer before suddenly letting go. The roots fell back in flimsy exhaustion.

She caught herself smiling. "Who can believe this exists in Bombay!" she sighed. With typical Mumbai cynicism she wondered aloud how it had escaped the eye of the eminent builder. "Don't you know," said Binny, whose grandfather had known some of the college trustees, "the college is tied up in a trust for 99 years. No builder, although plenty have tried, is allowed to touch it."

"That has never been a problem for them before. A promise of a brand new flat in the brand new building to a trustee, a 'donation' to a politician's 'Election fund' and the licence to build is in the builder's pocket," retorted Shalini, evoking smiles from the others at her worldly cynicism. Pleased that concrete hadn't yet marred the open section and the surrounding greenery, that it was still hers to enjoy, Lou took a deep breath. I'm lucky to be here, she thought. Almost immediately, she shook her head, changing her mind, Luck has nothing to do with it. I worked bloody hard. She remembered the maniacal drive with which she had remained glued to her books during her final year. As the exams loomed closer her schedule had become even more punishing. And the long hours of toil had paid off for they had ensured results even she hadn't dared hope for.

And now, I am at Gyan Shakti, were her exultant thoughts.

Soon, one of the young lads served them steaming coffee with a cheerful grin. Holding the scalding, shiny steel glasses by the rim, the three anticipated their first sip with relish. "Mmmm," said Shali, sipping the strong, creamy-smooth brew, "this is good." The snack was quality too and real value for money. They laid into it with obvious relish and Binny couldn't resist ordering a repeat. "You aren't making yourself popular with the crowd waiting for us to vacate our table," said Lou. Binny smiled unconcernedly as she continued savouring her idli with sambhar and chutney.

Before long, it was time to return to class. They hurried across the narrow stone walkway that ringed the field. Troubled by a slight stitch from having to walk fast after hurriedly gobbling down the last of her idli, Binny faltered as she walked past a bench overlooking the field. Shali and Lou, amused, slowed down as they saw her eye it with longing. Right next to the bench was a pink bougainvillaea spilling a splash of colour into the expanse of green within.

"I love this college," exclaimed Lou suddenly. The other two responded by pausing to look at the green field, the canteen with its wavy hedge, the ever expanding banyans and the thick wrought iron gates on the far side. A peepal tree, branches spread in wide disarray, stood by the gates, defying the neat orderliness of the ashokas against the far wall. The leaves rustled on a sudden breeze. As they hushed, so did the three girls, savouring the tiny second of silence before going back to class.

- LOUELLA –

The girls soon came to be recognised as a threesome at college. Wherever one was, the other two were bound to be. One day, Louella got off the bus on which she rode to college every day and went looking for her friends. She bounded up the stairs two at a time and ran headlong into one of the other students.

"Whoa," he said as he steadied her, "what's the big hurry?"

"Bhagu," she panted, "have you seen Shali and Binny?"

"Ye-es, they are probably drinking that disgusting concoction that Chacha passes off for coffee," he said, pointing to the two distinctly Binny and Shali figures at a table at the canteen. "Anything the matter?" he said, looking at her flushed face.

"Gosh, no. And thanks." Louella yelled, already half way down the stairs.

Bhagu stood watching as Louella ran all the way across the field. "Some exciting news...," he thought. 'I know, she's bought herself a new shade of nail polish."

Bhagu normally didn't think disparagingly of the opposite sex. It's just that he felt a slight touch of envy at the friendship between the three girls. He was a little taken with Shalini. In fact she had quite captured his heart. If he were honest he would have to admit he thought of her all the time. After that first startling and direct eye contact, she had studiously ignored him. He was surprised at how much that hurt. Stung, he'd reacted by ignoring her even more resolutely than she ignored him. But he longed to bridge the chasm they'd created. He saw Lou pull up a chair, leaning close to the girl who haunted his dreams. She is beautiful, he thought. Brooding, he turned to watch the trio. He could clearly see the warm welcome Shali and Binny accorded Lou. For a moment he tried to picture her greeting him as effusively. 'Who am I kidding?' he thought morosely. 'That isn't likely to happen. Not anytime soon.' Angry with himself for being weak, he determinedly turned away and went off to join his friends.

Lou was full to bursting with what she had to say. "Binny, Shali," she panted, breathing fast, "you'll never guess what..."

"What?" they asked, sensing something big.

Over the weekend my parents gave me...," Lou shook her head, as if unable to believe her luck.

"Yes," said her two friends breathlessly, sensing her excitement. Lou couldn't speak. She swallowed to clear the lump in her throat and whispered, "they gave me..."

Barely able to contain themselves her friends squealed, "What?"

"...a moped." Her voice sounded awed. "A moped?!" they squeaked in unison. "Yes..." Lou's voice was a bare whisper, so overcome was she. "Wow," Binny and Shali spoke with one voice. A powered two wheeler! Such a cool gift. Lou could talk of little else through the day and her friends were her most eager and captive audience.

"I knew something was cooking when the family started having these whispered conversations. If I walked in on them, there'd be sudden silences, ...guilty smiles, or," Lou smiled at the memory, "...warning looks followed by overly hearty conversations that sounded strangely out of context." Binny and Shali laughed. "I knew it was to do with a gift for me. I pretended not to notice but when I thought no one was looking I peered into all the usual hiding places. But they had locked it away at my aunt's." Binny and Shali, aware that they would never receive such a gift, not even in their wildest dreams, gave themselves up to the vicarious pleasure of listening to Lou's tale. Her weekend was completely given over to poring over manuals, learning all about the right mix of petrol and oil for the engine, the correct air pressure for the wheels and cleaning out spark plugs. "It is so easy to ride – easier than even a bicycle - no pedalling and no changing gears - just the accelera…"

"Lou," Binny interjected impatiently, "cut the chatter and let's have a look." Matching action to words she pushed back her chair and jumped up. Shali eagerly followed suit. Half out of her seat she realised something was wrong. For someone who had just received the best gift ever, Lou looked hopelessly crestfallen. "I was planning to ride it to college,' she said sadly, 'but the parents decided I needed a bit more practice before letting me lose on the streets of Mumbai."

"Oh," said Binny, her voice going small. Not knowing quite what to do with herself she flopped down again, looking as crestfallen as Lou.

Lou turned to her friends in obvious disbelief, "Can you believe it?" she said. "I ride everywhere on my bike. I even run errands on it but when it comes to riding my moped, my mum suddenly loses her nerve." Binny and Shali made sympathetic faces. They knew all about mums. Shali's mum would never give her a moped, wondering why she even wanted one, having a couple of cars and a chauffeur at her disposal. Besides, it wouldn't be proper. Binny wouldn't get one for completely different reasons. She would end up worrying for her mum worrying for her each time she took the moped out into the traffic. It could well give her only living parent's much too old and frail body an asthma attack or something.

For a while the three sat quietly, coming to terms with their disappointment. Binny's voice broke the silence. "What colour is it?" she asked softly. Lou's face brightened visibly. "A perky kind of yellow," she responded. "Oh," said Binny, falling more in love with the sound of it by the second. A wistful note creeping into her voice, Shali said, "I haven't ridden a bike in ages…" Lou looked at both for a second. On an impulse, she said, "Why don't you both come over after college to have a look?"

- An Invitation -

They jumped at Lou's invitation. Binny made a quick phone call home. It didn't escape Lou's attention that she conveniently forgot to mention the moped. For some reason, when Shalini made her call, she neglected to mention it too.

After their gruelling day at the college, the three were really eager to be off. Shali's mum had urged her to keep the car. Louella couldn't help wondering as she looked around the plush, air conditioned comfort of her friend's car, if Shalini might find her moped 'a bit of a come down' after this.

"Oh Lou" Shali protested, "Don't you know how lucky you are! I would give anything to be able to own a moped. Unfortunately," she said with a slight grimace, "I know what Mem would have to say about that!"

"Mem?" asked Lou, wondering if she might not mean 'mum'. "Oh no," Shali shook her head, "I mean my grandma who lives in Jaipur."

"I somehow assumed it'd be your mum and dad's objections that would matter," Binny tilted her head quizzically at Shali who nodded vigorously, "Theirs too," she said, "although I am not sure if their objections would be from personal conviction or because of what Mem might say."

"Your Mem sounds like quite a personality." Binny's eyebrow rose an inch as she spoke. Feeling that might be a bit rude, Lou quickly put in, "What an unusual name, 'Mem'. I mean, amongst Hindus, isn't your paternal grandmother 'Daadi' and the maternal one, 'Naani?'

"Correct. My Daadi is 'Mem' because she is such a m'emsahib[2]. Everyone calls her that. She has a very strong personality. In fact," Shali hesitated for a moment, giving the other two the distinct impression she wasn't sure if she should continue. Binny and Lou waited, hoping she would. Choosing her words with care, Shali said softly, "no one in the family, from my uncles and aunts to my parents, makes a major decision without consulting Mem first."

"Wow, really?" laughed Binny, slightly incredulous that her grandmother could hold so much sway. "What would happen if your parents went and bought you a moped without telling her?"

---

2 M'em for madam and sahib for sir; a gentleman's wife, term often used for the local 'landed gentry'.

Shalini laughed outright. "They wouldn't," she said with utter conviction. "If Mem had her way, I would already be married. Even as we speak, she is busy searching for a groom for me. She is worried there won't be any good candidates left to choose from if my parents leave it much longer. My dad was sixteen when she picked mum for him."

If her grandmother's boasts were to be believed, arranging a match for Shali's dad hadn't been easy. A string of parents of young hopefuls had started wooing Mem for his hand well before he had turned fourteen. She'd cannily kept all her options open but mentally had ticked them all off one by one. If a girl had beauty, she didn't have a basic education and if she had brains, she didn't have a dowry. Finally Shalini's stately and arrogant grandmother had settled on Shalini's mum, finding her suitable, but only just. Shalini enjoyed Mem's tales from the past. Mem brought them alive as no one else could. She was grateful she didn't live in those times. She couldn't imagine being married already. No doubt her granny was searching for a groom for her but she took comfort in the fact that these things took time.

Meanwhile she was busy enjoying life. It revolved around pretty jewellery, clothes, experiments with make-up, the next meal, a yearly visit or two to her ancestral home in Jaipur and on a slightly more serious note, and since it was expected of her, she supposed she'd best add education to that list. She hadn't done too badly at school but she was never going to be the star pupil at Gyan-Shakti. She would happily complete her bachelor's degree to please her parents. Besides, she did not really know what else she wanted to do. B.Com bought her time. She knew her grandma would search for a groom with renewed vigour if she were sitting idly at home. "And while Mem searches for a prospective bridegroom for me," she said lightly, "I am supposed to behave with much more ladylike decorum than gad about on mopeds." Her words might have been airy but her jaw was slightly set. Binny put a light comforting arm around her for an instant and changed the topic. She pressed Lou for more information on her moped. "Well," Lou divulged reluctantly, "she is a sort of bright yellow, slim and shiny and…" They looked at her, fascinated… "Yes?" they both said breathlessly. "And," added Lou with finality in her voice, "that's the third time I'm describing her to you. You'll just have to wait and see."

From the time they'd started out it had taken a good forty-five minutes, but the girls had hardly noticed. Lou began giving detailed directions to the chauffeur, which told the other two they were approaching her house. The street they entered was narrow and winding. Binny and Shali looked around with interest. They passed a school, obviously Christian because of the church in its grounds. "My junior school…," said Lou, as they drove past.

- *Snippet 1* - *Bandra*

Immediately after the British left India, the founding fathers of the Indian National Congress held tremendous sway with the common people. No one questioned their desire to do their best for the country[3] By pull, rather than push, they were able to influence events so that Bombay became less communal and more secular. Yet, there were a few pockets in the city where people from one community outnumbered the others by a sizeable margin - like the Muslims of Mohammedali Road, the Gujaratis of Wadala, the Marathis of Matunga, the Parsis of Dadar and the Christians of Bandra.

Bandra, on the shores of the Arabian sea, was initially home to the Koli fisher folk who worshipped the Hindu goddess Mumba Devi. The name Mumbai is derived from the shrine in another suburb of Mumbai, dedicated to Mumbadevi. As for the 'Good' or 'Bom' bay - the name came from the Portuguese.

People came to live in Bandra for many reasons - the proximity to the sea and the cool (by Mumbai standards) sea breeze, being a definite plus. Mrs. Charulekha, the old widow on the sixth floor of Louella's building had bought her flat in Bandra because many Indian film stars lived there. She was always hovering behind her windows peering through a pair of binoculars into the homes on Pali Hill and Carter Road. Although she may have caught a very rare glimpse of them, she basked in the proximity to the stars. When her relations came visiting from outside Bombay, one pucca item on the agenda was a walkabout on both Pali Hill and Carter road, with her knowledgeably pointing out the sealed off and heavily guarded homes of film stars.

Louella belonged to the minority Catholic community. Her parents, having migrated to Bombay from Goa, a Portugese colony till as recently as 1961, had chosen to live in Bandra. This is where they discovered the prettiest of churches and a great many of their own kind. Be-

---

3 Unbelievable in this day and age, but true. Today, the common people are extremely cynical about politicians in India. Words like corruption, bribery and sanctimony are synonymous with the word.

sides, their two-bedroom apartment in Bandra was half as cheap as the ones in South Mumbai;.

In those days, theirs was one of only a handful of buildings on their road. They lived on the fifth floor. From their balcony they could see a canopy of bright orange flowers atop the Gulmohr trees that seemed to flourish in their neighbourhood. When the flowers were in full bloom, the view was spectacular. It seemed like wave upon wave of orange rolling off into the distance. It ended in a tiny patch of blue in the west - a bit of the Arabian sea that was visible through the gap between the buildings of Carter Road. This gave them a soul satisfying illusion of space. If they looked east, they could see the beautiful bungalows of Pali hill. These bungalows too were fast giving way to high-rise. To the south was their long, narrow, winding ribbon of road with the old Koli village nestled in its curves. The village in those days had no buildings; only tiny little cottages that seemed to be stuck in time - some well maintained, but most, in an atrocious state of disrepair. But through their canopy of trees, and from that distance, one could easily avoid the detail. For Tony and Sherie D'Costa, Louella's parents, nowhere in Mumbai was it so pretty. It was a bit of Goa imported into the huge metropolis they called home.

But the view wasn't theirs for too long. Already, the spires of their church were hidden and on their west, a most amazing building, thin as a stick, with one room to each floor had come up slap bang into the face of their building. It not only blocked their view, the sea breeze and the evening sun, it robbed them completely of their privacy. The owners of the new flats, even if some of them didn't wish to, looked right into the homes in Lou's building. It was rumoured that the builder had been given permission to build on the tiny little patch of green adjacent to their building by none other than a politician. Permission by a politician! That was like an edict! It put paid to any protests about legal issues like the minimum distance between buildings. Nobody argued with God. In turn, the builder had built a bungalow for the politician at cost price. As far as they were concerned, a perfect win-win, back scratching, *law breaking, divide-the-pie-amongst-ourselves-and-screw-the-rest, situation…*

Lou's parents, rather than mope, took consolation in the fact that no ugly edifice could possibly pop up to block their view of the south. This was because the roads from the west and east merged into a single road at their building. Their building was at the apex of the road that meandered its way southward, through the village and beyond, finally joining up with Carter road by the sea. Surely no structure could come up in front of theirs - and yet, what if the impossible did happen? What if a building loomed out of nowhere to block their view of the south?

A Mumbaikar could easily take it in his stride, "Koi baat nahi, never mind…"

- Lou's -

The chauffeur signalled to the watchman that he wished to turn into Lou's compound. Feeling distinctly disadvantaged in a pair of shorts and a once-white vest, the watchman hastily donned his shirt as he hurried to open the gate. It was his job to warn the youngsters running around the compound – the garden, car park and playground all rolled into one – to stand aside whenever a vehicle entered the gates. To compensate for his lack of attire, Lou's watchman turned what would normally have been just a couple of short bursts on a whistle he wore around his neck into a volley of shrill blasts. The youngsters screwed up their faces and stuck fingers into their ears in protest as they ran to their pre-designated safe area. Lou, Binny and Shali couldn't help laughing, aware that Shali's chauffeur was amused too, but too well trained to show it openly.

As the sleek looking car turned into the gate, the youngsters turned curiously to see who the occupants were. The smartly turned out chauffeur was in the front seat. In the back were three fashionable young women. To their astonishment, one of them was smiling and waving to them. Suddenly, they recognised her.

"Its Lou," they yelled running towards the car. It was just good old Lou. The watchman gave another series of commanding blasts on his whistle but nobody paid him the slightest attention. The chauffeur hastily applied his brakes. The kids surrounded the car, peering in.

"Hey kids, move away from the door, will ya?" Lou yelled as she carefully eased it open. She laughed at the questions being hurled at her by the crowd of youngsters. Scooping her brother up, she turned to watch as her grinning friends stepped out too.

Five minutes later, when all the commotion had died down, and the kids were once again immersed in their play, the three girls made their way to the lift. Shalini had bid her chauffeur pick her up in a couple of hours and he'd driven away for now. Louella invited her friends up to meet her mum while she collected the keys to her moped.

As they walked towards the lift, they looked around Louella's compound with interest. It was mostly used as a car park by the residents. But with them away at work, it was a concrete playground. In one corner was a minuscule area marked off for toddlers - a seesaw, swing and two concrete benches. There was no garden to speak of except a two-foot border along the high wall that enclosed the property. Atop the wall was the usual barbed wire fence with sharp, twisted and protruding ends.

At first glance it looked like a fairly typical Bombay building – a concrete compound and a square block of high rise. Perhaps, compared to others, this one was a little less dilapidated – a relatively decent coat of paint, no leaky drainpipes.... As for the compound, the maali or gardener, had used every bit of his creative flair and ingenuity to make it pretty. He had planted bougainvillaea on both sides of the little side gate and coaxed the branches to intertwine in an arch on top. The braided and colourful canopy breathed life into the side entrance. He had decided on cannahs and lilies interspersed with a variety of willowy ferns and plump succulents for the two foot wide border garden - different shades of green interspersed with striking whites, oranges and speckled yellows.

The rest of the compound was, as expected, pure concrete bereft of flora except for a lone Gulmohr within the little play area. It was tall and its branches spread wide with hundreds of tiny green leaves fluttering in the breeze and giving the Gulmohr an almost ethereal quality. Sunlight filtered through the leaves, casting myriad, lacy shadows on the concrete below. Just before the monsoons, a brilliant canopy of orange flowers covered the top, which gave the Gulmohr its other name, "flame of the forest". Surrounding the tree was a two-foot tall, circular platform straight out of Malgudi days[4]. This is where the youngsters started all their games and the older residents sat and gossiped.

Louella cast a quick eye around the compound noting with satisfaction that they still had a good two hours before most of the residents returned from their offices to park their cars. There was plenty of room for the three of them to manoeuvre the little moped.

Energetically pushing the heavy grill gates of the lift to one side, she invited her friends to precede her in before clanging it shut. Pressing the fifth floor button and flexing her arm at the same time, a slightly embarrassed Lou joked, "Old fashioned thing," as the lift lumbered up ponderously, finally coming to a halt with a slight bump. This time Binny came to Lou's assistance exerting all her might and making the heavy grill door almost fly open. Lou went flying with the door, but managed to keep her balance by letting go of the grill and nimbly jumping out. With startled faces the other two followed her out. "What are you trying to do, kill me?"

---

4 Amusing and insightful stories by R.K.Narayan about typical Indian villages where the large tree – mostly a banyan tree, with a concrete platform surround is the epicentre of many an activity

Never Mind Yaar

said Lou. But when she turned to face Binny she was grinning. "She has plans to inherit your moped," said a laughing Shali. "I was only trying to help," protested Binny, her slightly blanched face looking relieved that Lou wasn't serious.

They were in a corridor with three locked doors, each leading into a flat. Lou headed for the one on the left and rang the doorbell. Almost immediately, a smiling Sherie, who'd been waiting impatiently since Lou's phone call, let them in. She didn't miss the initial wariness with which they greeted her. Now, why do I get the feeling Lou's indulged in a little grumble about the heavy hand of parental authority? she wondered with an inward smile. But they soon relaxed with her, their pleasant manner and obvious fondness for her daughter quite bowling Sherie over.

Soon, the three headed off downstairs again, Binny and Shali eager to discover the moped for themselves. It was everything they'd imagined it to be. It (or "she" as Lou called it) did look sort of feminine, standing there, delicately perched on its stand. They spent the next couple of hours having the time of their lives, admiring it, riding it around the concrete garden, even giving the little kids who pestered them, an occasional turn. Shalini and Binaifer shamelessly invited themselves to visit Lou again, threatening dire consequences if the invitations were not forthcoming at least once every weekend.

It was around six when Shali's chauffeur, loathe to interrupt his young m'emsa'ab[5] enjoying herself, showed up. Shali and Binny slightly flushed with exertion and the heat of the sun, reluctantly decided to call it a day. "If I don't leave immediately," Binny declared, "my

5 In this instance, master's daughter.

31

mum will send out a search party." Shali once more offered her a lift, which she accepted partly, agreeing to be dropped off at the railway station. If she hurried she could catch the 6:40.

- BINAIFER -

Standing by the door of the tightly packed ladies compartment, Binny lifted her face to the breeze. The long train snaked at full speed through the various suburbs and on to Grant Road where she lived in a modest two bed-roomed cottage.

As she neared home, her thoughts turned to the evening she'd spent with Lou and Shali. She decided happily that it had been one of those landmark days - the sort she would remember for a long time.

Alighting at Grant Road, she walked the five minutes it took to reach the Parsi colony where she lived. Entering through Gate E she immediately spotted the taut, anxious figure seated on their balcony. "Hi mums," she yelled out as soon as she was within hearing distance, "your daughter is home - safe and sound," she teased, spreading her palms out for her mum to judge for herself. Her mum smiled, the taut stance relaxing visibly.

From the corner of her eye Binny spotted her sister, Roshni, breaking away from the group she was cycling around the colony with and bearing down on her at breakneck speed. They often played this game, the idea being not to give way first. Binny stood her ground smiling as with perfect control, Roshni braked millimetres away.

"Roshni, Roshni" protested her alarmed mum ineffectu-ally. Binny and Roshni laughed although Binny's mouth looked slightly grey at the edges from Roshni having come too close. The two girls disappeared inside.

- *Snippet II* - *Zoroastrians*

As mentioned earlier, Binaifer was a Parsi. She knew she liked being one. That the Parsis were a minority in India made her feel special, not vaguely uneasy for being different. Perhaps she had the cosmopolitan nature of her city to thank for that; or perhaps it was the easy acceptance of the majority Hindu community...

Binny loved reading. One of the few stories she had read about a Parsi, written by someone other than a Parsi, was by Rudyard Kipling. She was fascinated by the story, not only because it made her laugh but because of how Rudyard Kipling had depicted the hero of his tale, an old Parsi known as Pestonji Bomanji. She felt Mr. Kipling hadn't quite got it right when he'd called his hero 'wily'. Being very young and vulnerable she took it to mean that all Parsis were wily. She much preferred the way Bollywood depicted Parsis – likeable, good natured folk with great, big, charitable hearts of gold who spoke Hindi with funny accents. A stereotypical Parsi in any Hindi movie was bound to amuse. Somehow Binny didn't seem to mind. Behind the laughter she sensed a tinge of affection and secure in that knowledge, she laughed wholeheartedly too.

Apart from the slight twinge she felt at Pestonji Bomanji being called wily, she delighted in Rudyard Kipling's story. It seems that one day, PB had just finished making a scrumptious cake. As he was getting set to eat it, a Rhino ambled towards him, lunged for the cake, speared it with his horn and walked away with his prize. After eating with great relish and entirely by himself, he undid the buttons on his smooth, soft skin, left it on the sand and went off for a nice, long, lazy swim.

While he was away, the Parsi put all the cake crumbs he could find into the Rhino's skin. After his swim, the Rhino put on his skin again. But he found it so itchy that he scratched and scratched and a great big fold appeared on his skin. Still feeling itchy, he went to a pine tree and tried to scratch himself against it. His skin folded over some more. Feeling itchier than ever and extremely fractious he lay on the sand and rubbed *and rolled. By now, his skin was full of folds and his temper ready to erupt!*

And so, thanks to the Parsi, to this very day, the Rhino has a thick convoluted hide and the worst temper imaginable.

Yes, the Parsis actually do exist. There are many tales about the Parsis of India, especially their idiosyncrasies. And it is they who seem to enjoy them the most. Binny and Roshni loved the one (recounted by their mum) about the Parsi who enlisted himself in the Bombay telephone directory as 'Rustomji of London'. It amused and even embarrassed them slightly, that the older generation of Parsis so readily stressed their vague 'English' associations. Their references to "aapri Raani" (our Queen) were mildly irritating especially because friends never passed up an opportunity to rib the two girls about such touching loyalty to the British Monarchy.

The Parsis form about 0.04% [6] *of the population of India. If the Parsis were any species other than homosapiens, someone would take on the noble task of saving them from extinction. For some reason, they are averse to marriage. If at all they do marry, it is very late in life. On an average, they produce one offspring - or in very rare cases, two.*

The Parsis came to India from Persia. In Persia they follow the teachings of Zoroaster. Zoroaster lived anywhere from 500 BC to 1500 BC. Very little is known about him except that he was a priest, he was married and had many children.

His Philosophy might sound familiar: There is good and bad in every human being without exception; that it is their own personal responsibility - individually, and by exercising their own free will, in every situation and throughout their lives - to choose one over the other. Individuals who chose good thoughts, good words, good deeds and charity over greed, violence and lies go to heaven...

---

6 The latest poll puts them at much less. By 2020 their numbers will have dwindled to so few, they will be referred to as a tribe.

Obviously, the rulers who believed that heaven was their monopoly by virtue of their importance and riches persecuted Zoroaster. His teachings were rejected and he had to go into hiding.

After about ten years, he finally made his first convert - his cousin. It was only after Cyrus, the powerful conqueror embraced his teachings that Zoroaster's message spread. The religion flourished for a long time. By the 1st and 7th century AD, other great religions like Christianity and Islam were the dominant religions in the Middle East. Zoroastrians were barely tolerated. Finally, rather than give up their religion, a handful of them left in a ship. After sailing for many months, they landed on the west coast of India - in Sanjaan.

Every Parsi knows the story of how they were refused permission to land by the King of Sanjaan. To make them understand how crowded Sanjaan already was, the king sent them a cup filled to the brim with milk. The Parsis sweetened it with sugar and sent it back to him. The King must have liked their similitude for he allowed them to drop anchor. But there were conditions... they weren't allowed to marry members of other communities, or to convert them. They had to speak the local language, Gujarati and, they could conduct their marriage and thread ceremonies only after sunset. The Parsis followed, and still follow, these dictums scrupulously. Even today, no one from another community is allowed into their fire temples although the irreverent ones smuggle in many a non-Parsi for a lark.

Over the centuries, there seems to have been a slight, inevitable blending. Parsis have kept their own identity and yet they've adopted many Gujarati traditions. This is because Sanjan, where they first landed, is in the state of Gujarat. The Parsis speak Gujarati, enjoy the myriad Indian styles of cooking and their women wear, amongst other things, sarees in the Gujarati fashion.

And so today, they are an integral part of the bewildering mosaic that is India.

- Shali's Secret Uncovered -

On Sunday evening Louella, as usual, was downstairs giving her moped a thorough waxing, cleaning out the spark plug and ensuring there was enough petrol in the tank. Tomorrow, for the very first time, she would be riding her moped to college.

The next day, feeling well pleased with life, Louella carefully crossed the traffic infested roads from Bandra to the other end of Mumbai. There was the 'Number 5' she would've been on. Cheerily waving to the driver, Louella left the red double-decker lumbering way behind as she wove in and out of the traffic along with all the other two wheelers. With one eye on the lookout for potholes and the other on drivers of larger vans, trucks and buses – mostly male - who, on spotting a female driver on a tiny little moped, had this irresistible urge to overtake her at all cost, she expertly manoeuvred her little machine into the gaps in the crawling traffic.

She rode into College Road, dark brown hair flying in the wind, dark brown eyes frowning in concentration behind transparent goggles which kept the dust from her eyes. She turned into the college gates and parked her little moped near the other two-wheelers. For the very first time, she took note of the various modes of transportation the other students arrived in. She decided with not a little satisfaction, that hers was really the best. Not even the slickest of cars, like the chauffeur-driven car Shalini came in, was a patch on her little yellow moped.

A trifle self-conscious she sensed that a crowd of students were watching curiously. She had this urge to blush and hurry past. Instead, she arranged her face into a cool mask and deliberately slowed herself down, keeping her mind busy trying to guess the makes of cars parked next to her moped.

When she approached the main gates, a shiny black Mercedes glided up and stopped by the footpath. Louella watched appreciatively as Shalini, looking fresh and lovely, stepped out. The chauffeur drove off after a respectful salaam to his young memsa'ab.

Shali spotted Lou and yelled out a cheery 'hi'. Lou waved back and waited for her to catch up. The two hurried into the college as they heard a single, resounding clang from the old brass bell. The pair was followed by many an admiring glance and Louella thought she saw Shalini glance more than once towards a quiet boy standing amongst his noisier friends.

She blinked and turned to look at her friend in astonishment. Am I imagining this or is something happening under my very nose, she thought as she saw her friend's slightly flushed and averted face. She did not say anything as both hurried towards their class. But just before disappearing inside the building she turned swiftly, wanting to see for herself if her eyes had not deceived her.

Louella almost missed a step. She couldn't believe her eyes. The boy was Bhagu! Caught unawares, he was unable to wipe the quiet longing off his face. When he saw that Louella had guessed his secret, he went a slow, dull, embarrassed red and turned away.

Louella's head swam at this unexpected turn of events. She had no time to gather her thoughts as the two girls hurried upstairs with a crowd of others. She longed to get Binny to herself to discuss what she had just witnessed.

- Binny and Lou on a Mission –

Binny's first reaction to Lou's disclosure was disbelief. Bhagu! She was stunned. Lou must have imagined that look. Bhagu was always clowning around and Shali did not look to her like someone languishing for love.

"How do you know what a person in love looks like?" challenged Lou. Binny laughed in acknowledgement. 'Love' was as yet an unexplored realm. Even if her feminine instincts gave her a tiny inkling, she was content to let Lou's dig pass unchallenged. Both girls finally decided that the situation warranted a little more observation. They decided they'd watch the other two carefully.

Not much later, the three girls were sitting on one of the benches overlooking the field, chatting idly when Shalini said, "Mem called yesterday."

"Oh!" said Lou, sitting up. "She is on her mission again. She says she's found a 'good boy' for me."

"Oh!" said Lou again. She and Binny exchanged a quick glance. "Are congratulations in the offing?"

"Of course not," Shalini burst out emphatically. The strength of her denial caught the other two by surprise and she added in milder tones, "I'm not ready to settle down yet...much too busy with my degree." In spite of her best efforts her voice quavered a bit. A part of her was aware that their antennas were up and sending frantic signals to each other. Lou and Binny exchanged another quick, meaningful glance which Shalini ignored.

"I think I know who Mem has set her heart on," she said after a while, desperate to talk and yet unable to decide how much she wanted to divulge. She was still mulling things over in her own mind. She had been brought up to think she would have an arranged marriage. She hadn't minded. She'd known she'd fall in love with the man of her parents' choice after the engagement. But what was happening with Bhagu was not according to plan. She felt the pull of his attraction and it left her feeling confused.

Aware Binny and Lou were waiting, she said, "She's obviously taken with him." Shali raised an eyebrow with an attempt at lightness which she was far from feeling. "She drops her usual imperious, superior manner when she talks of them ...such a khandaani family, so..."

"Who?" said Binny looking confused. "I mean ... whose family?"

Shali gave a weak smile at her friend's confusion which ended on a sigh. "His name is Rajinder," she said, "He's that same scientist I spoke about earlier. According to Mem," she continued bitterly dropping all pretences, "things are progressing swimmingly. Mem likes them and they like Mem."

Lou laughed incredulously. "And you?" she asked the obvious question. Shali tried to shrug lightly. The helpless dejection in her face told another story. Feeling sorry for her and slightly angry with her unknown granny, Binny said for the second time in the space of days, "Your Mem sounds like quite a character. Sorry," she said immediately contrite, "I don't mean to be rude." But unable to contain her thoughts she exclaimed, "But she can't force you to get married, can she? You aren't even eighteen yet."

"Mem got married when she was eight. As far as she is concerned, eighteen is practically over the hill. She has already started using overt pressure on my parents.

40

They know I don't like that stuffed shirt and avoid mentioning his name in my presence. But she doesn't give
up easily. She tells my parents if they leave it any
longer, there won't be any decent Dayal boys left for
me."

Lou and Binny pooh-poohed the idea. Shali shook her
head saying, "No, it's true. It even scares me a bit and I
can imagine what it must be doing to my poor parents.
It won't be long before they'll succumb and start pres-
suring me."

Lou, more to provoke Shali into revealing her feelings
than for any other reason, asked, "Shali, if you think
there won't be any good Dayal boys left and if your
Mem is so impressed with this boy, why don't you at
least meet him once?"

"You haven't met him in over a year and he might have
changed," said Lou softly, trying to elicit a response
when none was forthcoming. Binny turned to watch
Shali in silence. The question hung in the air between
the three. Shali, surprised at the strength of her dislike
for the suggestion, struggled to hide her reaction from
their curious eyes.

With a guileless expression and a half-wink at Binny
Lou added, "If you meet him and like him, why, everyone would be happy." The wary expression back on her
face, Shali tried not to be provoked into saying more
than she ought. Yet her lower lip jutted out slightly at
the suggestion. "You must be joking," she said, trying to
keep her voice light. "He can never change. I can't stand
his superior airs - you know the type…"

And with a supercilious look in her eye, she proceeded
to say in a slow deep drawl, 'Our PSLV is putting another satellite in space. The scanners will provide im-

ages for agriculture, environmental - environment......'
Binny and Lou laughed as Shalini struggled to remember the uses of a satellite. With exasperation, she gave
up.

"...whatever!" she said scornfully. "Who wants to know
about his PSLVs anyway?" Binny and Lou laughed
again.

"But I know Mem has set her mind on him," Shali continued, beginning to feel a bit cheered by her friends, in
spite of herself. "For all I know, she's already boasting
about her future son-in-law Rajinderji," she infused her
voice with mock reverence. This time, when the other
two laughed, she joined in reluctantly.

Binny said it reminded her of an old aunt of hers. "She
broached the subject of marriage to me when I was fifteen, saying she knew of this 'handsome'," it was
Binny's turn to imitate her aunt rudely, "young Parsi
doctor, who was looking for a nice young Parsi girl."
And, as if she were putting the icing on the cake, my
aunt said he lived in Canada. He was specially flying
down to choose a bride. The thought of having a
stranger come to check me over was so repugnant I told
my aunt not to ever bring him over or I'd..." Binny
stopped, looking slightly sheepish.

"You'd what?" asked Lou. "Well, I couldn't think of an
insult rude enough to hurl at him on the spur of the
moment, so...," and Binny hesitated again. ".....so?"
prompted Lou. "...so I said I'd stick my tongue out at
him," Binny finished lamely.

The three girls were unable to stop laughing at that. Lou
shook her head sadly at Binny. "You are crazy," she
said. "Is it any wonder your race is almost extinct?!"

Binny laughed unabashed. "I was only fifteen," she protested laughing. Turning her face to the heavens she
said dreamily, "Perhaps we should tie the doctor and
the scientist to the ABCD – that space thingamy - and
blast them off into outer space," she said which con-
jured up an image so amusing that it entertained them
for the rest of the recess.

Shali had come close to confessing the true reason for
not wanting to meet Rajinder, or any other boy for that
matter. But not just yet, she thought as she laughed with
her friends.

- Two Unlikely Cupids –

Lou's parents shook their heads. She had been stuck to
the phone this past hour. They knew Binny was at the
other end. "What's there to discuss after they've spent
the full day together?" Tony D'Costa wanted to know of
his wife, eyebrows raised. Binny and Lou were dissect-
ing Shalini's every word. After a week, Shali had still
managed to keep them guessing. She spoke of her dislike for other suitors but never about her attraction for
Bhagu. "She knows we know. Why won't she tell us?"

"Doesn't she know we want to help? Why keep it so
secret?"

"It's hardly a secret. It's obvious."

But Shali was confused. And not knowing what to do,
she decided she'd do the next best thing. Nothing.

"Was it our imagination after all?" Binny asked Lou on
Monday. "Are we mistaken?" Lou wondered on Tues-
day. But now and again, for a split second, Shalini's pretences slipped. Especially when he was around. It was
in the quick - too quick - spin of her head as she looked
away. And yet there was a stillness to her, a strange

43

breathlessness in his presence. Then there was the way she tried to veil her eyes from them... "No," they decided, "the body language won't let her hide her feelings. She is fascinated with Bhagu."

"She's in love," they sighed happily. "I am not surprised she resists her old grandmother's pressures to get married to someone else," declared Lou. "I know," agreed Binny, "she can't seem to stand this other bloke."

"I can't stand him either." said Lou, half serious, which set the two giggling. Lou and Binny were in love too. With love. And they felt the situation warranted their help. Bhagu was perfect for Shali.

Everything Shalini said or did took on a new meaning. They were both agreed she dressed with even more care. And the biggest change - the absolute clincher... Earlier her appetite had been a joke between the three. She'd often promise herself she'd go on a diet soon, then eat till she was good and full. "And now," said Binny, almost pouncing on the fact as the most telling change, "she toys with her food."

As for Bhagu, the two girls knew he was besotted with their friend. They had discussed "The Look" as they called it, often and had kept an eye on Bhagu ever since. "It is obvious to anyone who cares to notice that he is smitten."

"Yes, he seems almost mesmerised as soon as she appears."

"And she seems to reciprocate, although it's almost in spite of herself - against her better judgement."

"Perhaps that is why she doesn't do anything about it."

"I know," agreed Lou, "I tell you Binny, if we wait around for her to make any moves, it will be forever."

"Let's not wait," said Binny impulsively. "Let's you and I do something to bring the two together." That seemed like a brilliant idea. But do what? After a lot of discussion, they came up with a plan – "why don't we make friendly overtures? Start a conversation between lectures; or invite Bhagu for a cup of coffee" – only to discard it again – "No, not that yet; Shali might take it into her mind not to join us; But if we were already seated at the canteen, she couldn't very well up and leave, could she? She might…"

And so, much to Tony D'Costa's exasperation, the two unlikely cupids plotted away, blocking the phone for hours on end.

- A Day at the Movies -

The next day Binny asked her friends if they'd go shopping with her. "For what?" asked Lou, pretending she didn't already know.

"A salwaar kameez?"

"Where?" Lou tried to look innocent.

"That's just the problem. I don't know."

"Shali would know," said Lou triumphantly. "I agree," said Binny and both turned to Shali.

'Oh, oh,' was Shali's sceptical reaction, 'why does it sound like some badly rehearsed plot?' But on thinking about it she realised it wasn't such a bad idea. A day over the weekend with her friends might be just the

---

7 Salwaar kameez – North Indian outfit consisting of loose pants gathered at the ankle and a top that reaches below the knees. A chunni or long scarf completes the outfit. The entire ensemble is known as a suit, for short.

thing to cheer her up. 'What's more,' she thought, 'it will reassure mum.' She knew she had her mum worried. Even Rajubai, her cook, complained that she hardly ate and was thin as a stick. But what could she do? Her guts seemed to twist at the very thought of food. She felt raw inside and lived with a constant ache which she tried to conceal from everyone. When her mum broached the subject of marriage, she almost recoiled and when Mrs. Dayal mentioned Rajinder - the man from Sri Haricota, she kicked up such a tantrum that her mum could only stare. This was so unlike her daughter. Previously, if her parents gently teased her about marriage to a young, handsome man of their choice, she simply blushed, delicacy preventing her from saying that she didn't dislike the idea. And now, to be faced with such vehement objections! It startled her parents, to say the least.

Determined to put thoughts of Bhagu aside, Shali impulsively turned to Binny, "O.k. Binny, let's do it."

"Ya'ay," said Binny . The three set to making plans.

That night Binny and Louella were back on the phone. The plan, hatched a day before, had been to get Shali out, cheer her up, get her defences down and then confront her. Binny said happily, "I'm really looking forward to our outing on Saturday, aren't you?"

"Yes," said Lou. "It was nice of Shali to invite us home for lunch."

"And for me to try on some of her own suits," said Binny excitedly. "It's really the most practical thing to do. It'd be nice to know whether they'd look good on me." Eventually, they decided to go the whole hog and take in a movie as well. The plan, changed many times over, was finally to meet at the movie theatre and afterwards, go home with Shali for the day. The girls were crazy about the actor as were a hundred million others. They happily discussed the reason for his appeal. Shali realised she was beginning to feel happier already and looking forward to the weekend.

On Saturday, Shali and Lou were the first to arrive. As they waited outside the theatre for Binny, they chatted idly, watching the melee of people and the illegal vendors doing brisk business. The posh shops looked relatively quiet. There was no sign of Binny which wasn't unusual. She was normally the last to arrive. Suddenly, Lou spotted her in the back of an auto rickshaw. As she paid off the autowalla, Binny smiled at her two friends weakly, looking pale and disturbed. Feeling concerned, Shali and Lou looked suspiciously at the autowalla. With a leer at all three, he drove off. "What happened, Binny?" Lou asked, not taking her eyes off the disappearing auto. "Oh nothing to worry about," said a slightly wan looking Binny "The autowalla and I started chatting about things in general. Towards the end of the drive, he was telling me about his personal life. You know, things like his having a wife and seven children, how old his kids were and which school his son went to. When he said with obvious pride that his robust and healthy wife was strong enough to have delivered so many kids - no complications, I was amused." Lou and Shali laughed too, despite themselves. "I told him we were a family of three sisters and a brother. That's when the conversation started going wrong. He wanted to know why my brother was letting a young girl like me gad about by herself. I was taken aback and lost my smile which he didn't seem to notice because he said the girls of today were much too free, gadding about by themselves and wearing clothes that showed their ankles."

"What?" said Lou in disbelief, "Who does he think he is?"

"Quite honestly, I didn't mind what he said as much as the bold way he started staring at me in the rear view mirror. It was so at variance with what he said. Sort of creepy and ….bold," she repeated again, unable to think of another word in her present state of mind. "I don't know what it was about that look but it made my flesh crawl." Unable to help herself, Binny shivered at the memory before continuing, "That's when alarm bells really started ringing. I did not want to be alone with this … this person"– Binny conferred the status unwillingly – "for even a second longer than necessary and it was wonderful to spot your impatient faces in the crowd." The remnants of fear still clung to her insides but Binny was fast getting back to normal. Not her friends though. They were all wound up. "Who does he think he is," Shali repeated Lou's sentiment, "the lech…" she added, leaving her friends in no doubt as to what she thought he was.

"…the low life," said Lou. "Did you notice the leer he gave us before driving off? Why don't they do something about insects like him?" she wondered out loud, looking accusingly at a group of youth standing not too far away who seemed to have witnessed everything and who, as usual, were unwilling to interfere. "At least FROWN. Let them know their behaviour needs changing, not our dress code," Lou addressed the young men directly, making them feel uncomfortable. Binny felt good as her friends rallied around. She smiled at them both, finally managing to shake off the dirty feeling that still lingered.

The three girls suddenly realised the crowd outside the theatre had dwindled to a handful. For a moment they had forgotten the movie. It would still be the ads. Not wanting to miss out on even a bit of their hero, the three hurried into the theatre.

The next three hours were sheer bliss. They came out of the theatre, replete, the very core of their beings touched by the sad love story. It was almost lunch time, although, right then, they couldn't bear the thought of food. Not after such a noble, enriching and soulful experience. But very real hunger pangs soon put paid to that exalted state of being. They hadn't eaten for a full three hours, not counting the ice cream and popcorn during the interval. They suddenly felt starved. Binny hopefully suggested a snack before hurrying to Shali's but Shali said they could wait till they got home as Rajubai had been cooking up a storm since morning. The sleek car and chauffeur were waiting for them outside the theatre. Lou and Binny couldn't help feeling thrilled as once more, the chauffeur respectfully held the door of Shali's Mercedes open for them.

"Can't decide if I should look superior," Binny whispered to Lou, "or thank him graciously," as she got into the car. The two giggled as Shalini instructed him to take them home and got in with a distracted 'thanks'. Of the three, she had been the most profoundly moved by the story of young, unrequited love.

- Shali's -

Binny and Lou knew Shali was rich and weren't surprised when they arrived at a building of marble, stone

and concrete. It overlooked the sea. Each flat had a ter-
raced-garden of its own, yet each remained totally private from the others. Downstairs, there was the inevitable concrete compound but at the back of the building
were a huge garden and playground. Shalini informed
them that a famous architect had designed it. A watchman silently appeared by their sides. Unlike Lou's
watchman, he was dressed in a khaki uniform deco-
rated with plaited gold braid, whistles and walkie-
talkies in hip pouches. He recognised Shalini and immediately executed a metallic click of his heels and a
respectful incline of his body, arms stiff by his sides.
Lou and Binny tried hard to look like they received
bows everyday of their lives but their awkward smiles
gave the game away. He held open the lift door and the
three got in with him following closely behind. On the
way up, Lou commented to Shalini that her watchmen –
there were at least half a dozen - looked very professional in their starched khaki clothes. Shalini, never one
to flaunt her good fortune, accepted the compliment
with a vague smile. She didn't add that these weren't
ordinary watchmen. They worked for a security agency
and underwent heavy training before they started work.
"Compared to them," Lou muttered, "Govind, my
watchman, was positively underdressed and overloud."
Binny pretended to ponder for a moment and then
nodded vigorously in agreement. Lou dug an elbow
into her ribs for agreeing so readily. She knew Govind
made up for his lack of finesse and professionalism by
being extremely obliging. Sometimes he'd disappear
from the gate for a good fifteen to thirty minutes, taking
care to leave it open to let cars in or out as old Mrs. Charulekha got him to carry her shopping upstairs or shift

her furniture around. Nobody had the heart to stop the old lady from using his services for herself although it did mean the gate was left unattended. Koi baat nahi, never mind. Besides, they might need his services to run personal errands too. The kids ran around happily, the older ones looking out for the younger ones and all was well.

Within what seemed like seconds, the lift came to a cushioned halt on the 15th floor. The doors slid open soundlessly. As they stepped out, Binny couldn't help teasing Lou that her lift had definitely taken longer to reach the fifth. Immediately Lou shot back, "I bet your lift has a single yellow light bulb and a ninety year old Bawaji[8] liftman who falls asleep before we reach the first floor." Binny laughed good naturedly, not bothering to explain that her low maintenance Parsi Colony didn't even boast a lift.

Soon they were standing outside the highly polished door of Shali's flat. Judging by the smells wafting out at them, Shalini's cook seemed to have prepared a banquet for them. Forgetting everything else they realised once more how hungry they were.

Nothing prepared the two girls for the lovely flat they were let into. As for Rajubai, she was smiling from ear to ear as she almost bowed her favourite *chota* (little) *memsahib[9]* and her 'highly-learned' friends in. Shalini turned to her mum who had stepped into the lounge and said in typical fashion, "Mum, meet Binny and Lou. What's cooking? We're hungry." Louella and Binaifer joined hands in awkward "Namastés". Mrs. Dayal smiled. "Hello," she said softly. "Come in, come in." She

---

8 Bawaji: a parody of a Parsi.
9 M'em for madam and sahib for sir; a gentleman's wife.

turned to her daughter and said, "Give us a few minutes, Shali dear, lunch won't be long." With another smile that included both Lou and Binny, she was about to bustle away when her daughter yelled after her, "Tell Rajubai to make it quick, mums. We are all starving…" Lou and Binny felt slightly embarrassed. Binny muttered to Shali, "We've barely been introduced for goodness' sakes, Shali. Will you stop mentioning our appetites so persistently?" But their rumbling tummies could hardly let them disagree.

The three headed as one towards the balcony. They sat there enjoying the cool sea breeze, a glass of fresh nimbupani[10] each and the smells wafting at them from the kitchen, chatting about any and everything - the movie, their fellow students, the professors, college, Mumbai, life….. Soon Mrs. Dayal caught Shali's eye and gestured for her to go to the table with her friends. The three washed their hands at the basin in the passage and sat down to lunch served in shiny steel dishes. Each girl had a large stainless steel plate with an array of little steel bowls arranged on it. Each dish was served separately in these bowls. Everything was absolutely delicious and piping hot. The rotis (chapaatis) were steaming hot with melted ghee[11] on them. These were brought in one at a time, all puffed up and straight from the stove, exactly as Shalini liked them.

"I could get quite used to this". That was Louella breaking a long silence. "Mmmmm!" agreed Binny, her mouth full.

---

10 Nimbupani – lime juice, sugar and iced water
11 Ghee – Clarified Butter

- A Lazy Afternoon -

After eating to their hearts' content, the three went to Shali's room. While not large, it had everything a girl could ever wish for. Shali drew the curtains and plonked herself on the bed. Binny and Lou are like a tonic, she thought. However miserable I am deep inside, their company cheers me up. She stretched lazily. It would be so perfect, she sighed to herself, if Bhagu were here with us. Then, 'later!' she admonished herself and determinedly put thoughts of him aside, ignoring the dull ache that began welling up inside. Binny sat in the wooden rocking chair, loathe to talk. She surveyed the room. She decided she loved everything in it - the counterpane, the curtains, the dressing table with nail-polishes, lipsticks and bottles of cream and kohl, the mirrored wardrobe with ceiling to floor and wall to wall sliding doors, even the pale green colour of the walls. Lou smiled at Shali. "That was a scrumptious, delicious meal. Your Rajubai is a great cook."

"Yes," agreed Shali, adding humorously, "chapattis dripping with ghee and all."

"Mmmm," said Binny rubbing her tum in blissful satisfaction, "… that's what made them so tasty." Even as she laughed, Shali's thoughts found their way back to Bhagu. She realised how much she'd changed. She knew he was responsible. Earlier, she complained if Rajubai wasn't generous with the ghee on her chapattis and now she complained if Rajubai was. For a moment she hovered dangerously between day dreaming about Bhagu and talking to her friends. Giving herself a mental shake she jumped out of bed. "Well Binsi," she said, heading for her cupboard, "let's see what we can do for you before the heavy meal takes its toll. Lou is half asleep already."

"Mmmm," replied Lou from the cool tiles, her head resting on an arm flung out on the bed. Binny gently rocked her chair, looking on. She would happily have dozed off too but was looking forward to trying on Shali's beautiful outfits. Shali slid open a cupboard door. It was crammed full of clothes.

"I'll never be able to pick one out from that lot, Shali, why don't you?" she said lazily. Shalini brought out half a dozen outfits for her friend to choose from. "Here's a variety," she said. "These, by the way," and she held up what appeared to be a shorter *kameez* (top) than usual, "are kurtis, the latest thing." Binny loved them immediately. She picked an elegant ensemble in a riot of pastel colours, locked herself in the bathroom and put it on. The material was chiffon and lined. As she put on the trousers she saw that the lining stopped at the knees with only the gauzy material falling in soft folds to her ankles, a tantalising shadow of her long shapely legs showing through. She wound the long, flowing dupatta, the scarf, around her neck. The outfit fit her slim figure to perfection and she stared at herself in the bathroom mirror, fascinated.

With slight trepidation she opened the bathroom door. It was Shali and Lou's turn to stare. It was such an amazing transformation. A teenager had gone in through that bathroom door but a young lady had stepped out. Binny couldn't help feeling pleased.

"Wow, Binny, is that you?" squeaked Lou, sitting up. Binny, awkwardly aware of their stares, took refuge in making a face at them. "You look great," said Shali. "Why don't we pile up her hair?" she said to Lou as the idea struck her. She held Binny's hair off her neck. "Maybe a touch of lipstick?" she said, beginning to feel quite taken with the idea.

"Kohl..," said an enthused Lou, standing up and almost dragging Binny to the dressing table. She pushed her down on the low stool. Then, more to tease Binny, who had begun protesting mildly, than anything else, she continued, "and foundation..."

"Aah yes," said Shali, opening the dressing table drawer and producing two bottles. "The bronze, I think," said Lou, pretending to study Binny's face. "Hmmm, the dark pink," said Shali, still in earnest as she held the bottle close to Binny's face, "it will blend in more easily with her complexion." Binny watched her friends-turned-makeup-artistes. She understood Lou's little game and her eyes squinted to slits even though a little smile played on her lips. "Don't forget the purple eye shadow," she said with heavy sarcasm. Shali, watching the two, caught on at last. "Toe ring," said Lou, ignoring Binny completely. Shali laughed outright. "Nose ring....," she said, managing to outdo the toe ring, her lips twisted in an effort to look sincere. Grabbing a long metal rod with a flattened head, she pushed it down with her thumb in a jabbing motion. It was what she normally used to paint on her bindi on her forehead. Feeling the thin, sharp point of the wrong end gingerly with the tip of her index finger and aiming it at Binny's nose, she supplied the information, "...the lance." Binny, knowing her friends were having her on, jumped up and said, "Oh sure, and this," pretending to strangle Shali with her bare hands, "is a choker." But the slightly alarmed look she gave the metal instrument before hurriedly moving her face out of its reach did not escape

Shali and Lou. They collapsed, laughing, on the bed. Binny's instincts, when it came to self preservation, always had her running scared. Shali and Lou could never pass up an opportunity to tease her. The way she crossed the street, for example, was a treat, for she never walked across boldly, as they did. She waited till the coast was reasonably clear and then scuttled across for dear life.

Having had their little joke, the two, with total absorption in their faces and quite unaware of the fond look she gave them, went back to the makeover. Binny surreptitiously touched wood. Her friends meant such a lot to her. As they got busy with the makeup, she wondered about life's unexpected turns. She had been through a very rough year, losing the two men she loved - her father and grandfather - in quick succession. When cancer took her dad, with all the turmoil at home, she barely managed to get a 55% aggregate in her Secondary School Certificate exams. She thought it might be best for her to go through a short horticulture course and start earning. Her mother and grandfather would have none of that. They were determined to give Binny the best education possible. With her kind of results Binny had little chance of getting into a good college. But one of the professors at Gyan Shakti, a client of a good friend of her grandfather's, introduced her to the Principal - Dr. Naakwa. He asked Binny to fill in the application forms and said he'd see what he could do. And then another blow struck the family. Unexpectedly, Binny's grandfather passed away. The family was devastated. The lines of sorrow on their mum's face seemed to permanently deepen.

Dr. Naakwa heard of the terrible tragedy and made sure that a seat was reserved on his college rolls for Binaifer Desai. Binny was petrified on the first day. Everyone seemed to know everyone else except her. She seemed to know no one. She went to the far corner and stood next to someone who seemed as alone as she. Closing her eyes, Binny said a little prayer. When she opened them, she still did not feel any better. Her heart felt as if it was sunk way down into her keds. And then Binny stared. It couldn't be--- It wa--s.... "Louella," she yelled. She did not even realise but her feet were already hurtling across the room. "Lou," she shrieked, uncaring that everyone had stopped whatever they were doing to stare at her. In her heart, she thanked her dad, her grandfather and Lord Zoroaster ardently. The tight band around her heart melted away.

- A Makeover –

While she was busy with her thoughts, Shalini and Louella had put her hair in a neat chignon, clipped on long earrings and lip-gloss. The youthful teenager had all but disappeared. In her place was a young woman. Putting on the finishing touches, the two finally stood back and watched their handiwork with satisfaction. They would never look at Binny with the same eyes again. Shalini found her voice first. "Gosh Binny," she said, "you look absolutely ...stunning!" Binny blushed. "Its amazing what good clothes and a little makeup can do!" she said, trying to cover her confusion. Shalini brought her mum in to see the transformation. Mrs. Dayal was amazed. "Why," she said, "put on a bindi and she could easily pass for a beautiful young Hindu girl." Binny went home that night, determined more than ever to buy herself a kurti just like Shali's. On the way to the train station, she and Lou discussed Shalini again. They had been unable to 'confront' Shalini as they'd planned. "But," said Lou, "we have softened her up a bit."

"Yes," said Binny, "ready for the kill." But jokes aside, they wished they could help. There had to be a way. They'd have to think of something fast as *Holi*[12] was approaching and the college would remain closed for ten whole days.

Today's Special –

The following week started off uneventfully. They were once again immersed in their books. Shalini locked herself away in her room all the time under the pretext of studying. But all too often, her thoughts drifted to Bhagu. She realised that her studies were suffering. Her youthful exuberance had given way to a more serious mien. Mrs. Dayal and Rajubai both noticed how serious she looked, and in their eyes, thin as a reed.

Sometimes Shalini stood back, surveying her mum, Rajubai, Bhagu, her two friends, even herself. It is like some silly soap she would think, smiling sadly, and I am the unfortunate heroine. How do I get away from the whole sorry mess, she wondered. Maybe Bhagu should simply fall in love with someone else. Oh no! she'd think almost immediately, quite sickened by the thought, anything but that. She knew everyone worried about her, which in turn made her anxious. I wish they would all leave me alone, she'd think, uncomfortable with their furtive scrutiny. This whole matter had to be brought to a head or she would go silently mad. "I

---

12 Indian festival

know," she said, suddenly, "I need to get away. Far away. Maybe a visit to Jaipur ..." The hardest part was knowing how much he liked her. The almost certain knowledge made her heart ache with longing. But her mind told her that Mem would never accept Bhagu. A mere student with no job for her first grand daughter? She would probably throw a fit. But more devastating than that was her strong suspicion, that her own parents wouldn't accept him either. Shali didn't have it in her to simply disregard her family's wishes. She wasn't even sure if she was capable of sacrificing her own lifestyle for love. There were so many question marks; she always came back to the same conclusion. She had to get away. The whole thing would have a better chance of blowing over. She knew her parents would enjoy the trip, rediscovering family, their ancestral home and the inevitable social whirl with the entire extended family. With a plan to follow, where earlier she'd felt completely lost, Shali, with almost feverish determination, willed herself to put everything else from her mind and gave herself up fully to her neglected studies. Later that night, she and her parents reserved their seats on the plane.

Sometime during the middle of the week, as her car approached the college, she noticed vaguely that the traffic had slowed to a crawl. Her eyes searched for Bhagu and her treacherous heart beat fast as it neared the spot where she knew he always stood waiting to catch a glimpse of her. He did not say or do anything. Simply gazed on her as her car passed. It had become their secret tryst, well away from the inquisitive eyes of others. It was also like a progression in their relationship, an admission of her growing attraction in spite of her better judgement. He was not there! Shalini cast her eyes about in blind panic. Why wasn't he there? She twisted around in desperation. Had she missed him? And then she saw him. He was across the road, on the opposite side, and she could tell he'd understood her momentary panic. But she was so relieved to see him there, she didn't care. She gave him a brilliant smile of pure happiness. "He still likes me," she thought, blind with relief. Her chauffeur noticed the sudden desperate movement of her head from left to right and the relieved smile. Without turning his face, he manoeuvred the car till he could clearly see Bhagu. "Hmmm, what's all this about?" he wondered as he gave his young m'emsa'ab a thoughtful glance through the rear view mirror. Shalini did not really pay attention to the traffic. Eyes downcast, she toyed with her handbag, a slight tremble in her hand betraying her highly emotional state. She focused all her energies into coaxing her hands to be still and stop their trembling and her agitated heart to slow its frantic beating. Lou or Binny could very well be at the gate and it wouldn't do to let her friends guess at her utter state of discomposure. The turmoil of a few moments ago still raged inside her - the blind panic at first and then the sheer joy of discovering that it was unfounded. When they were almost at the gate, it finally dawned on her that something unusual was happening. A bigger than usual crowd of students was gathered outside. They seemed amused. Curious, she looked to see what all the fuss was about. What she saw there actually made her forget Bhagu for an instant. She blinked and looked again.

A huge banner hung outside the boy's common room on the second floor, proclaiming to the world,

HAVE A COFFEE OR A CHAI INSTEAD
AT GS IT'S PIPING HOT AND DILUTED.

A couple of office executives tooted in appreciation as they drove past. A nice start to another high-pressured day. Apparently, things hadn't changed much since their own college days.

Shalini joined Louella, Binny and the crowd outside. Everyone seemed to be enjoying the commotion, even adding to it. The banner had opened up the floodgates and they spoke of their own experiences at the canteen. Lunchtime at Chacha's canteen had started becoming quite a dicey affair. The quality of his food had gone down considerably and where previously, he'd made the purest of South Indian coffees with hand roasted and freshly ground coffee beans in pure milk, he now used milk heavily diluted in water. His attitude toward female students still remained rude and brusque. He could barely stand their presence in his canteen, especially the ones who dressed outrageously. He seemed to think all women – whether they were from his community or not, belonged in *purdah*[13]. They ignored him, celebrating their youth and having a great time. But where previously they preferred eating at the canteen, they now ate at the Udipi[14] joints outside the college. They always wound up at the picturesque canteen afterwards, their meeting ground. To justify their presence there they grudgingly shelled out for a coffee. At least, it was affordable and piping hot. The banner, to everyone's surprise and delight, went unnoticed by the

---

13 veil
14 Udipi joints: no-frills restaurants selling affordable South Indian fare.

faculty for a full day. The next day, the novelty hadn't quite worn off. Professor Billimoria, from his office with the prime view, noticed the larger than normal crowd outside the gates. To his astonishment, even cars seemed to slow down and sound their horns - not like the everyday, irritated blast at youngsters to get out of the way but more, sort of, appreciative. And they all drove away smiling. He was completely baffled and phoned Dr. Naakwa. Together, they went down to investigate. Putting on their most dignified faces, they slowly walked past the suddenly silent but watchful youth and into the bank across the road. Once inside, they turned with haste to look at the college. The huge banner with the bright red lettering sprang out at them. The words rose and fell on a fresh breeze and were maddeningly elusive "...che appi pingho tand ilut ed."

As the words fell into place, their eyes couldn't help mirroring the amusement in the youthful faces outside. After a reasonable wait, the two professors returned to college. Without glancing at the offending banner and lost in a discussion of great import, they walked past the youth with another effort at dignity, aware that this time the youngsters' amusement was more abandoned. The banner was pulled down that same morning.

- SHALINI -

Shalini and her family reached Jaipur within a couple of hours. The entire clan seemed to be there to meet them. Shalini's mum drew a half ghoonghat[15] and bent over to touch Mem's feet. Mem blessed her daughter-in-law, "Jeeteh raho, long life". Then Shalini followed suit. "Jeeteh raho," Mem said to her granddaughter, her autocratic face softening into a smile. Then, on an impulse, she patted Shalini's cheek. "You are thin as a stick. Doesn't your mum feed you? Never mind, we'll nurture you back to health – put some meat on your bones," she said, managing to make Shali feel special, size her mum down and compliment herself, all in one breath. The three Bombay Dayals were fussed over and made much of by aunts, uncles, cousins and neighbours. There was much feet touching depending on where one fit in the hierarchy. Everyone spoke and nobody seemed to listen. Bombay was already a world away.

Shalini's dad went across and shook hands with his brothers and cousins. Soon they were lost in some discussion. "Probably politics," Shalini thought to herself, happy for her dad. She grinned at her cousins. She was the eldest and their ages ranged from three to seventeen. "Sharad has grown," she thought, holding out her arms to the shy four year old. "Shali *didi*, (sis)" they all greeted her, clamouring for her attention. Soon it was as if she'd never been away. The late evening air was cool and crisp and the low airport building and red earth looked unusually lovely. With a sudden lift in her spir-

---

15 Ghonghat: A veil made with the part of the saree that hangs from the shoulder.

its Shalini thought, "I'd forgotten how beautiful Jaipur was."

Shalini liked her two Chachis, wives of her dad's younger brothers. That they were such good cooks was definitely a point in their favour. Their ages ranged between the early thirties and late forties. To her, they always seemed to be bustling about happily. Only their mother-in-law could sober them up, but never for too long.

Shalini's dad was the eldest of three brothers and hence the head of the household. Every one jumped to do his bidding when he was in town. He wasn't even allowed to fetch water for himself. He only had to comment rather vaguely that the heat made one thirsty and a servant appeared at his side with a copper-lined silver glass of cool water on a tray. He was a good sort really. In Mumbai, before they'd found Rajubai, it was he who made the first pot of tea every morning. Except, of course, when they had overnight visitors and never, when his mother was visiting. To her it was clear as day that the kitchen was no place for the man of the house, especially since he happened to be her son. If she ever found out that Mr. Dayal made tea for her daughter-in-law, she would have a fit. The ripples of her indignation would be felt throughout the world as some of the family were scattered far and wide. Oh no, in Jaipur it would be more prudent for Mr. Dayal to sit back and enjoy all the attention. Besides, to be quite honest, it wasn't too hard to slip into the old ways... He was the eldest male and that made him head of the family. But for all practical purposes, his mum was the undisputed head of the household. Her word was law. No one dared upset her strong sense of tradition. She'd be most offended - especially since, with her knowledge and authority on the subject, she mostly seemed to reap the benefit of those traditions. Mem couldn't quite understand why everyone thought her such an ogre. She didn't see herself like that at all. Take the T.V. serial she avidly watched everyday, "Ji Meh Jaan", Soul within the Heart. It was the age old battle between tradition and love where love won in the end against all odds. The characters were beloved household names and the cast almost as famous as the Indian movie actors. So often, the Dayals would have a spirited discussion about the fate of the characters of that soap. Mem was the most vociferous in her impatience with a capricious boss or a cruel father. She left no one in any doubt about what she would do if she were the heroine. But real life was another matter... When Mem's second grand daughter fell in love, her parents were keen to get her engaged to the young man of her choice, especially since both sets of parents were good friends. Unfortunately, Mem disapproved. The boy's family weren't rich enough. Shali was soon put in the picture but came to know about Mem's feelings on the matter only when her grandmother and uncle had a blazing row.

"Shali didi," It was Sharad. "Didi," he said even louder, "sis". Shalini jumped. Her thoughts were miles away in Bombay. Sighing inwardly she thought, 'I've put such a lot of distance between Bhagu and me but somehow, he manages to sneak into my thoughts.' She smiled at her cousin affectionately. "Didi," whispered Sharad, his little mouth trembling, "Mem is scolding Prakash Chacha." Although she led Sharad away, Shali could clearly hear Mem shouting, "A bank clerk? A clerk?" she repeated, incredulous and scathing. "Are you out of your mind?" she wanted to know. Shali could hear the murmur of Prakash Chacha's soft reply. "We'll be the laughing stock of Rajasthan," Mem bellowed in response. "How could you even think of such a match?" And after some more murmurs, Mem's biting reply, "Is that how high you aim for your daughter?" With each word Shalli's heart sank a bit more. "The two have grown fond of each other, ma." Shali clearly heard her Chacha say. "That kind of 'fondness' doesn't last long," was Mem's scathing retort. "It will if we let it, ma," Shali couldn't help cheering at her uncle's words. 'Trupti is lucky,' she thought. "We won't announce it till Shalini is engaged," she heard her own name, which made her sit up. Of course, thought Shali, realising immediately that her being the eldest grandchild meant that they would have to get her engaged first. If not, her chances of finding an arranged match in the community would diminish. Everyone would start wondering if something was wrong with her if Trupti got engaged before her. Shalini was uncomfortably aware that even her uncle had a vested interest in ensuring she was spoken for. And it would be rather convenient if it were a man of Mem's choice. That might soften Mem up for Trupti's choice.

If only they could get me engaged to Bhagu, Shali sighed to herself. It would be perfect. She went into a reverie, something she seemed to do quite often these days. Bhagu, seated in her lounge, making polite small talk with her family; his eyes would keep wandering to the door separating him from the depths of the house. Soon, she would be led out through that door by one of her aunts (not because she'd forgotten how to walk but because a girl who was being presented to a boy could do with every bit of moral support.) She'd wear a chiffon sari – yes, the one with the blue paisley, as it was simple, yet elegant and showed off her figure to perfection. She imagined stealing a glance at Bhagu. At that very moment he would glance at her too. Their eyes would meet for a brief second. She'd hastily lower her lashes and he'd look away. But it would be enough. Both families would know they liked each other. What a perfect arrangement.

What a pipe dream. Shalini shook her head with a wry grimace. In reality, her situation was similar to Trupti's. If anything, it was worse. Bhagu was a stranger. Besides, Mem had already found her first grand daughter the perfect match. She was eager, as was everyone else, including her uncle, to clinch the deal. Neither Shalini nor Bhagu would be allowed to stand in Mem's way. She would be very angry, probably enraged, if she ever found out about Bhagu. When Mem raged the world trembled. The truth of that statement was never more apparent than at that very moment. The whole household seemed eerily quiet. Only her grandma's loud voice and her uncle's murmured response could be heard. "You'll wait till after Shali's engagement to announce Trupti's?" Mem was only just beginning to understand how far the 'affair' had progressed without her knowledge. "This is getting WAY out of hand. You will put a stop to this nonsense AT ONCE," she commanded. When Prakashji didn't respond, Mem realised what it meant. He was letting her know that the engagement would go through with or without her blessing.

She knew her son was a Dayal and a male, at that. By tradition he made all the decisions ...even if he doesn't know what he's doing, she thought scathingly.

"We are supposed to be from a khandaani reputable family. Do you realise how much people will talk?" she said, incredulous that he didn't. When even that elicited no response, she yelled, "You have to find her – *I* will find her - a more suitable boy."

Finally, her son had to go. His wife, taking pity on him, sent one of the servants to call him away on a false errand. Mem, enraged but helpless, watched him go. Couldn't he wait while I finalised things for Shali, she fumed angrily. It was probably that empty headed Sarika who encouraged him. She's never liked me, she thought darkly of her daughter-in-law. See how craftily she called him away. Well, she thought, she won't get away with this. After all, I am her mother-in-law. Mem's claim to her hierarchical birthright seemed to calm her down a bit.

As always, everything came down to her poor daughters-in-law. Pretending to be unaware, they bustled about, chattering about ingredients and recipes, seemingly busy as they prepared the next meal. Look at them, she thought watching them with a dark scowl. They are much too free and easy. Things were different when I was a bahu, a daughter-in-law, in this house. I knew how to conduct myself with decorum. Mem often indulged in her favourite pastime, comparing herself to her bahus, to the detriment of the bahus. I *never* let my ghoongat, veil, slip. I *never* spoke to my husband in the presence of others, she thought, heaping scorn on her bahus for doing just that.

There is no grace in today's bahu, she thought with a toss of her head. When her bahus saw that contemptuous toss, they knew her thoughts bode them no good. That is when they wisely kept a wary distance.

Perhaps the only saving grace in mine is that they have given my sons such lovely children. Yet, she thought disapprovingly, unable to be too generous, Prakashji's wife could only produce a girl. Her eldest son and daughter-in-law had also produced a mere girl but she chose to ignore that fact right now as bahu number two was more out of favour than number one. And they are ruining her reputation, thought Mem, allowing her to run around with some clerk. A clerk! she snorted derisively, whatever next.

She loved her two eldest grand daughters devotedly of course. That was a separate issue altogether. But she blamed her first two daughters-in-law for not giving her an heir to the Dayal khandaan - a male grandchild to carry on the name. That her sons might in any way be responsible, she chose entirely to ignore.

She thought with pride of her three healthy, intelligent and handsome sons. She had done well. No one could fault her. Not even her own mother-in-law. Each birth had been like a victory. Another male child! It had immediately given her added clout. Every family in Jaipur and beyond wanted her sons for their daughters. And the dowries they had brought into the family! She hastily covered her smug expression with her usual look of haughty displeasure.

Her reverie was interrupted by Shalini, looking very pretty, as she walked past to join her cousins. Immediately Mem's face softened into a smile. Anyway, she unconsciously tossed her head; the kids definitely look and behave like our side of the family!

I am going to give Shalu such a grand marriage, it will be the talk of the town, she determined, feeling slightly happier. And Prakashji is going to come round to my way of thinking before long. A clerk! she thought disgustedly for the nth time...

- Mem -

Shalini and her cousins found Mem a contradiction. They knew she could be extremely unpleasant and yet, if she so desired, very charming. They could spend hours with her and never get bored. She enjoyed and spoilt them. Yet, on another plane, they were aware of her darker side – especially her feelings for their mothers.

Mem had lived in this house for so long, she was part of its history. They lived in the same house, but her stories of their ancestors were so different from the reality of life now, that she might as well have lived on another planet. The cousins loved nothing better than to remain at the table after a meal, or to sit outside snacking and enjoying the cool evening breeze, listening to their grandma's tales. Mem's stories both amused and repulsed. But they never failed to fascinate. Take the story of Sonny. Every time he passed them, Mem and her sister-in-law would have to squat, for he was male. And if they addressed him, they had to add the respectful suffix "ji". Sonnyji was the family's pet dog. The cousins could not believe their ears. "Mem, you didn't."

"You couldn't." And on being reassured that she did and could, "Mem, he was, after all, only a dog!"

"So?" she teased with a fond look towards Sonnyji's son, "what's wrong with good, old fashioned respect for a dog?"

"But Mem," Shali challenged, "what if Sonny had been female?"

"Then we wouldn't have called her Sonnyji now, would we?" she laughed gaily, easily evading the issue. They couldn't help laughing too. All their attempts at cornering her proved futile.

They loved the story of her fairytale marriage to Da.[16] She had been devoted to him. He was the only person she had loved, protected and obeyed all at once. When he had passed away after a short illness, she had been inconsolable with grief. She was eight and Da – fourteen, when they were married. Five thousand guests had been invited for the first day of celebrations when Lord Ganesh was formally invited to attend and bless the wedding. The celebrations had lasted a week. Mem never tired of describing the innumerable lunches and dinners, the ladies sangeet (singing) and a mammoth mehendi[17] session. Mem claimed that as a young bride, the mehendi on her hands and feet had been so dark, it had almost been reddish brown - the myth being that the deeper the orange, the more adored the bride. "I've yet to see a deeper shade of orange," she boasted. And of course, she had yet to witness as grand a wedding as hers. In the evening, the groom, covered in garlands of flowers, rode to her house on a magnificent white horse.

---

16 Da (pronounced Daa and short for Daadaa or paternal grandfather).
17 Mehendi or Henna, a vegetable dye, is valued for its myriad properties by Indians. Safer than chemical dyes, it has a cooling, soothing effect on a nervous bride. After it is washed off, it leaves a faint reddish aura, which looks attractive on dark hair. It is also used to adorn hands and feet in fine, intricate patterns. Once dried, the green leaf paste is washed off leaving an orange dye behind for about a fortnight after which it fades.

His silk suit with its sherwaani and achkan and a beautiful, bejeweled saafaa - Rajasthani turban - made him
look like an Indian prince. Behind him, as was the tradition, rode a young, unmarried girl. A long procession of
friends, relations, elephants and camels followed them
on foot, the humans dancing to the strident tune of the
'shenai' from the liveried band. The path was lit by
bright halogen lamps balanced on the heads of four
strapping young men, smartly decked out in starched
white and gold braid, and walking at the four corners of
the procession.

The traffic obligingly gave them right of way, the cars
slowing to a crawl. Soon they formed a procession of
their own behind the wedding party. There were one or
two desperate attempts to extricate themselves from the
procession of automobiles as drivers tried winging for
the nearest exit. But on the whole nobody seemed to be
in a rush. Everyone smiled benignly.

The pundit (priest) calculated the auspicious time of
marriage - between 8 p.m. and 4 a.m. Mem always forgot to mention that she slept through almost all of the
actual ceremony. She fell asleep in her mother's lap and
was gently nudged awake from time to time during
parts of the ceremony where her participation was im-
perative. The next day, when she awoke, they were law-
fully wedded man and wife.

Every action from there on in, was geared towards the
day she would finally leave her parents' home to go and
live at the bungalow. There were the hot oil massages
for her hair and haldi (turmeric) paste for her skin before every bath... Today's new brides might not have the
patience to go through those unending massages but
they couldn't help noticing that even now, at the ripe

old age of sixty-five, there was something wonderfully soft and supple about Mem's complexion. Finally, when she'd turned fourteen, her weeping mum and other members of the family had taken Mem to the Dayal residence. And here she had stayed ever since.

Not wanting the tales to end, the kids begged Mem for more. "Tell us about the time you dropped the box of spices."

"That's enough for today" she would suddenly become unapproachable again. She did not wish to be reminded of the telling off she'd received from her mother-in-law. The children, aware of her sudden mood swings, left her strictly alone, getting absorbed in some other fun.

- A Nudge in the Right Direction -

The ancestral home, a huge rambling old place, with the sitting and dining rooms running through the centre, had bedrooms on each side. The smooth, white marble tiles lightly speckled with black, and air coolers installed through the house, helped keep things cool in summer when Jaipur reached temperatures beyond the forty degree mark. A huge storeroom next to the kitchen at the back was where the winter gear - the *dhurries* or carpets and coal burners - was packed away, to be brought out each winter.

When Shalini and her parents came to stay, the servants prepared their rooms by folding away the dust sheets. Almost immediately, they slipped into the busy social rounds - entertaining and being entertained, trying to meet up with the entire extended family.

This time they were caught up in preparations for Holi, celebrated in March on a full moon day. At the old bungalow the preparations were in full swing. The servants were making a straw effigy of Holika. It would be set alight in a huge bonfire, a night before Holi. Shalini, a bit apprehensive, was aware that she would be meeting the parents of the prospective, hand-picked-by-Mem, groom that night. At least she didn't have to meet Rajinder yet. He had been unable to get away from Sriharicota, where he worked. On the night, as they all waited for the bonfire to be lit, Shalini sat with her cousins, feeling self conscious. The couple smiled at Shalini and she smiled back nervously. But she needn't have worried. Without Rajinder to contend with, it wasn't too difficult. In fact, if she were honest, it was quite flattering. They sought her attention at the smallest excuse and hung on to her every word. Her likes, her dislikes, her philosophies, her favourite T.V. programmes, her college, her studies, her friends, books - nothing Shalini said, thought or did was too insignificant.

It's not like I have to marry Rajinder tomorrow, she reasoned, beginning to enjoy herself. She even ventured to test them, tentatively mentioning her desire to complete her college degree before contemplating marriage. They, in turn, let her know they understood, even approved. "Rajinder, after all, is a Nuclear Scientist," they said, letting her know, equally subtly, about their hopes for a connection between her and their son.

Shalini blushed, hastily veering away from the discussion. That gives me a grace period of a full three years, she couldn't help thinking. Anything is possible between now and forever. I just have to be pleasant to his parents while I am in Jaipur, she concluded. That was easy enough. It was unthinkable she would be anything else, after all, they were nice and they were her elders.

She gave herself up to the Holi celebrations, watching her dad set Holika alight. The tiny blue flame looked hopelessly inadequate as Mr. Dayal coaxed and nurtured it till it could cope on its own. It spread almost lazily, a lick here, a flicker there until suddenly, it roared into life and spread to engulf Holika. The Dayals moved back instinctively as the heat reached out to them. Dwarfed by the mighty flames the entire clan stood around in silence, watching until they tired of the heat and the roar of the fire.

Shalini and her cousins turned their attention to passing around snacks, munching and chatting, as they waited for the grownups to organise whatever came next. The story of the victory of Prahlad over Holika[18] was an absolute must - the highlight of the evening. Any one of the ladies recounted it. The long, dancing shadows thrown up by the bonfire were the ideal backdrop to the tale. The grown ups might have heard it often, but every year it was the little ones - three and four years old - whose fascinated faces they watched. Through their eyes and their expressive faces, it was like listening to the story for the very first time...

---

18 The story of Holi is many thousand years old. Prahlad and Holika were the children of a wicked king. Holika had magical powers that let her walk through fire, unharmed. The deeply religious Prahlad worshipped Lord Vishnu. But the king, who had been blessed by Lord Vishnu in his youth, had begun believing himself to be God and wanted everyone including Prahlad to worship him. Everyone except his son complied. The king tried to get him killed but every time, Prahlad escaped by a miracle. He decided he would get Holika to hold Prahlad as he lit a bonfire around him. He told Prahlad that his God could not save him but if Prahlad asked him - the King, he might consider a royal pardon. Prahlad declined. Whilst in the fire, Lord Vishnu transferred Holika's powers to Prahlad. Holika perished in the fire. The villagers rejoiced at the victory of good over evil by setting alight a huge effigy of Holika and playing 'Holi'.

Mem took it upon herself to recount the tale, an extra sparkle to her entire demeanour. This Holi was finally turning out to be as good as she'd hoped. The fact that the Rais had accepted the invitation at all was a clear move, from her perspective, in the right direction.

- A Double Celebration? -

What followed the next day was even more important to the kids. That's when everyone played 'Holi.' The Dayals, after an initial reticence, warmed to a good game of throwing coloured water at each other in their own backyard. Then, soaking wet and coloured from top to toe in brightly coloured gulal or powdered colour dye, and armed with bags of the same, they continued the game with their neighbours on the street.[19]

At night, the Dayal family met for a very special family puja or prayer, and a traditional dinner. The Dayal men, as the brothers liked to boast privately, normally ate anything that flew, swam, crawled or walked. But for religious days such as today, they were pure vegetarians.

A few days later, Shalini, fed up of wearing tatty old clothes for Holi and looking forward to the farewell dinner party to which the whole clan was invited, stood in front of the bedroom mirror, longing to get into all her gear. She had bought an expensive salwaar-kameez at Aarohi's - a trendy boutique in Bombay. She ran her hands lightly over the silk Kameez. Her *chunni*[20] looked elegant in cream organdy with tiny silver sequins glint-

---

19 All of India celebrates Holi for at least a week, when kids and grown-ups from every community, aware of the legitimacy of dousing others with colour, jump on to the band wagon.
20 Long scarf

ing in the overhead light. She wore a silver bindi to
match the outfit and rust nail polish. Her lipstick was a
pale, shiny russet and her platinum and diamond set
complemented the entire outfit to perfection. She knew
she looked good as she stepped into the hall.

The Rais looked slightly stunned, then delighted. Mr.
and Mrs. Dayal looked at the smiling young woman -
where was their little girl! - their hearts simply bursting
with pride.

- Mumbai and its Travails A Distant Memory -

And so Mrs. Dayal watched her daughter, happily
aware that whatever ailed Shalini had been left behind
in Mumbai. Shalini whiled away the last days of her
holiday idly flicking through magazines, feasting and
enjoying the company of her cousins, aunts and uncles.
On the last evening of her stay, Shalini and her cousins
decided that before the cool evenings disappeared altogether, it would be a good idea to sleep on the huge terrace atop the bangla. They had done it often but not in a
long while. That evening, the servants washed the dusty
terrace. The water not only cleaned it but cooled it down
as well. Within an hour everything was dry. Then they
spread charpoys[21] out under the brightly starlit sky, lying down in the company of langur monkeys and pea-
cocks who eyed them from a respectful distance. Mem
and the other grown-ups joined them for a little while,
with the younger kids begging Mem for a story. She
tried sending them away to one of her sons who only
teased them with the story of the great storm that blew
the roof off a granary. "The rice was stacked high in that

---

21 Cot with wooden frame and woven jute instead of slats

granary. A sparrow flew in through the blown roof, picked up a grain of rice, went back to its favourite perch on the tree and ate it. It then flew back to the granary and picked up another grain of rice, went back to its favourite perch on the tree and ate it. Then it flew into the granary..." till the little ones caught on, protested and went back to Mem. Her stories were really the best.

- *Bhabuti Naaie [Bhabuti the barber]* -

Once there was a king. He was mighty and powerful but at the same time, he ruled his kingdom with justice. He had a great secret. Nobody knew this but the King had only one ear. The other ear was missing. The King always kept it covered with magnificent 'saafaas' - turbans. It had been easy to keep his secret for all these years. But now, the King needed a haircut. He was in a quandary for the barber would surely discover his missing ear.

He sent for Bhabuti Naaie. Bhabuti Naaie was pleased. To cut the royal tresses was indeed an honour. He presented himself at the royal palace in his best dhoti and armed with his sharpest scissors. As he trimmed away at the royal locks, he was full of praise for their magnificence and shine.

Suddenly Bhabuti Naaie went silent. His hand hesitated and then stilled. He looked closely, and then looked again. The King had a missing ear! Bhabuti was utterly surprised. He stared at the King through the mirror - his mouth and eyes wide. The King looked back at him solemnly. Then the King turned around to face Bhabuti and in a stern voice swore him to secrecy.

"What you just saw Bhabuti, is for only you to know. Never tell any other person - not even your own wife." Then he added in a menacing voice, "If ever word of my missing ear gets out, you will be severely punished."

Bhabuti Naaie trembled with fear and swore to the King that he would never breathe a word to a single person. Then he went away.

But on his way home, he thought and thought about the King's missing ear and desperately wanted to tell someone. He thought he might burst if he didn't share his secret. So he went deep into the woods. He looked around and spotted a tall tree. He thrust his face through a hole in the tree and whispered his secret. He whispered good, and long and hard. Then he laughed and laughed and went back home.

A few days later, some woodcutters chopped down the same tree. They sold it to a man who made musical instruments for a living. This man made a harmonium, a sitar, a violin and tablas from the trunk, and sold the instruments to the court musicians. The King was a patron of the arts and invited his entire kingdom to come and listen to the fine new instruments of his court musicians. When everyone was seated, the musicians got ready to tune their brand new instruments. Everyone fell silent.

Suddenly the tablas went "Dhumak-a-dhumak". The tabla-walla was surprised because he had not even touched the instrument. The violin sprang to life making the violin player recoil in fright. It wailed on a thin note, "Rajaji ro ek kaan." [The King has one ear] The harmonium sang, "Thaney koon kahiyo?" [Who told you?] The tabla boomed back, "Bhabuti Naaie kahiyo" And with a great cacophony of sound, all the musical instruments laughed and laughed.

Mem reproduced the conversation between the musical instruments in perfect imitation. Even the grown ups listened appreciatively. She acknowledged their admiration with a raised eyebrow and a half smile before continuing...

"The entire gathering was thunderstruck, not least the King. He was very angry and sent for Bhabuti Naaie. A very frightened Bhabuti Naaie was brought before the King. He told the King how he had whispered the secret only to a tree deep in the woods and to no one else. The King realised that the musical instruments

must have been made from the same tree. Bhabuti Naaie had indeed, kept his promise. He hadn't told any person.
The musical instruments were still laughing. The King found their laughter so infectious that he suddenly joined in. All his subjects were relieved, for they were holding themselves back with great difficulty. And everyone laughed and laughed ... and laughed..."

As she lay on her charpoy, Shalini realised that Mumbai seemed far away. She heard the watchman's stick hit the concrete pavement twice or thrice as he walked slowly past. Finally she drifted off, listening to the familiar sounds of childhood - safe in her own home.

- A Plot -

The next day, they were all up early to see her family off. Shalini had been overwhelmed with gifts and needed a couple of extra suitcases. She agreed with her mum and dad that it had been a good break. Thoroughly refreshed, they were ready to get back to their academic and medical worlds.

While Shali was away, Binny and Lou had been extremely busy. They had discovered that Bhagu had a passion for tennis and played regularly at the local gymkhana (gym plus club). They'd requested that he introduce them to the badminton coach since they wanted to sign up for lessons during the holidays. After sweating it out on the court, which both girls enjoyed immensely, they fell into the habit of spending time with Bhagu, chatting comfortably and sipping coffee before heading home.

One day, whilst chatting, Bhagu said, "Did you know Dr. Naakwa has taken over the debating club at the college?"

"Really," said Lou, surprised. "Doesn't he have enough on his plate already," said Binny.

Bhagu nodded. "Perhaps," he said, "but he is so much better than the previous man, who was a lawyer and who tried to confuse the members with too much legalese." Binny and Lou laughed.

"Is he planning to employ someone else?" asked Binny.

"I'm not sure. He rather seems to be enjoying it. It's been a while now and he seems in no hurry to find a replacement."

"How do you know all this, Bhagu?" asked Lou

"Oh, I've become a member."

"Hmmm, interesting," said Lou, a glimmer of a plan beginning to form in her mind. On the way back, on her little moped, the two girls yelled out a conversation to each other over the roar of the air rushing past. "Binny," yelled Lou. "What?" Binny, who was riding pillion, stuck her head over Lou's shoulder and as close to Lou as possible to enable her to hear better. To anyone approaching them from the other side, it looked like one body with two heads. "Why don't we join the debating club?" Lou yelled. "No way, Lou," shouted Binny. "I wouldn't be able to argue to save my life." Lou was silent, letting Binny get used to the idea till they reached the station. When she stopped to let Binny off, she said, continuing the earlier conversation, "All the more reason for us to join Binsy. Besides, Shali would be forced to meet Bhagu all the time." Binny, having alighted with a smiling wave of thanks was already half way to the station. She stopped and turned back. "Lou," she said, admiration in her voice, "sometimes you surprise me. This is one of your best ideas yet!" Lou gave her a mock bow before riding off.

They waited impatiently for Shali's return. She was barely back before they told her unceremoniously, "We are joining the debating club."

"Congratulations," said Shali dryly, sensing another of their 'schemes'. "Not just us two Shali, I mean you as well. And no," Lou added as she anticipated Shali's objections, "you can't duck out of this one!"

"I can't?" Shali's lower lip started jutting out, always a dangerous sign. They hastily changed tack. "Shal, how can we do it alone? We need all the moral support we can get."

"Oh really," said Shali laughing, not in the least convinced. "Come on, Shali, it simply wouldn't be fun without you. Besides, everyone needs to do something besides study. Something, ..umm, stimulating" Eventually, they wore down her defences with cajolery, flattery, threats and determination. She reluctantly gave in.

It was the Saturday before college reopened. The three girls, slightly nervous, waited outside the auditorium till everyone started trickling in. "Will we be asked to say anything?" asked an anxious Shali, thinking worriedly that if they did, she'd make a fool of herself. And then, everything else went from Shalini's mind. Her heart almost missing a beat, she realised she was face to face with him.

Her resolve to end it all finally and irrevocably with Bhagu had been made with steely determination in Jaipur. Surrounded by Mem, her parents and the entire extended family and the Rais, it had almost seemed possible. Coming face to face with him so unexpectedly, she realised how hopeless her case already was. Her treacherous heart let her down at the very first sight of Bhagu. For a tiny moment, the two gazed at each other, almost mesmerised. How could this deep emotion between them simply be wished away? 'But it can only bring us grief,' she thought hopelessly as she turned away. And Bhagu felt the familiar twisting pain in his guts, barely responding to Binny and Lou's cheery greetings. Everyone trooped into the auditorium. The girls went in and sat behind everyone, trying to be as inconspicuous as possible. Dr. Naakwa, recognising newcomers, walked over to hand them forms to fill in, stating he was delighted to see them. Eventually, he presented them to the others. As it turned out, they didn't have to say much. All they needed was to stand up, introduce themselves in a standard format, (Name:---; the degree studying for:----; which year:--------; and the most difficult part, one interesting fact about themselves.) and sit down to encouraging applause from the more seasoned members. Bhagu, a relative new comer himself, was picked to do a sample introduction so they could emulate his example. He made it sound incredibly easy. For the one interesting fact about herself, Lou declared she was originally from Goa and that her parents had come to Mumbai in the early seventies. Shali followed suit saying she was originally from Jaipur and had come to Mumbai in the early sixties. Binny said she was originally from Mumbai and had come to Mumbai from … "

Her voice trailed away as she realised what she was about to say in her haste to get it over with. The audience could barely conceal their mirth. And then they generally overdid the encouragement bit, clapping thunderously and smiling warmly. Embarrassed, Binny said a quick 'thank-you' and rushed back to her seat, vowing never to return to the podium again. Later, reliving the agony of that moment for the hundredth time, she railed at her friend, "Lou, its one thing trying to bring the two lovers together, but quite another making a fool of yourself in the process." Lou giggled. Binny had somehow helped dissolve the tight knot of nerves in her stomach. "Come on Bins," she cajoled her friend, "forget it. It happens to the best of us. I bet some of the audience were as nervous for their own initiation and understood perfectly. Besides," she said, "even Shali and Bhagu found it hilarious that you travelled from Mumbai to Mumbai...." When Binny made as if to strangle her, Lou backed away, laughing.

"… but listen to this, Binsy," she said urgently, something in her voice making Binny forget her mortification for a moment. "When you said what you did, they turned to each other without even realising it…"

"…and Binny," said Lou softly, knowing she had her friend's full attention, "almost of their own volition … their eyes met in a smile." Binny, her embarrassment definitely forgotten for a moment went silent. Then, "Oh," she said. A few moments later, "Oh," she repeated, looking at Lou with interest.

Lou nodded her eyes wide as she waited for Binny to absorb the full impact of what she was saying. Then she added, "After that, they kept glancing at one another. They couldn't stop, Binsy."

"Really?" said Binny, beginning to feel Lou's excitement. Their plan to bring the two lovers together was finally showing the first signs of success. Lou was nodding vigorously. "Oh," said Binny again, slightly sheepish, her role of cupid clearly battling with her embarrassment. Lou was almost dancing with excitement. "Mmm," Binny conceded finally, a reluctant smile spreading across her face, "I'm not too sure I'll ever live it down but some good does seem to have come of it."

- Project Shali -

Project Shali had become one of their top priorities. And with the smell of success so close, the two girls were unable to relinquish it. The club figured in all their conversations. The last topic of debate, the next. And innocuously, or so it seemed to nobody but themselves, they often brought Bhagu into their conversations. It was easy, for they often read in the agenda that Bhagu was to be in a debate - yet again! Perhaps Dr. Naakwa was impressed with his abilities too. "I wish I could talk like that," said Lou, a touch of envy mingled with her admiration, watching Bhagu as he smiled and chatted with Dr. Naakwa. "I mean everything he says seems so logical - so obvious..."

"...after he's said it," agreed Binny, grinning. Even Shali couldn't help smiling. "O.K." conceded Lou, "It seems obvious in hindsight..."

"Just kidding," said Binny. Then, ladling it on a bit too thick for a wary Shali, she continued, "I agree about Bhagu though. He makes it seem soooo effortless!"

"Yes," gushed Lou. "The words just roll off his tongue...Any ordinary person would spend ages trying to put together all those brilliant observations." Lou was unable to resist a quick look at Shali. "... and probably not even succeed!" supplied Binny, watching too. Their comments elicited no response from Shali who simply smiled. They raved on, ...the command... the mastery...the easy confidence..."don't you think so, Shali?" Shalini, cornered so brazenly, felt her cheeks flush as she gave what she hoped was a nod of agreement. But she too was impressed. And dare she admit it, deep down inside, there was this tiny touch of pride. She knew her steely resolve had all but disappeared. It had been borne of a feeling that the whole affair was doomed from the start; that she had to protect Bhagu from her family. Her parents wouldn't dislike him as an individual. They would welcome him as they would welcome any of her friends. But Mem's strong hopes of a match between Shali and Rajinder were now very much their hope too. He had a job! Prestige! It made him a much stronger contender than Bhagu. Besides, he was a Dayal. The meeting with his parents in Jaipur had gone off smoothly. Both sets of parents and her grandma had been delighted. Shalini was the only hitch in those carefully laid out plans. And Bhagu. She understood all too well how speedily and politely they'd freeze him out if they ever discovered her secret. And Mem! She hoped Mem would never guess. She'd been thwarted by "a mere clerk". But, to be thwarted a second time – and by a mere student! She'd be very angry with her grand daughter and her daughter-in-law. Coldly furious with Bhagu she'd cleverly humiliate him and then extend the same treatment to his family as she constantly did to Trupti's future in-laws;

Shalini was scared. She was scared to thwart Mem. She was also left wondering if Bhagu could stand the treatment he would inevitably be meted out. What if he ended up hating her because her family despised him? Could she take that? 'No!' she decided, taking matters into her own hands. Feeling she had no other option, she tried to deny her feelings for him.

'Coward,' her heart screamed as she tried giving weight to her decision. "What if they have a point?" said her mind, immediately contradicting her heart. "What if Bhagu won't be able to provide the creature comforts I take for granted? Will my love withstand that? My family aren't my enemies. They simply want what they think is best for me. They are definitely more experienced ...they understand human nature and are wiser than me. Won't it be safer to bow to their judgement? It will certainly be easier."

But her feelings for Bhagu proved to be persistent. They were such a formidable foe for her resolve. There was the look in his eyes. How could she resist what she saw in them? the love? the hurt? the pleading? It made that resolve very shaky.

On the other hand, it was easy to resist Lou and Binny's efforts to worm any admissions out of her. If they tried to broach the subject, she backed out of the conversation. Clammed up. Withdrew. No, she simply wasn't ready to speak. She needed time to sort things out in her own muddled mind first.

But when everyone was busy watching Bhagu as he took the floor, she felt safe enough from their sharp scrutiny to steal a few glances. And each time, she couldn't help admiring more and more, what she saw. She was obviously prejudiced, and knew her friends' accolades were a touch too enthusiastic. Yet, it couldn't be denied he was good. The others, Dr. Naakwa, his opponents - surely everyone couldn't be wrong?

It was hard not to appreciate his tact with them. 'Even as he cuts incisively through their arguments he manages not to offend them,' Shali thought with a burst of pride.

- The Debate -

Shalini recalled the last debate. Bhagu had been pitted against a seasoned debater. The topic -'Is Mumbai truly secular?' was well researched by the savvy final year student, Bharati. She stood at the podium looking poised and serious. Her frame was petite but her presence commanding. "It would be a fair comment," she stated, "that we all react differently to different cultures. Most of us accept that whilst we follow our own traditions, we need to let other communities follow theirs; that the common umbrella we all share is that of our humanity, guided by the laws of our city. This helps provide order, peace and justice through which we share our city's resources. This umbrella covers all of us in our diversity; all of us have to obey its dictates to be able to live and prosper together, under its shade."

"And then," Bharati paused before declaring, "...there are *the others*."

Dr. Nakwa couldn't help noticing that the audience was riveted. Another, slightly longer pause ensued. Dr. Nakwa made a quick note to award Bharti a point. It amused him to note that it was a rather hurried scribble as he was anxious to hear what she had to say just like all the rest. Her soft voice permeated the silence as she continued, "They are but a handful but they exist in every community. They feel threatened by the very presence of other communities. They feel their own culture is being swamped and overshadowed. In their minds, secularism, or a tolerance for another religion, another culture, other ways of doing things, seems to pose a threat to their own. It might be a perceived threat, but to them, it seems very real. They long for the 'good old days' when they lived within their own community without having to contend with the strange ways of others. Their very identity, the identity of their community, is wrapped up in their own rituals, habits, traditions and language," said Bharati, adding with slow emphasis, "If any one of these is under threat, then who they are is under threat."

She instinctively knew how to make the right moves, using every trick the club had taught her to make her arguments effective. She knew it was time to let her line of reasoning lead to its obvious and logical conclusion. "That is why," she said, "they resist even a slight divergence from their own culture.

Their argument is that 'civilisation' is represented only by their culture. They are keen to preserve everything about that great culture for it is their rightful heritage - their khandaan."

"They perceive the desire for change as criticism ... criticism," Bharati emphasised, "for their ways. How can anyone call themselves a true Hindu (or a true Muslim, Sikh, Christian or Parsi),' they ask, 'and still desire a change from our norms and traditions?'

"And yet they see it happening all the time. They see others in their own community openly keen to join the modern world and all the changes it brings; to an extent they accept changes too - changes in communication and travel, science and technology, and in modern medicine. What they can't bear is to witness their own kind enjoying differences in rituals, habits, in how they work and behave. They feel stung. Almost betrayed. Everything they stand for seems to be falling apart before their very eyes. They feel vulnerable."

"Still, apart from these good folk, is Mumbai secular? Let's see. The liberal minded go ahead and experiment. And we feel really sorry for our traditionalists. It must be difficult to live in this fast changing world. The traditionalists are a mere handful and yet, here's an amazing fact, their opinion is slowly gaining the upper hand in Mumbai. Why?"

"Why, when they are the minority," she rephrased her question slightly, "is their opinion gaining the upper hand?" The audience waited wondering what theory Bharati would put forward. "I'll tell you why," she finally said. "The reason is simple. They have ... organised."

"They have organised under the leadership of someone who understands their fears and wishful thinking; someone who promises our traditionalists a chance to return to their previous days of glory. The plan is simple. It is consistent and it is universal. The first part of the plan is to ridicule the traditions of others, so different from their own refined ones. The leader is strident and loud in his or her condemnation. This emboldens our traditionalists to voice their feelings of murmured discontent; to let off steam; to believe that here is a person who will protect their faith, their community and their very identity. And is there a price our traditionalists have to pay? Of course there is. There always is. That is the second part of the plan. The leader lets it be known that he or she can make good their promise only if voted to a position of greater power and authority in the field of their choice. This leader's motives aren't my concern today. Let it suffice that the traditionalists do not look beyond the promise to ask what the leader's actual plans are. How does one make good a promise to return to the 'good old days'? Force the others to renounce their own culture or religion? Or send everyone back to where they came from? Or the more liberal minded from within their own community to stop experimenting?" As mentioned before, the traditionalists do not look beyond the promise. Bolstered by the strong front behind which they stand, they become strident in their own verbal attacks."

"Unfortunately it doesn't take long for those verbal attacks against a whole community to become an attack against individuals. They might have a neighbour or a co-worker who belong to the hateful 'others'. How long before one or two verbal attacks spark off physical abuse? When that happens, what do our traditionalists do? For the sake of the glory that was and which they want back so badly, they are willing to accept that some individuals from other communities - decent though they might be - could sometimes get hurt. They turn a blind eye."

Bharati paused and with deliberate movements, picked up her glass of water and drank from it. As she put her glass down and covered it with a beaded doily, she was aware that all eyes were on her. Nobody in the audience stirred. There was complete, hushed and mesmerised silence. She paused for a long second, looking directly at her captive audience before continuing, "Incapable of hurting an ant under normal circumstances, our traditionalists' attitude has undeniably hardened." Bharati let that sink in before continuing. "So where have we, the tolerant majority, gone wrong? We aren't the ones hurting others so why are we to blame? We might not like some of the things they do in the name of tradition but what can we do? Disapprove of someone's grandfather or an old aunt? Take a stance against our own?"

"So we turn a blind eye."

"Others amongst us prefer to distance ourselves from the whole thing - why stick our noses into something that doesn't concern us? One way or another, we all take a vow of silence."

As for people from other, mostly minority, communities – whether here in Mumbai or anywhere else - they feel they have two options. Either get completely cowed or unite in retaliation."

After letting the audience absorb that Bharati said, "This is where our silence has led us. We are beholden to, and victims of, the organised actions of a small proportion of people from our own communities. Or, from a different perspective, we are victims of the inaction of the tolerant majority. Either way there is extreme mistrust between communities. Already great cracks have appeared in our secular umbrella, in one law for all, in peace and harmony, in live and let live. If things are allowed to carry on as they are, then in all probability, this secular umbrella is going to crumble. Now you tell me," Bharati murmured softly, "are we truly secular?"

- The Proponent -

It was Bhagu's turn.

He started off in a light and humorous vein. As he groped in his mind for the right words, Shalini was able to gaze on him to her heart's content. "Everyone knows the diversity of thought and belief that exists in Mumbai. What is amazing is that we have managed to co-exist at all. "Live and let live, Koi baat nahi or No Big Deal" are some of the attitudes that have kept this great big melting pot peaceful on the whole."

"But are we *truly* secular?" he murmured, exactly as Bharati had done. Only a slight, incredulous shake of his head as he glanced toward his opponent indicated he found it preposterous she doubted it, even for a second.

With deliberate movements he picked up his glass of water and had a sip. It was such an accurate imitation of Bharati that a slight titter went round the audience. The mood in the room brightened visibly. He felt, rather than saw, people straighten in their chairs. They were hardly won over but at least, they were prepared, even eager, to listen.

Bhagu knew how important it was to get them in the right frame of mind before he presented his case.

"Bharati," he continued with a slight bow of acknowledgement toward his opponent, "would have us believe we are not!'Not only that,' she declares, 'entire commu-

nities have become intolerant … entire communities de-
spise and scorn the habits, religion and culture of others.' Bhagu knew that wasn't strictly what she'd said but
the moment called for high drama and he gave it everything he had.

"Let's see if she is right," he said, and so saying, raised
his hand high for all to see as he started counting on his
fingers. "Don't we all - Hindus, Muslims, Christians,
Parsis, rich and poor - each and every one of us - without exception, burst phutakas[22] during Diwali? If we
didn't, our kids would want to know why! Don't we all
throw coloured water on poor, unsuspecting, innocent
folks with cruel relish during Holi[23]?

We have school holidays for Id, Navroze, Buddh
Jayanti, Diwali, Christmas and important festivals of
every community that lives here. Any more holidays
and there'd be no school. Hands up who's been to the
Bandra fair[24]? Or for a Langar on Guru Nanak's[25] birth-
day? Or a lunch at ISKCON[26]?

Bhagu put up his free hand. Shali's hand shot up, but
halfway, it hesitated, stilled and then was hastily with-
drawn. She cringed as she saw Binny and Lou exchange
a telling look and a half wink behind her back but was
thankful they didn't say anything.

Luckily for Bhagu, more than half the audience had no
such reservations and their hands popped up everywhere over the tops of their heads. He smiled at the
slight commotion he'd created.

---

22 phutakas – fire crackers
23 Diwali and Holi – important Hindu festivals
24 Bandra Fair – a fun fair after Easter.
25 Guru Nanak – most important Sikh prophet
26 ISKCON - International Society For Krishna Consciousness

"What about our marriage ceremonies?" he continued when the noise died down. "We are one nation that has been privileged since centuries to have witnessed and enjoyed a wide variety of wedding ceremonies. As for our receptions - a feast ...for the eyes and stomach. While on the topic of food, let us see what our restaurants have to offer. Russia may have its Beluga caviar - we have bhelpuri![27] France has its wines, we have ganna juice," he declared facetiously, aware of it going down well with his audience. "The list goes on. Mughlai, Goan, South Indian, Bengali and Gujarati fare - on any given day, the only real dilemma we face is, to pick one over the rest."

"Then there are our movie stars, television soaps and plays. Don't we all, from every strata of society watch those? Why, I would be justified in stating that even the Arabs are hooked."

"The list goes on," he repeated, "...our beaches - the sound of the sea - if we can reach it, that is, through the obstacle course of vendors and beggars; our parks and playgrounds ... ...taken over by," he shook his head ruefully, "... the same vendors and beggars;"

He stopped. He did not wish to get too deeply into the deplorable state of his city or he'd get his audience depressed all over again, which would be a pity after the effort he had put into lifting the pall of gloom cast by Bharati and her prophecies of doom.

"The list does go on. But I'll settle for one more," and a grinning Bhagu delivered his final sixer, "Who celebrates when Gavaskar hits a century? Is it only the Maharashtrians (Gavaskar's community) or us Indians?"

---

27 Popular Indian snack

The audience went wild as he knew they would. There were wolf whistles and thunderous clapping. He stood there grinning. He knew he didn't have to, but after the noise had died down he clarified it further, "Is there any denying this peculiar pride we feel in being Bombayites or Mumbaikars - call us what you will."

By now, the audience was eating out of his hand. He sensed it. Smiling as he savoured their approval he mimicked Bharati again, "Now you tell me, are we truly secular or not? - and cupping an ear with his hand he leaned forward expectantly.

He was gratified when "YES!!!" they yelled as one. They seemed to feed off each other's highly infectious mood. Bhagu grinned, looking at them with great satisfaction. "Why," he threw out his exit line, "we even have our own song," and so saying, Bhagu proceeded to sing it, "Bom, bom, bombom, Bombay meri hai…(is mine…)"

With great gusto the audience took up the refrain, "Bom, bom, bombom, Bombay me - e -ri hai."

When Dr. Naakwa, with a slight smile, held up his hand for silence, the voices degenerated once again into loud laughter. They felt sorry for his opponent. But when they looked at her, even she was smiling….

Dr. Naakwa had the final word. He found Bharati's argument compelling and thought provoking. Bhagu's had emotional appeal. It was a tie.

- Posters -

The three girls looked at each other with satisfied smiles. Binny stretched out her cramped feet and looked at the time. Bhagu had held them in the grip of his argument for a good ten minutes. It had left them all on a high somehow...

Later, during a short break, he had come across to speak to them. Lou and Binny had congratulated him. "You even managed to make us feel privileged to have our beggars on the beach," laughed Binny. "How do you do it?" said Lou, laughing and shaking her head at the same time. Shali just smiled, unable to address him directly. And in her presence, the normally articulate Bhagu seemed to lose his tongue too. He simply smiled his thanks. Binny and Lou felt it incumbent upon themselves to keep the conversation flowing. "Wasn't it funny when Dr. Naakwa and Professor Billimoria walked back from the bank - their pretence of being lost in conversation ..." said Binny to the trio. "We are so immersed in our discussion we haven't noticed the humungous, bright red banner staring us in the face," said Lou. Binny and Bhagu grinned. Shali smiled too. For the second time that day, her smile lingered when her eyes met his. Lou and Binny pretended not to notice. But goose bumps crawled up their skins as they witnessed the softness in Shali's face. Later, elated by their success, they said to each other, "Let's just relax and let things take their course."

The rest of the year passed uneventfully, with only the second banner creating a slight commotion. This time it appeared as mysteriously as the first and at the same spot.

"COME ONE, COME ALL
CHACHA'S FARE AND SAT-ISABGOL"[28]

---

28 Sat-Isabgol: Centuries old, popular ayurvedic roughage, made from psyllium husk. Many Indians swear by it and have a teaspoon added to their cereal or yogurt etc., everyday, claiming it cures stomach disorders and has no known side effects. It looks like wheatgerm and is tasteless.

Ever since the posters started appearing mysteriously in their college, the youth got a huge kick out of inventing some of their own. The canteen had become a pet peeve of theirs. The messages were everywhere - on black boards, on pages torn out of books and even on darts that glided past the girls.

STOLEN SECRETS FROM OUR FAMOUS CANTEEN
INGREDIENTS FOR PAPER DOSA - PAPER AND KEROSENE

Under normal circumstances, the female students would studiously ignore those darts but of late, Dr. Na-akwa was startled to see some very self-possessed young ladies make an inelegant grab for them as they glided past.

"Hmmm...Totally out of character," he thought.

Shalini, Binny and Louella do not know exactly when the rumour started, but soon it was whispered all over the college that the posters had been put up by none other than Bhagu. But when they confronted him, he just grinned. "Bhagu," said Lou, "everyone says those banners were put up by you. Is that true?" He neither admitted nor denied it. The girls let it go but felt slightly uneasy. Chacha was a dangerous man to pit oneself against. He was the representative of the slum he lived in and there were rumours that he had connections with the underworld. Shali looked worried too, although she didn't say anything.

Binny and Lou felt pleased with the success of their campaign. Joining the debating club had been a great idea. They almost felt that exposing this brilliant dimension of Bhagu's to Shali had all been their own work. And the other payoff was that they were getting to be good at debating too. But their progress was pitifully slow. They openly admitted that they would never be as good as him. "He is a natural. He does not even apply his mind," said Lou, openly envious. "The rest of us come prepared with reams of notes and he just stands there empty handed"

"...as if he's simply enjoying an argument with friends," added Binny. "He almost seems to pluck information out of thin air," gushed Lou. "Imagine singing a song during a debate," said Binny with incredulity. "Only he could get away with it..."

The two girls were only slightly off the mark. Bhagu's resourcefulness stemmed from his love of knowledge for knowledge's sake. He could not help satisfying his curiosity by delving deep into vastly varied topics. Throughout his life, Bhagu would hear the admiring refrain, "Is there anything you don't know..." He was also blessed with a photographic memory and an instinctive ability to convey exactly what he wanted to say without being offensive. Bhagu was born to take centre stage. When he spoke, people listened.

– A Dilemma –

That night, as she lay in bed, Shalini recalled the precious moments she'd shared, what if with an audience of fifty or so, with Bhagu. How perfect it would be if I could have him all to myself, she sighed. She lay there lulled by happiness, daydreaming. Suddenly, she sat up in bed. A daring thought, one that had hovered tantalisingly on the outer edges of her consciousness, pierced her mind. Why didn't she call him? She pushed the thought away. Nobody she knew ever did things like that. It was much too bold.

She knew Bhagu's telephone number from the first day at the debating club. While introducing himself he had revealed information which she had tucked away in the deep recesses of her brain. Once home, she'd locked herself in her room and with fast beating heart and hands that shook, she'd turned the pages to 'B'. There were at least a hundred Bhagus but only one who lived at the sea-face. There it was, clear as day. Not that I ever intend calling him, she had hastily reassured herself.

But, with the desire to call him taking root in her mind, she felt restless. After that debate everyone had milled around, complementing Bhagu. It was churlish of me not to offer my congratulations, she thought, trying to justify what she was about to do. The very next instant she ruefully shook her head. Who was she trying to kid? Ignoring the part of her that urged caution, she threw off the covers and jumped out of bed. As she walked to the writing desk the voice implored, Don't do it. Don't even think about it. It is way too imprudent. Reaching for the phone, she noted with a kind of curious detachment, that her hand trembled slightly as it hovered centimetres from the receiver. Her mum and dad would simply think she was dialling either Binny or Lou.

But suddenly, her hand stilled. The voice inside her was screaming, *what* are you doing? Have you gone mad? Jerking her arm away, she ran back and almost fell into bed. Breathing very fast, she shut her eyes tight, waiting for the reaction to pass. After a few minutes she felt calmer. Turning over with a sigh, she decided to call it a day. But sleep eluded her. A wild desire seemed to have her in its grasp and wouldn't let go. She tried to rein it in for what seemed an hour but was barely a few minutes. Finally, throwing off her blanket once more, she resolutely went to the desk, picked up the receiver and dialled the number which was carved out in a large font in her mind's eye.

She could hear her heart beat as she waited. On the third ring, her eyes tightly shut she thought, Why aren't you picking it up? and on the fourth, What if someone else picks it up? That was such a horrifying thought, her free hand swiftly reached for the disconnect buttons.

When the phone rang, Bhagu thought it was perhaps his dad calling to say he would be home late. He was a businessman and ever since his wife had passed away, he'd become a bit of a workaholic. Bhagu understood perfectly and did not resent being left to himself. It wasn't exactly like he had to fend for himself. Ramu, their resident old bachelor manservant made life reasonably comfortable.

But, he *had* waited dinner...

Feeling slightly dejected, Bhagu picked up the receiver. "Hello," he said, surprised there was no answer from the other end. "Hello," he repeated, slight impatience creeping into his voice. He was about to disconnect when he heard her voice. "Bhagu, I - I.. It's me, Sha - Sha - lini." Her voice was barely audible. He was stunned. "Shali..." His heart started racing. Having called him, she was lost for words. "Bhagu, I - I...," Bhagu was equally lost. He'd never expected this - not in his wildest dreams... His firm grip on the receiver slackened and he stared at it in disbelief. Am I dreaming? he thought. Is she really at the other end? he wondered, his heart starting to do its familiar wild tattoo all over his chest. For a second Shalini panicked. Bhagu seemed so quiet. Perhaps he doesn't want me to call him at home, she thought. The awful realisation started somewhere deep within her, snaking upwards slowly before piercing her mind with a stab of conviction. "I hope I'm not disturbing…," she said, stung and ready to disconnect. "You aren't, Shali." That was almost wrenched out of him. With an effort he tried to compose himself. "I think I'm a bit stunned," he admitted with a shaky laugh. Bhagu collapsed into the nearest chair. He willed his unresponsive body to sit up straight, loosen his grip on the receiver, his mind churning out thoughts by the second - think of something to say; something clever; not too clever or you might scare her off; I hope I don't scare her off' which made him more tongue-tied than ever. To date, he had never been sure where he stood with her. She gave him very conflicting signals. Sometimes he felt she really liked him. But whenever he did try to approach her, she always shut him out. This phone call was the first real sign of hope she had given him. He jumped out of his chair, suddenly too wound up to sit still.

"I - I see." Shali said into the long moment of silence, with a nervous little laugh. She couldn't think of anything intelligent to say. Her mind seemed to have deserted her completely. But the quiet desperation in his voice was strangely reassuring. "I wasn't expecting a call from you." He said that quietly too, but a tiny throb was evident in his voice. Shalini could not ignore it. She felt her treacherous heart give an elated lurch.

"I …I see," she said again. "I called because…," she hesitated for a tiny moment. Then, her voice sounding a little stronger she said, "You know the debate today?"
"Yes?"
"I really enjoyed it," she said.
Everyone had said so to him. He'd been pleased with their compliments but hers simply bowled him over.

Without even realising it, his face broke into a smile. "Thanks Shali," he said. "Why thank me, you are really good," she said admiringly. "It was only a debate," he proclaimed modestly. "Only a debate?" she couldn't help exclaiming. "Honestly Bhagu, do you realise what it does to us mere mortals to hear you say that? We toil for days preparing notes, practising… and then watch you walk up to that podium, pluck sentences, seemingly out of nowhere, string them together – and it all makes perfect sense…"

"Umm….," she could hear the beginnings of a smile in his voice, "am I being accused of inventing my facts?".

"No, of course not," she protested, smiling slightly.

"Of not researching them, then?" he said.

"Maybe," she laughed. "No, definitely," she amended, feeling an inexplicable lift in her spirits. "Bharati had a fat wad of notes. I didn't see yours," she challenged. "How can you say that, Shali?" he protested, pretending to feel hurt, "I took pains to prepare."

"Really?" she laughed. "Don't spare me," he said. "I can take it. Tell me honestly, did I get the words to 'Bombay Meri Hai', wrong?" Shalini laughed out loud. "You refuse to take anything seriously," she accused. "Oh I dispute that Shali. I take mealtimes very seriously"

Bhagu felt that wasn't particularly clever and winced at what she might think. But Shali seemed to enjoy his words for she gave a little chuckle. "Is that why you put up all those banners?" she asked.

"Me?" he asked innocently, "Banners?" and without admitting or denying anything he added, "although, to get Chacha[29] to serve us better fare isn't such a bad life-

29 Chacha – Indians like to confer, out of respect, relationships to everyone. Bhabhi or sister-in-law, Didi or sister, Bhaiya or brother are terms

mission, is it?" She smiled. Bhagu was beginning to sound like his old, irrepressible self again. Then she sobered up. "That's downright dangerous Bhagu. And foolish. You won't even listen to us when we tell you..."

"You haven't spoken to me till today Shali. I might not listen to others but I'll listen to you." Shalini hadn't felt so light hearted in months. "Then listen good and hard Bhagu," she said, "I want you to stop all those banners and one-liners. I feel scared for you."

"It's nice to know you worry for me Shali."

"Oh, I d-do," Shalini stammered slightly as she made the confession. "All your friends – including Lou, Binny and --- and I," she stumbled over the first person singular, "worry for you." He heard her hesitation and understood she wasn't ready, not yet, for a personal note to enter the conversation. He sighed. At least, she had called! For now, he would have to be content with that. "Thanks!" he said, feeling strangely moved. He was used to fending for himself – he even liked it. It was unusual to have people express concern for him. Unusual, but surprisingly nice. Feeling she'd said too much already Shalini said a hasty, "G--goodnight Bhagu." He could sense the softness in her voice. "Wa-it." He panicked, afraid she was going to break the link between them and be gone as unexpectedly as she'd called. He sought wildly in his mind to keep the lines open just a bit longer. "Can we not discuss this - I mean, the - the canteen a bit more tomorrow?" When she did not reply immediately, Bhagu dropped all pretences and said, "Please, Shali, will you call me again?" Shalini was suddenly overcome by the way things were moving. It all

---

used for friends, cousins, strangers. Chacha or Chachi – young uncle / aunt.

seemed to be beyond her sphere of control. 'After all, things haven't changed in my family,' she thought. 'Mem would almost certainly throw a fit if she knew what I was doing right now.' But she couldn't listen to the little voice of reason any more. She knew what Bhagu was really imploring her to do. "Yes," she whispered and before things spiralled totally out of control, she quickly disconnected.

Goodnight Shali." He spoke to the sound of the dial tone. Slowly he put down the receiver, loathe to completely severe the unexpected avenue of contact. Please God, don't let her change her mind tomorrow, he prayed fervently, feeling anxious and elated at the same time.

- Will She? -

In spite of her feeling that things were moving too fast, Shalini found she was singing softly to herself as she prepared for bed. The next morning, the feeling of exhilaration persisted. With a cheery "Bye Rajubai" and smiling at the unintended play on words, she almost sailed out of the flat. Rajubai thought to herself that she'd have to tell Tai, elder sister, their little girl was back on track - the Shali they'd always known.

Today, as her car passed the spot where Bhagu always stood waiting to catch a glimpse of her, she expected the usual emotion to assault her. And today, for the first time, when he looked at her, she was unable to look away. She was still reeling from the tangible emotion that had passed between them when the car reached the college gates.

This time her chauffeur was as alert to whatever was happening in front of him as behind. With incredulity he realised that the romance between his young mistress and the young man seemed to have progressed. Goodness, he thought, taken completely by surprise. He had known her since she was little and she was growing up. I'll bet Rajubai and her parents do not know. He wondered if he should tell.

Lou and Binny were at the gate. They prattled on happily before it registered that their friend wasn't listening. In fact, she looked somewhat dazed. "Are you alright Shali?"

"Ye-es I - I 'm fine."

"You look sort of peaky," said Lou.

"I-I'm fine, Lou. I've even eaten breakfast today." It wasn't such an irrational answer. Shali simply meant she wasn't sickened by the thought of food, something she'd always loved but had been put off lately. Slightly nonplussed by her reply, Lou looked at her friend queerly. "R ....ight," she said dubiously. Later, discussing their friend, Lou said to Binny, "If this is what 'love' does, I hope I don't catch it."

Shali and Bhagu really couldn't concentrate on their studies that day. It had been hopeless for a while but today it was simply unbearable. When she thought nobody was looking she stole a quick glance at Bhagu. Their eyes met for the second time that day and as before, it stopped her heart. Her eyes widened and then darkened with emotion. She did not look away for a long moment. Then, saner thoughts prevailed. The last thing she wanted was to be the subject of speculation in her class. Not yet. With a quick, weak little smile at him, she turned away.

That night, Bhagu, for the first time, hoped his dad would come home late. He waited impatiently for nine o'clock. And as the hour approached, tiny darts of anticipation winged through his body, affecting his breathing and making him feel light headed. At two minutes to nine, his stomach felt like it was permanently left behind on some giant ride at the fairground. And his heart pumped blood so loudly, it echoed in his mind. Would she call? What if she had changed her mind? He was nervous, elated and despondent all at the same time. At twenty seconds past nine he was convinced she had changed her mind. When the phone rang, his nerves were already jangled. He grabbed it off the hook with nerveless fingers and dropped it. Feeling embarrassed, yet full of anticipation, he grabbed it off the floor.

"Hello"

"Woa Bhagu, you O.K?" It was his dad. "Go ahead with dinner son. Mr. Mukherjee is coming over for a meeting. We might go out for dinner."

"Ye-es dad, fine." For once he was relieved. He looked at the clock once more. It showed one minute past nine. Why hasn't she called? he wondered. What if she tried while dad was on the line? he agonised. The minute he disconnected, the phone rang. For a second he stared at the receiver in shock, his eyes unseeing. Then, willing his nerveless fingers to reach for the receiver, he picked it up carefully. "Hello," he said for the second time within the space of a minute. "H-hi Bhagu." It was her. "Shali" His voice sounded so glad she smiled. "How are you?"

"I'm fine now!" Shalini couldn't help laughing. "Why, what was the matter earlier?" she asked, surprising herself with the archness of that question. "Guess," he said, a bit short of breath for this was the first time she'd flirted back.

Binny and Lou, had they been listening, would have wondered if their friends were right in the head. But then, they weren't in love - not yet.

- A Campaign –

It was the pretext of the canteen that provided the perfect excuse for them to meet almost thrice a day. Bhagu said he was planning a signature campaign. Finally the cat was out of the bag. It had to be him who had put up those posters. "I knew it," said Binny. "All those pithy one-liners….. But," she continued, "a signature campaign? We thought the banners and one liners were a nice way to get the message across. Isn't this taking things a bit too far?' she asked of Bhagu, full of misgiving. "I said exactly same thing to him," said Shali distractedly. "He scares me - I mean Chacha." Lou and Binny exchanged quick, triumphant looks. When had Shali said 'exactly the same thing' to Bhagu? Shali blushed, realising the implications of what she had just blurted out. Luckily for her, the two girls didn't pursue the matter. Bhagu said there wasn't any real harm in a signature campaign. Not in a democracy. Lou turned to him, saying bluntly, "What hi-faluting democracy are you talking about? Has anyone with any kind of clout ever been convicted of their crimes in our 'democracy'?" she challenged. "I can't help feeling there's real danger in crossing Chacha," said Binny worriedly. "He and his ilk don't play by the rules of …of, …"

"democracy?" supplied Lou dryly.

"The debating club," said Binny. "I mean," she added, "this is real life"

"I am not advocating anything drastic," said Bhagu mildly. "All I want is to start a signature campaign…" Shalini, in a rush of love immediately decided she would champion his cause. "That sounds harmless enough," she said, total support shining out of her eyes. Lou and Binny, totally unconvinced, didn't have the heart to dim the light in her eyes and reluctantly supposed it did. So the three girls, more with their hearts than with their heads, promised Bhagu their support.

Perhaps because he was aware of how shaky their support really was or perhaps because it was the best way to spend time with Shali, Bhagu quickly plunged them right into it. The canteen campaign took on a momentum of its own. It threw the four together often. Bhagu could have drafted an appeal in a jiffy but he reasoned that, four heads being better than one, he needed to meet with the three girls to discuss the wording. And all the time Binny and Lou could see Shalini walking on air. It was plainly written on their friend's face - she thought the world began and ended with Bhagu. Shalini did not bother to hide her feelings any more. Not at the college anyway. The time had come when she needed to listen to her own heart. Her fear of what her grandmother, her parents and the entire clan would say took second place. They had such a lot to talk about that sometimes Louella and Binny felt awkward standing around waiting for them to finish. She often monopolised the willing Bhagu in discussions that allowed her to discover a tiny bit more about him. And sometimes, they were both totally lost in the sight and sounds of each other.

Louella and Binny began to feel decidedly uncomfortable at having to be mute witnesses at such close quarters. Sometimes they had this inexplicable desire to giggle. Couldn't they just get on with the matter of the canteen, for heaven's sake?

They decided the next time the four met to "discuss the canteen", they would keep Shali and Bhagu on track about the p.o.a. and then sort of fade away.... The first time they made their getaway, they drifted off to admire the new plot of cannahs in the college grounds. After studying the flowers for a while, they kept waiting for Shalini to finish talking and join them. That was a mistake. Shalini, a sparkle in her eyes and a bounce to her step, joined them some twenty minutes later. Next time they did not even bother to wait. Binny and Lou felt a mix of emotions. Playing cupid had been fun. Those plots and schemes to help the cause of love had served their purpose. They were happy for their friend, but there was a slight feeling of loss.

Shalini and Bhagu were unaware of the buzz their romance was creating at Gyan Shakti. It wasn't that the two even so much as held hands. Yet, there was something so palpable in their awareness of each other as they walked side by side, completely in step, eyes smiling even as they looked straight ahead, that it somehow suffused the world around them with a warm glow. It was sort of nice to look on and bask in, what everyone sensed was, the beginnings of a romance.

And so, on the day Bhagu started his signature campaign, perhaps for all the wrong reasons, the two attracted quite a crowd. "I'd heard such rave reports about the previous Chacha," Bhagu said earnestly to his fellow students. "His coffee was supposedly better than Starbucks...If this Chacha learnt all he knows from his uncle, why do we get coffee that is so badly watered down?"

Everyone milled around the young couple, smiling at Shalini and listening to Bhagu, albeit warily, as he tried to convince them to sign up. They agreed with him that lunch at the canteen had become a dicey affair. They told him a few others had tried complaining before him. "Ah," said Bhagu, "individual complaints aren't as effective as a mass campaign." One or two students saw the handful of signatures he had collected and wondered at the rather emaciated "mass" he spoke of. Not having the heart to point it out to him, a few of them read his petition, willingly put their signatures to it, earned a smile from a grateful Shali and went off, happy to have done their deed for the day.

Binny and Lou, the other team, were a completely different story. The two had secretly talked it over and decided they were going ahead with the campaign only for their friends' sakes. Couldn't they get coffees at any number of Udipi joints a minute away from GS, for heaven's sakes! This was a complete waste of time. With an attitude like that, their campaign wasn't half the success Bhagu's was. One of the students reminded them that others before them had tried, that they weren't the first. Lou told him to shut-up and sign up. "It will cost you," he laughed.

"Ye ..es?" challenged Lou, a hand on her hip, one eyebrow shooting up to meet her hairline. "Join me for a cup of watered down coffee at the canteen," he said, unable to stop grinning. He included Binny in the invitation.

"Ha ha, very funny," said Lou. But in spite of herself, she found herself grinning back. "On one condition...," she said. "Well...?" the young man was surprised he might have pulled it off. "Help us collect a few signatures?" Lou meant that to be as cheeky a demand as his but couldn't prevent her voice ending on a hopeful, even slightly desperate, note. The young man laughed outright. "That way, we finish the damn thing faster and then we can all go across for that awful coffee," she finished quickly, aware with a slight blush that she was shamelessly holding out a bribe. "Sorry Lou," he shook his head. "You know where to find me if you change your mind." Lou and Binny looked after his receding figure regretfully and then with a sigh, went back to the business of collecting signatures. "God, I'm thirsty," muttered Binny to Lou, her eyes wandering with longing towards the canteen. But later, when they saw the pleased expression in Bhagu's eyes at their (admittedly dismal) effort, they felt gratified. The ever optimistic Bhagu was sure that before the week was up, the faculty would be forced to sit up and take notice. Between them, on their first day, they had collected about forty five signatures. There were only a couple of thousand more to go.

- Ostriches -

On the third day of the campaign, on his way home from college, Bhagu was accosted by four goondas (thugs). Unable to believe it was him they were after, he stood rooted to the spot looking at them enquiringly, almost politely, as their car with no number plates screeched to a halt at his bus stop. They got out of the car, laathis (sticks) in hand, and advanced at almost a leisurely pace on him, so confident were they that no one would dare stop them. Finally it dawned on Bhagu

111

that they were, indeed, after him. He tried to run for it but it was hopeless. He was beaten almost to a pulp. It took exactly one minute but was efficient and merciless. Everyone, except the four were frozen to the spot and soon they vanished in their getaway car. With several ribs, his nose, an arm and a leg broken, he was simply left in his own pool of blood and an agony of pain. People looked on, frozen with horror. Many melted away from the scene in haste.

Finally, having witnessed the brutal beating of a fellow Mumbaikar – and that too, one so young, troubled someone's conscience enough to summon a scared cabbie. Together they took him to the nearest hospital. They knew what their reward would be for being good Samaritans. They would be peremptorily summoned to the police station several times over the next few weeks, probably kept waiting, their own time, effort or money of no consequence, as the police meticulously recorded as many details of the case as possible – perhaps to be able to solve it but more, so their backsides were completely covered. But for the moment, luckily for Bhagu, they ignored the knowledge of the harassment that was to follow or indeed, even the fact that they might be beaten up by the same goons for daring to help.

There were several witnesses, including the cabbie and the kind gentleman. But, as the police well knew, nobody was crazy enough to describe or identify the four men. It was an 'open and shut' case for the 'standard' police enquiry.

Underneath the seeming appearance of normal life, Bombay was a hotbed of unrest. Almost everyday there were stories of fights between rival gangs and someone getting killed. Everyone suspected the collusion of politicians and the police with these gangs. Decent people lived with the uneasy knowledge that there were sinister things happening in their city, things they didn't wish to delve too deeply into. They felt threatened from all quarters, watching with horror and helplessness as the bad elements crawled out of their hidey holes, bolder by the second. These criminals had links to a politician who they might have done "personal favours" for and who, for fear of his own links to the gang being exposed would rather let their crimes go unpunished. In such an atmosphere, not knowing who was linked with whom, decent people effaced themselves as much as possible, quietly going about their own business, aware that if they volunteered any information, they might well be the next victims.

At the college suspicion fell on Chacha. But no one dared voice it openly - not because they believed in the maxim that a man was innocent until proven guilty but because God alone knew who Chacha had links to.

Prof Naakwa, on hearing of the incident felt vaguely uneasy. Why was the young man, Bhagu, beaten up? he wondered. He seems a likeable young chap. Is someone trying to get at his father? Or, thought the professor, his heart full of misgivings, is it anything to do with the last Student Council meeting and this signature campaign I've been hearing about?

He invited his most trusted colleagues to discuss the matter.

- Dr. Naakwa Assesses the Situation -

Very little that happened at the college escaped Dr. Naakwa's attention. He had known the current Chacha since he had first arrived in Mumbai – almost ten years ago. His cousin had approached the faculty for an assistant. They could've picked anyone from Bombay but he requested they consider his cousin from the village. The cousin had had a run of bad luck. He had lost his eldest child. It would be good for him. "Besides," he said candidly, "I would never be able to trust anyone as much as my own clansman."

From the start Dr. Naakwa had misgivings about the second Chacha. His cousin had been with the college right from the word go and was an affable, likeable chap. He enjoyed the students and they, him. This Chacha somehow didn't fit in. For one, he believed women belonged in the kitchen and academia was no place for them. He was rude to the point of being offensive with them. The faculty and students were mildly amused. They thought, given time and his cousin's influence, he would change.

The college gave both the Chachas a generous salary. When the elder Chacha started getting his horrific headaches, the college decided he would continue receiving his full salary while he was ill.

When he died, the entire college was shocked. They had expected him to get better. Everyone mourned his loss. It was expedient to let the second Chacha carry on as, after his cousin's training and two years experience at the college, he knew the trade. To Dr. Naakwa's surprise, he continued looking after the first Chacha's young family.

Today, Dr. Naakwa wondered if he had made the right decision. I blame myself for letting the matter of the canteen get to this stage, he thought. There have been so many indicators. I should have been alerted when the banners started appearing; the light hearted jokes in the college Patrika, the talk in the teachers' room; the messages on blackboards and darts...

The faculty had discussed the matter in an amused and desultory manner. They had even declared it was healthy and democratic to let the students have their say. And they had maintained the status quo, hoping the problem would resolve itself. Chacha's action jolted Dr. Naakwa out of his complacency. There was no proof, of course. But it was a possibility he couldn't ignore. It was worse than anything he could have imagined. Professors Billimoria, Sapre and Dr. Naakwa closeted themselves in a room to discuss the matter. After an hour of looking at the problem from all angles they realised there seemed very little they could do. They couldn't give Chacha a warning. Where was the proof? He would simply deny all knowledge of the beating and probably laugh all the way back to his canteen. To see them so utterly powerless and ineffective was one satisfaction they couldn't allow him. They had to rule out the police. They didn't trust them. They were easily bribeable. Some of them would probably be in Chacha's pocket already. He was the unacknowledged leader of his slum colony. They couldn't approach Mr. Khanna - the local M.P. To even get an appointment, they'd have to bribe everyone to the hilt – from the doorman to the secretary. And donate generously into either Mr. Khanna's private funds or towards the party election funds. Or both. They were willing to do anything, even that, if there were any guarantees of success. But they had to conclude that course of action wouldn't produce anything useful. Mr. Khanna would institute his own special brand of enquiry into the incident, like, would it

115

cost him a block vote[30] - Chacha's slum colony's block vote - if he decided to bring the culprits to justice. Dr. Naakwaa and his allies had absolutely no illusions about the outcome of that inquiry.

That left ... them. They had dithered too much already. They'd have to think of something fast before everything snowballed out of control. They decided, even if they were lashing out in the dark, it would be worth their while to spend money on an investigative agency. For starters they would collect a dossier on Chacha. Surely they'd find something they could use against him. At the end of the meeting, Dr. Naakwa remained where he was, thinking about young Bhagu, imagining his brutalised body lying in the hospital bed. When he gets back to college, he thought with a slight shake of his head, I have every intention of knocking some sense - hmm, unfortunate choice of words under the circumstances, he smiled to himself - into this idealistic, likeable, totally impractical and impulsive youngster.

Putting on his calm, inscrutable expression, Dr. Naakwa went for his next lecture.

- The Student Council -

It was the beginning of a new week. Chacha felt omnipotent and smug. He had made his point. He was bustling about busily, preparing for the morning break. The canteen was still one of the most popular places to hang out and socialise. It would soon be packed. Chacha did brisk business and wasn't concerned about intangibles like 'potential' income. He sincerely believed it was

---

30 Block vote – an entire group voting for the party of their leader's choice.

good business practice to dilute the cold drinks and water down the milk. It was no easy task. But who said making money was easy?

He often had to come in after the college was deserted. He had keys to the back gate but had scouted around to see if he could use other means to get in undetected. He didn't want the gate squeaking open when he wasn't supposed to be there. His efforts paid off as he discovered that the bark of a mango tree formed part of the boundary wall. Carefully prising out the bricks right next to the tree he had made a barely visible gap which he could squeeze through to carry out his nefarious activities.

He never pushed his luck when it came to the faculty. Their drinks were undiluted. But he did pretty much what he wanted with the studentlog[31] and now, they knew what happened to the ones who tried to complain. Today, as usual, he was ruling the roost, the ultimate don of his domain, when he realised it was 9 am. The morning bell had gone. 'Strange!' he thought, 'where are the early birds?' By mid-day when still nobody had turned up, Chacha understood they weren't coming. "Ah well,' he thought, still pretty smug, 'they're sulking. They'll keep away for a day or two but they can't keep away for ever.'

After news of Bhagu's horrific beating spread through the college, students, completely of their own volition, deserted the canteen. No one wanted to even look at it, so sickened and put off were they. Their footsteps led them instead, to the union office. There they sat, whispering, wondering and hoping for some news of Bhagu...

---

31 Log pronounced logue and meaning folk

There never were so many students at the union office before. Most preferred to keep away. To be honest, the union and its activities were anathema to most of them. They weren't at the college to upset any apple-carts. They were here to study. Period. But today they were hurting for the young man who had almost single-handedly, with only his girlfriend, and two other unlikely volunteers in tow, tried to do what they themselves had often itched to. Where they had been too apathetic, he had had the courage to try. As they put it, "One has to admire his guts for attempting the impossible."

Binny, Lou and Shali were given their fair share of credit too. Shali was distraught after hearing of Bhagu's ordeal. Binny and Lou really regretted giving in to him about the signature campaign against their better judgement. Whenever they stepped out, it was with trepidation as they couldn't help wondering if the same treatment would be meted out to them. But they were reasonably convinced the Mumbai *junta*, public, wouldn't tolerate ladies being beaten up on the roads.

For the first couple of days Shali couldn't keep away from the hospital. To lend her support, Binny and Lou stayed with her. They didn't witness the impromptu meeting at the union office. They heard about it the next day.

The number of students gathered at the union office swelled to overflowing, spilling out into the corridors. Some of the students gathered there had witnessed Bhagu's beating and their whispered description of what they had witnessed added poignancy to the outpouring of sympathy for the likeable young man. And slowly the sympathy turned to burning anger.

The Union members saw their opportunity, one they were determined not to squander. They had tried so often to recruit members, but most students preferred to keep away. The president spoke to the crowd.

He said the canteen wasn't just a place to eat. It was where they met to socialise, to discuss and even to study. "Chacha doesn't own it," he said, a slight tremor in his voice betraying his controlled anger. "If we want it back, if we wish to show any respect for the one courageous person who tried, we must all take the same stance he did."

"We are all united and determined right now. BUT, are we going to let off steam and then let the whole thing fizzle out? If we want RESULTS, if we want Bhagu's courageous, almost single-handed action to be worth the beating he took for it, we need to follow this up with an action plan." He then asked for suggestions as to what unified action they wanted. The response was overwhelming. The suggestions, some good and some not so good, came hard and fast. With everyone speaking up, nobody was afraid any more. It was heady stuff. Finally, after much discussion, it was decided that a space would be reserved in the weekly union newsletter – the Patrika - for the latest inspired quote; that they'd take up where Bhagu had left off - continue with his signature campaign; that to match action to words (of the memo), they would go nowhere near the canteen for seven days, after which they would monitor daily, what every student had to say about the coffee. Where there were four volunteers earlier, this time, there were two hundred. Everyone present was eager to put their names to the memo. To strengthen their resolve and commitment the union leaders ended the meeting with a march. Self conscious but enthused all the same, students filed out of the union office.

"2 4 6 8, who do we appreciate?"
"Bha --- gu."

"Nahi haarengey, nahi haarengey (Won't be defeated)
Canteen mein mazedaar coffee piyengey" (we'll drink choice coffee at the canteen)

Pretty unoriginal, but all the union wanted was a show of strength. Everyone except the union leaders dispersed after that rush of adrenaline. The ones left behind drafted the memo and came up with yet another brilliant idea. Photographs. One of them rushed to the hospital, gaining entry by claiming to be Bhagu's brother, which he justified to himself by asserting that he felt a certain kinship to the brave young man. Developed overnight and enlarged to a decent size, one was of the now conscious Bhagu –an arm and a leg in plaster, face a swollen mask of pain, nose hidden in a plaster, eyes mere slits, yet smiling for the camera. And the other, Shalini and her two friends captured unawares in the hospital corridors, anxiety writ large on their faces. The next day the crowds were back in full force. Everyone had heard there were photographs. They wanted to see for themselves. And what they saw left no one untouched.
Within a couple of days, armed with a couple of thousand signatures, the president, committee members and 15 members of the union general body approached Dr. Naakwa. They were jubilant for their plan was working.

No one had yet been anywhere near the canteen. They handed in their memo and spelt out their plan.

The experienced and worldly wise Dr. Naakwa, not convinced of the continued success of the latest campaign, gave it a much needed shot in the arm. He and some of his trusted colleagues summoned a relatively chastised Chacha to his office, one who had had a bit of a quiet week. When the faculty sent for him, for the first time he felt the stirrings of fear. He wondered if his job was on the line. It was a sobering thought. Everything took second place to his ability to feed his family and that of his dead uncle's. A relatively cowed Chacha presented himself at Dr. Naakwaa's office. The four professors sat there looking grave and imposing. Dr. Naakwaa's voice was surprisingly kind when he started talking. Mentioning that the students had complained about the food and with a great show of concern for Chacha's time he said, "Two years ago, our Chacha, your uncle requested that you be brought on board to help him cope with the increase in volume. It is only fair we do the same for you now. We know how difficult it is, managing on your own." Chacha nodded, eager to grasp the excuse they handed him. "We have found just the man to assist you," smiled Professor Billimoria. "And he seems anxious to help." Chacha waited expectantly. "Maaroji from Chinchpokli," Professor Reddy said softly, almost casually. Their expressions carefully pleasant, they watched him closely. Chacha paled. Feeling cornered for the first time, he tried to think coherently. The name they mentioned didn't belong to any old person off the streets – someone he could bully and keep in his place. It belonged to the leader of the slum in the next suburb. "Do ...do you mean Meethuram

121

Maaroji," he said hoarsely. They nodded. He knew what that meant. The faculty had somehow found out who his bitterest rival was. Wondering what else they knew about him he recognised the threat, couched though it was in words of concern. It was so much worse than anything he had expected. The crook from the rival gang would not only swallow every pai[32] of his profits, having him interfere in the canteen would completely erode his - Chacha's - power base at his own slum. He would be reduced to a laughing stock.

He was ready to comply. Hands joined in supplication he pleaded with the faculty. He hastened to assure them he could cope. He had been busy trying to get tap water for his slum and might have neglected the canteen.

"We hope you've been successful," enquired Dr. Nakwa.

"Yes sir," said Chacha, "it is all done."

"In that case," interjected Dr. Nakwa warningly, "I hope you will never neglect the canteen, serve anything substandard *or* threaten anyone who reports it. I personally am going to keep tabs through not just one but many handpicked students." Chacha almost protested but Meethuram Maroji's threat was too real. He bit back his objection and instead, promised humbly. He begged for a second chance.

In truth, the faculty hadn't and wouldn't even dream of speaking to Chacha's rival. Gang warfare on their territory – no thank-you. But Chacha wasn't to know that. They realised what it cost him to be humble and decided to give him another chance. Only, this time, they were the ones with the trumps and that is how it was going to stay.

---

32 Pai: Old Indian currency – term still in use.

After a relieved Chacha was gone, Dr. Naakwaa grimly locked away the thick dossier titled, "Chacha" hoping it was for good. What he'd read in it had given him an insight into Chacha's psyche as nothing ever would.

From the very next week things changed for the better. From the students' perspective, it was an unprecedented victory. They found Chacha's fare doubly delicious for it had the sweet taste of success. The students had their canteen back and Chacha seemed to be the winner. In his absence, Bhagu's stature at the college grew. The odds had been stacked against him. Nobody had wanted to take part in his campaign. He had been pounded to a pulp. Yet, undaunted and unshaken in his belief, he had taken the first, singlehanded, courageous steps.

- BHAGU –

It would be another month before Bhagu went back to college. At first, his dad, with the help of the extended family who came over from other parts of the country, looked after him. Within a few days, grateful but relieved, Bhagu and his dad were on their own again, with Ramu, their resident manservant, looking after Bhagu's needs at home. From witnessing his son incapable of moving, to being able to hobble around the house with the help of a walking stick was immensely reassuring. Soon, work claimed Mr. Bhagu Sr. as well.

One day, a young lady paid off an autorickshaw – a three wheeler taxi, and rang his doorbell. Ramu opened the door, amazed. The young lady said she had brought Bhagu his homework. Never had Ramu seen Bhagu so glad to see his homework. Shalini started dropping by everyday. Rather than visit him after college in her car, she preferred missing lectures every afternoon. She didn't want her chauffeur, who picked her up in the evenings, to mention her afternoon jaunts to her parents.

Within two weeks of returning home from the hospital Bhagu longed to get back to his active lifestyle and the college. His entire day was built around the hour Shalini spent with him. Ramu, his live-in manservant, let her in every afternoon. She did not know what he really thought of her lame excuse of bringing Bhagu his homework but since he didn't mention it, she held her peace. The house so lacked a woman's touch, Ramu couldn't be happier. He watched her closely. She nursed Bhagu with tenderness. Neither his slight limp, nor his slit like eyes in the slightly swollen face seemed to bother her. She did not cringe nor show any revulsion. Just a deep pity and often, if Bhagu winced with pain when his ribs felt sore, he saw her quietly suffer for his master. And, old Ramu smiled toothlessly to himself, she is quite pretty. Ill though he was, Bhagu couldn't help noticing the effect her presence had on his manservant. He let her in before she knocked. And before he (Bhagu) had time to greet her, Ramu was there again, a glass of cold water on a tray. A tray, thought Bhagu, amused. Something Ramu had never bothered with for him or his dad. Before long, Ramu doddered in again, smiling ingratiatingly, a snack he'd obviously taken pains to prepare and make visually appealing, on another tray. Amused at first, Bhagu started feeling that Ramu had started vying for her time with him. And he hovers, he thought, slightly vexed. He, who had always shuffled about sloppily, started treading the floor softly. It made Bhagu jump. "Why are you creeping about so," he accused Ramu when, without any warning, he felt Ramu's presence in the room again. Ramu blushed, feeling slightly exposed by his young master's petulant observation. But he was gratified by the young lady's soft 'thank-you.'

With the resilience of youth, Bhagu was fast getting back to normal. His limp had all but disappeared; his ribs weren't so painful any more. As for the swelling on his face, it seemed to have vanished completely. His broken nose had healed somewhat crooked, giving him a slightly hawkish look. Shalini said it suited him. He laughed at her obvious prejudice.

Soon, Shali was spending her last afternoon at Bhagu's. He was going back to college the next day. The hour simply seemed to fly. Shali looked at her watch and declared it was time for her to go. "What?" asked an incredulous Bhagu. "Already? It seems like you've barely arrived, Shali," he complained. "Ramu shadows you around like some lost puppy and I hardly get any time with you.' She spent some time cheering him up, reminding him that from tomorrow, they'd be able to spend all their time together. As she made to leave, Ramu was already racing as fast as his old limbs could carry him, to open the door. Bhagu made a face behind his back. Smiling, she waved to him, thanked Ramu gravely and left. Bhagu watched his manservant grin idiotically, join his hands in a namaste and shake his almost bald head from side to side with delight. He thought with a slight shake of his own head, Ramu has never behaved so ... so... and after searching for the

right word for a while, could only come up with 'besotted.'

It had been wonderful having Shali. He would have
gone slowly mad without her visits to look forward to.
But, he thought with relief, from tomorrow, I won't
have to worry about dad returning home unexpectedly
in the afternoon and my having to explain Shali's presence. It was a prospect that had haunted him constantly.
That wasn't how he wanted to introduce her to his dad.

Surprisingly Ramu had kept his own counsel. Bhagu
didn't know if it was because he thought it might stop
her from coming around or because he'd sensed and
respected Bhagu's wishes. God, he was happy. He
closed his eyes...I wish it were tomorrow already, he
thought. Ramu looked at the blissful expression on his
face.' My young master is …..besotted, he thought with
a shake of his head, quite besotted!

Bhagu went back to the college to a hero's welcome.
Everywhere he went, people wanted to shake his hand
or thump him on the back. He quite enjoyed all the attention. They dragged him off to the canteen. A rather
subdued Chacha served him a cup of the thickest,
creamiest of coffees. Bhagu, gratified, thanked him with
no vestige of hostility. He was more than willing to
meet Chacha's offer of a call for truce.

But Chacha couldn't help thinking it was this very person who had challenged his leadership and almost
made him lose his livelihood. Threatened by the effects
of a deserted canteen and by the prospect of a rival taking over, he had been willing to be amenable to almost
anything. But deep down inside, now that the students
were back and his livelihood wasn't at stake, he had begun to feel sore and resentful. Although the students

were back he somehow felt he had lost face. He was the leader of his slum. Everyone respected him there. They did his bidding. He was used to calling the shots. Over here, these youngsters looked at him as if they had beaten him at some game. He blamed only one person for that. When he thought no one was looking, he darted Bhagu a quick look of pure malevolence. He might be cowed but he'd bide his time. One day he'd take his revenge. He knew he did not dare have Bhagu beaten up again. If he had his way, he'd beat everyone who had forced his hand. Only one thing kept him toeing the line. Fear. What if the faculty made good their threat of bringing in that goon from the neighbouring slum?

Shali, who had looked up to order a plate of ragda-pattice, saw the look on his face, a chill crawling up her skin and into her heart. Later she told Bhagu about it. Bhagu, ever the optimist, pooh-poohed her fears. Chacha might feel resentful now but he, Bhagu, had wonderful ideas for the canteen like advertising space in the college patrika; value meals. Chacha would see his turnover doubled within days and realise he didn't really need to waste time adulterating milk or cold drinks with water. With a great inward sigh Shali smiled shakily and let it go.

- CHAPTER II –

And then one day, like a jolt from the blue, it was brought to bear upon them, how insecure their relatively safe little world at Gyan Shakti really was.

Binny, with a light and happy step, headed straight for the canteen. The aroma of freshly ground coffee hit her when she was half way down the narrow stone path. Sniffing appreciatively, she thought, 'Ummm, this can be sooo addictive.' Lou had hers strong and she loved hers in a glass of pure, undiluted milk.

The two young women had long adapted to their routine a deux at the college. Binny was full of anticipation, certain that Lou, Partha and the rest would already be crowded around their favourite table drinking Chacha's delicious coffees. "Ah, here she comes - all set to save Kurien,[33]" yelled someone from the crowd. "Chacha, ek coffee with jyada milk," said another, a coffee with more milk… "Nahi *yaar*, ek milk with…" said Lou. "Yeah-yeah!" Binny interrupted good humouredly, "it is better than the bitter brew you poison yourself with every morning." There was a loud cackle from the group - the kind that would have set Dr. Naakwa's teeth on edge.

And so she was welcomed into the familiar fold.

Reasonably content in their beautiful canteen, their little patch of green in this city of concrete, Binny, Lou and friends discussed the travails of life in Mumbai. The discussions were purely academic - the corruption! the

---

33 Kurien – A mini Indian icon who, in spite of government restrictions and licences, managed to fill the shelves of Indian shops with tetrapacks of milk in a move known as "operation flood". Milk has never been a scarcity after that.

crime! They were privileged youngsters and to varying degrees, relatively untouched by it all. As they philosophised and celebrated their young lives, time ticked away inexorably towards the moment when a sinister event was to overtake them with a vengeance. It crept closer as they sat there, enjoying themselves, unaware. It hit the city so suddenly it left them reeling. The first bomb went off at the Stock Exchange building. And by the end of the day, there had been ten more[34]. As people tried to vent their grief and anger, they looked for someone to blame. Angry mobs quickly took over the streets of Bombay. They were brutal in their desire to exact revenge. Some had their own hidden agendas for the violence but all seemed to have only one thing on their minds – hurting human beings from another community by any means - beatings, killings, destruction or looting. Even after their anger was spent, many of them, drunk on their complete power over their city and her residents, were reluctant to relinquish control. The ordinary Mumbaikar went into hiding.

With their usual agonising slowness and ineptitude and after many thousands of lives were lost – economics always having more sway than ordinary Indian lives - the authorities decided to send in the Indian army to restore confidence and order. The ordinary Mumbaikar slowly emerged out of hiding.

- 2 -

I stood at the door of the class. The silence was almost eerie. Could these be the same spirited youngsters? Where was all the incessant chatter? Their faces seemed

---

34 Based on a real event, probably the first simultaneous, synchronised bombings ever, that took place in 1993. Though reported internationally the deliberately planned and organised incident did not cause much of a ripple in the rest of the world.

to have aged with grief. Nobody had anything to say. There was the young Parsee girl - what was her name? Ginny or something. What a different face from the one ablaze with happiness on that very first day, almost three years ago. Today, Binny was white faced and silent – as were Shali, Lou, Bhagu and all the rest. They were still in shock. And nobody was sure if the violence and hatred had spent itself or if there was more to come. They looked wounded and bewildered, the question uppermost on their mind, "who could hate us so much? And why?"

I realised it was weighing them down to such a degree it would be pointless to try and deal with things academic. This unspoken issue needed addressing first. It will be a long healing process, I thought grimly. And it had fallen on me to at least attempt a beginning. Once more, I walked quietly into the room. Once more I put a couple of books and the class register down on the side of the polished wooden table. I touched the edge of the sturdy long table for a long thoughtful moment before I finally looked up. One or two senior students looked at me expectantly. Their silence hurt. They were like helpless, rudderless, stricken and wounded young children. As I began speaking in grave tones, I knew they listened, even if their young faces looked down at their desks. "A terrible tragedy has hit our city and we are all reeling under its aftermath. We are all in shock." I paused, selecting my next words with utmost care. "But we would do our city a grave disservice if we let it cripple or divide us."

"Whoever wanted that to happen," I continued, suddenly knowing what I must say, "is being sought by our city fathers. We can only hope that they will succeed in their quest to bring the culprits to justice."

And then, spacing my next words, I carefully spelt out a possible course of action. "Let - them - deal - with - their - side - of - things - and - we - will - deal - with - ours."

I knew I had to talk about the dead. Many of these youngsters would have witnessed death for the very first time. But it was difficult, even for me. "We owe it to the innocent victims who lost their lives to show that whoever committed these cowardly and horrific acts, will not triumph - not in crippling our city nor dividing it. We owe it to the victims to make every effort to go on as before, …undivided, …united, …as Indians."

"I now request all of you to stand and observe a two minute silence for the people of our city whose lives were lost so tragically and so needlessly by the actions of others. They might have been young or old and they might have been from any community - it matters not. We grieve for them and we honour them because first and foremost they were human beings - and also because," my voice cracked slightly but I held on grimly, "they were from Mumbai."

- 3 -

At break, Binny and Lou decided to have one of Chacha's decoction coffees. As they were heading towards the canteen, Shali hurried to catch up with them. She had time to spare as Bhagu was busy with the college union. None of them had the stomach for anything solid. The girls sat sipping their coffee in silence. Lou was the first to break the silence. "I still can't believe it," she whispered. "Can you?"

131

"No," Shali shook her head slightly, eyes moist and wide.

"Up until now, even the word 'bomb' simply meant noisy fireworks to me!" said Binny, her voice shaky. Lou and Shalini couldn't help smiling at that but Binny didn't even notice - so disturbed was she. She continued distractedly, "And now, to think we suddenly have to deal with not just one but eleven of them! All in one day! And those riots!" Binny kept exclaiming softly and shaking her head as if she were still in denial.

"I wonder who did it," whispered Shali. The newspapers were already throwing up possibilities. What was gnawing at all of them was the fear that another explosion could go off anywhere, anytime. Even going home on the train was a scary prospect for Binny.

"I always thought we were safe in our city while the rest of the world was going mad. And now," she said, sounding sorry for herself, "I don't feel so safe any more."

"No one is safe any more," said Lou, feeling sorry for herself, for all of them ...for Mumbai. "Ours isn't such a safe city any more," said Shali glumly. Lou and Binny shook their heads in agreement. A long, thoughtful silence followed. Then Shali leaned forward as if she didn't want others to hear what she had to say and started confiding in whispers, "When Bhagu, with the sheer power of his words, convinced the club that we were one big happy family in spite of our differences, I believed him because it was the happier image and I wanted so desperately for it to be true. I ignored what my mind told me - that it simply wasn't true about many Mumbaikars. Bharati, on the other hand, said very uncomplimentary things about our bigotry and the majority taking the easy way out and I resented that. But I can't help thinking now that she was right." The thought had long been a tiny niggling worry at the back of her mind. Today, it desperately needed airing. There! She had finally said it! It was a tremendous relief to get it out into the open at last. As for Binny and Lou, so finely tuned were they to what she felt, they had no trouble hearing her whispered words. They had this sense of discomfiture about their city too and Shali's confession opened the floodgates. Lou and Binny almost tripped over their words - so eager were they to share their thoughts. "I feel all the positive things he pointed out do happen," said Binny, "did happen," she amended, uncertain if they would continue happening, "but I don't know why we avoid voicing our unease about the intolerance between communities…"

"That's easy, Binny," said Lou, "we would rather pretend it didn't exist. But it simmers under the surface all the time."

"We sit up and take notice only when it erupts," said Shali, which brought their thoughts back to the riots. They were silent once more.

The destruction and violence had been on such an unprecedented scale that each of them knew of at least one person - an acquaintance, a neighbour, friend, even family - who'd been affected. It was one thing reading about bombs going off in far away places which they had up until then. But now finally, regrettably, they had been set off in their own city. There were stories of blame, revenge, settling of old scores, even killings. They whispered the stories to each other – disturbed that there were such stories to tell at all. They heard each other out, believing what the others said completely, but unable to come to terms with the horror of what people from their own city had done to each other. As they grappled with what Mumbaikars were capable of doing Shali, a genuine desire to understand in her voice said, "How can their prejudice blunt their sensitivity to another human being's Physical Pain?" The other two looked at her, unable to help her out with any answers. "Wish we could simply pick them up and throw them back into the dark ages or something," Lou burst out in frustration. "Then they could fight away with each other to their hearts' content." The other two smiled wanly. "We can't seem to do a thing to stop them," said Binny hopelessly, after a long silence. "We are such cowards really, all we can do is go into hiding," she added sadly. "Yes," said Shali, "and emerge only after the destruction is complete."

"Like worms out of wood," said Lou in disgust, eager to confer the lowliest of sentiments upon themselves. "…sweat out of pores," agreed Shali, understanding Lou's emotions. "…kids out of class," said Binny, keen to agree with the general consensus but unable to come up with anything quite appropriate.

For a full twenty seconds Lou and Shali made genuine efforts to understand. Finally giving up, they looked at her blankly. "You know," she said, and when it was clear from their faces they didn't, launched reluctantly into an explanation which sounded as convincing as a Parsi teaching Marathi, "how a school looks almost deserted during class time and when the bell goes for recess, it's suddenly full of … rowdy kids…" Her voice trailed away.

"Oh," her friends digested the information with serious faces. Then, their natural high spirits getting the better

134

of them, they laughed helplessly at Binny's strange metaphor. But their laughter was tinged with nervousness. Darting quick glances at the other tables to see if it had been noticed, the girls hastily quashed it. At such times it might seem crass and insensitive.

It was a harsh judgment they inflicted upon themselves, albeit in seeming jest. It was much easier not to have to come face to face with one's own weaknesses. But at times like these, some soul searching was inevitable. And what they saw didn't make the girls feel exactly proud. "But," said Binny, continuing the conversation as if it hadn't been interrupted, "we all know what would happen to us or our families, if we tried to stop them."

"Besides," said Shali, "where are the police at such times? It is exactly as Bharati argued," she said with a shiver. "The goondas know their power is so complete they'll never be caught or punished."[35] The media had often decried the 'nexus between the politicians, the police and the underworld', Bharati had spoken about it at their debating club and scores of movies from Bollywood had made it their central theme. The villains in these movies were so brutal they were grotesquely inhuman. But the tragedy of it all was that everyone had begun to accept that such villains existed in real life too; that they were organised into Bombay's underworld, the mafia and gangs. It was hard to accept and yet impossible to ignore. What else were they to believe? For the second time after Bhagu was beaten up, Binny, Lou and Shali had witnessed firsthand, acts of extreme violence that were well thought out, planned and executed.

---

35 Their confidence seems to have been justified for even today, years later, the culprits have yet to be caught or punished.

After a while, even the worst memories fade and the normal sights and sounds superimpose themselves on peoples' minds. But each time, events like these always leave a little indelible mark on Mumbai's psyche. It says to them that somehow, Mumbai isn't working as it is supposed to; that in times of trouble, ordinary Mumbai-kars have no recourse to justice. The Indian armed forces are the only agency that all decent and ordinary Mumbaikers still feel relatively safe with.

This last spate had been so intensely savage and brutal, its memory would take a long time to fade.

- The Young Lovers -

A few months passed. Mumbai was slowly limping back to normal. The riots were already a bad memory. At the college, professors had started calling the final year students for extra coaching. The extra classes were a great excuse for Bhagu and Shali to spend even more time together. Their trysts were often behind the broad trunks of the banyans. They especially loved the quiet solitude of the college in the early evenings after almost everyone had gone home. That's when they spent some time sitting on one of the thick, over-ground roots. After she'd seen the look on Chacha's face, Shali ensured they were out well before the gates were shut and the college completely deserted. Bhagu felt she was a little too nervous and that given time, Chacha's hurt pride would heal.

Feeling utterly content in each other's company they talked softly, their heads close together. Sitting with Bhagu, Shali suddenly remembered her conversation with Lou and Binny after the riots. She couldn't help smiling as she remembered Binny's comparison of cowardly Bombayites coming out of hiding, to kids rushing out of classrooms. Watching her, Bhagu couldn't help admiring the tilt of her nose, the dusky smoothness of her skin and her even, white teeth showing through the slight smile on her lips. She turned to him, her smile growing wider as she decided she'd tell him about how Binny had missed the point. It had completely slipped her mind until today. Bhagu listened quietly as she talked. "And Bhagu, your argument was so much more palatable, it was almost as if we wanted to believe in it. Although immediately after the riots," she couldn't help shuddering as she mentioned them, "we felt Bharati had a point too. Bombay does seem to be full of goondas and bigots who have no tolerance for anyone or anything even a bit different." Bhagu went quiet. Finally he said softly, "You know Shali, at that time it was simply a debate I wanted to win. I was out to impress a girl," he half kidded, making her bury her face into his shoulder. He hugged her close and was silent for a moment. Content, she listened to his heartbeat. After a while she heard his voice mingle with the heartbeat. For a moment it was the timbre of the voice she took pleasure in, not really taking in what he said. "But even I can't help thinking Bharati was right. I wish we could have another debate. I'd argue it differently."

"Oh no Bhagu!" The exclamation was torn from her. She looked up to find him looking sombrely at her. Doesn't he have any concern for his own safety, she thought, slightly alarmed that he might just go ahead and organise one at the club. How would he argue it differently? Talk about the riots? Whatever could he hope to achieve? Didn't he understand it was still too early to speak on such sensitive issues? What if he said something to upset someone? Anger someone? He's already been roughed up once, she thought. Does he want it to happen again? He isn't thinking straight right now. What she didn't realise was how much Bhagu being beaten up, coupled with the look she'd caught on Chacha's face, had affected her. She looked so alarmed for him that Bhagu felt a sudden wave of tenderness for her. It felt good to have her worry for him. Unable to help himself, he pulled her to him and held her close for a second. He was about to let go when she moved closer, burying her face in his chest. As she snuggled up to him, his arms tightened around her. Her senses felt alive to his touch, and unable to help herself, she gave a deep, yearning, consoling, lingering kiss close to his lips. It was so close he only had to turn a fraction…

A long moment passed. Her fingers unconsciously trailed a slow, tremulous path down his arm. "I must go," she said reluctantly, aware that the driver would be waiting. Bhagu watched her fingers, mesmerised, "You must," he agreed shakily, his entire being rejecting the words. For another long moment the two sat there, lost. Finally, slightly happier, Shalini jumped up, waved, smiled, and was gone.

Bhagu remained there long after she'd left. The depth of his feelings for her did not surprise him. He had been attracted to her from the first day when her beautiful eyes had accidentally looked into his. He leaned back and closed his eyes, wanting to hold on to the memory of her presence for as long as he could. Slowly, he let it envelope his entire being. Thankfully, her rejection of him was a thing of the past. She accepted now that they belonged together. She had told him about the doubts that had assailed her - doubts she still had. He knew they could only carry on seeing each other if her family were kept in the dark. He wished it didn't have to be like that. Well, sooner or later, they would have to know. What was important was that she had promised she would marry him - that she couldn't and wouldn't marry anyone else. With her by his side, he could face anything. An image of her in his home, his dad and Ramu smiling on with approval, flashed through his mind. It was so real, he sat up, transfixed. His eyes flew open. Then, unable to contain himself, he jumped up and walked out of the college through the barely visible little gap he and Shali had discovered between the trunk of the mango tree and the brick wall. He walked fast, holding on to those images of Shali in his home. His face wore an idiotic look of pure happiness. Then, simply to keep up with his happier frame of mind, his feet broke into a run. Heart soaring, he jogged for a good twenty minutes. He did not know or care where he went. He had found the girl of his dreams. He wanted to marry her and she him. Even the thought of her grandmother couldn't put a damper on his happiness. She was too far away in Jaipur. Panting, he stopped to catch his breath. Looking around, he saw he'd reached the suburb of Haji Ali[36], named after a Muslim saint whose white Darga (mausoleum) was in the middle of the Arabian sea. It was one of Bombay's distinctive landmarks, its white-domed silhouette especially beautiful against the back-drop of the ocean. Its clean, smooth lines were some-what blurred as, in recent times, another building, a square block, had been erected behind it. Bhagu, still breathing hard, went and sat on the parapet along the

---

36 Anyone who knows Bombay, knows Haji Ali woud take much longer to reach. Author's licence

sea. He watched the trail of devotees walking the barely visible narrow path, seemingly into the water. From where he sat, the sun was a huge red orb, hovering over the sea. As it lowered itself to perch on the distant waters, it threw out arrows of white light into the cyan and orange colours of sunset. He sat watching for a long moment, quiet and at peace. The light dimmed making his city glow in its muted colours. A cool breeze started up in the sea, playing with the waves and quickly invading the promenade. Bhagu lifted his face to it, watching it flap rapidly through the clothes of scores of Mumbaikars. The distant sound of the sea got louder and as the waves started rising, devotees of Haji Ali hurried back to land. Soon the path to the Darga would be completely submerged. The sun was almost gone. As he watched it disappear over the horizon, the people of his city bowed their heads and joined their hands to the sun in its final moments. And many Bombayites, clearly non Muslims, turned to the white Darga too, heads bowed and hands joined, as they paid their respects for a few short seconds to the Muslim saint.

The last dart from the sun rose out of the sea and straight into Bhagu's heart. I wasn't wrong, he thought, his heart full of hope and elation. "Shali, I wasn't wrong," he said softly, his mind on the debate. "We do respect all religions. What's more," he exulted," the respect is not simply lip service. It is genuine and it is deep. It simply cannot be ignored." Smiling happily he jumped off the parapet and began heading back home. As he passed them, he sensed rather than saw a couple of kids staring at him. They'd clearly witnessed him talking to himself and jabbing the air. He grinned and they dissolved into helpless giggles.

- *Snippet III* - *Mumbai's Psyche*

Today, we know there is nothing unusual about living with diverse cultures. It is a world wide phenomenon. But there is this other dimension to Mumbai, which makes it so unique. Except for scholars of religions, no other people in so many numbers seem to know so much about the philosophies of different religions. The knowledge almost seems to be acquired by symbiosis. If analysed, it may, no doubt, be very superficial and even inaccurate. But borne out of this has been a slight blending of faiths. Thus, it isn't unusual to see, a Parsi lady paying her respects to Sai Baba - offering Indian sweets and praying fervently for all things most human beings pray for (health of a loved one, success in an exam) - without losing her devotion for and prayers to Zoroaster; a non-Buddhist declaring a fast on Thursday out of respect for Lord Buddha; Many Mumbaikars, irrespective of the religion they were born in, believe in putting garlands of Marigold at the entrance to their homes for good luck during Dusshera - the day Ram returned to his kingdom, victorious, after defeating the evil rakshas or demon, Ravan, who had captured his wife Sita; And many believe in the Hindu Goddess of Wealth - Laxmi, (the word is now synonymous with wealth in many an Indian vocabulary) who, it is said, only enters brightly lit places during Diwali.

Rachana - Mrs. D'Costa's maid - being a very devout Buddhist, celebrated Lord Buddha and prayed to him through the year. But she also went on foot for seven continuous Wednesdays, to attend the 'Novenas' at the Church of Mahim, about 5 km from her home. Over there she prayed to the Virgin Mary to turn her alcoholic, wife-beating husband into a new leaf, which was asking for nothing short of a miracle.

Perhaps it is sights like these - the willingness to gain succour and strength from saints of other religions without feeling one is letting down one's own - that has made Mumbai so unique in the eyes of her residents. And perhaps, that is why, so many of them seem to have this implicit belief in the truly secular nature of their city.

- Female Logic –

The next day, Bhagu was full of eager anticipation. He couldn't wait to get to the college. Shalini too had the same thought as she hurried to the lift. She was aglow with happiness. Rajubai stared. Her chota memsahib was growing up to be a very beautiful young woman. The chauffeur had, for some reason, held back the information. Perhaps his instinct told him the parents weren't ready to hear about Shali's secret romance.

The months that followed were idyllic. The two lovers were blissfully happy. Binny and Lou sometimes missed their threesome terribly. Occasionally, they went off on their own. One day, sitting and gloomily stirring their coffees, they saw Partha come over. "Hi Binny, hi Lou," he said cheerily, reasonably sure of a positive response. For a long moment both girls looked at him, unsmiling. Couldn't he see they wanted to be miserable by themselves? Lou was the first to snap out of it. "Hi Partha," she said, smiling uncertainly. But 'to hell with them' written all over his face Partha walked away. What did I do to upset them? he puzzled, once out of sight. It was beyond his comprehension. Girls! he shrugged, raising his eyes heavenward. Binny and Lou looked after his receding back in dismay. "Why were we unfriendly with him, Binny?" said Lou. "I don't know. Maybe because he was too cheerful and we wanted to be miserable?"

"Maybe because his kind came between us," suggested Lou. "Gawd that's childish," she said, shaking her head. She looked down at the table. "Worse," she changed her mind. "…it's like temperamental Prima Donnas who've lost the limelight."

142

"... spoilt Opera Singers stamping their feet and yelling in song," said Binny, cheering up slightly as she always did when they played their game.

Lou's lips turned up at the edges. "Something like that..," she smiled. She couldn't decide if Binny was being brilliant or mixing up her metaphors again. Then she lost her smile. It wasn't half as much fun with no Shali to share it with. That was exactly the point. "It just isn't the same without Shali," she said sadly. Binny lost her smile too. "She's busy and all, which is great isn't it?" she said brightly. The two girls tried to smile without much success. Then, dropping all pretences of trying to appear positive and upbeat, Binny said in abject misery, "She seems to have forgotten us completely." "Thank goodness," said Lou, "there's only about nine months to graduation."

The two girls stared at each other. "Nine months to graduation! Was that all??" That Shalini was fickle and did not seem to care about their threesome any more was difficult to accept. But what was to become of their twosome?

"Hi Binny, hi Lou." Shalini wondered at the two slumped figures at the canteen table. Two very despondent looking bodies shot up in their seats, faces bright. Shali...," they cried out gladly. "How are you," Lou jumped up to hug her friend. "You look lovely," said Binny, unable to stop smiling. Shalini smiled at them both. "I knew I'd find you here. "Where's Bhagu?" they asked, puzzled. "I don't know," she said, her face looking stubborn and set. "Oh, oh!" Lou mouthed to Binny, "Lover's quarrel." With a faint nod of agreement, Binny rubbed her two index fingers against each other behind Shali's back. Their own misery completely forgotten, they turned their attention to their friend. Shalini was grateful. She still felt the shock of his accusations.

- A Lovers' Quarrel? -

Bhagu was committed to so many activities, it wasn't easy for the two lovers to meet. If it wasn't tennis, it was the debating club and if it wasn't hockey, it was a student and his woes. It was almost as if he couldn't help himself.

Even Dr. Naakwa said so. Within a month of returning to college, Bhagu started getting more and more involved with the Student's Council. The canteen wasn't the only burning issue - now settled so satisfactorily. There was plenty to keep him busy and he thrived on the challenge.

About the end of term, he was summoned to Dr. Naakwa's office. Dr. Naakwa came straight to the point. He was concerned his young student was dividing his energies between far too many other activities and not expending enough on his studies. "It is a pity," he said, "that in spite of your obvious intelligence you choose to be such an average student." Dr. Naakwa rarely presumed to advise students about their grades. But he was really soured off by the lack of effort from one of his brightest stars.

Nobody had called him 'average' before but Bhagu was aware that by being so singled out by Dr. Naakwa, he was, in fact, being paid a huge compliment. With a guilty start he noticed his last assignment on the professor's table and managed to mumble a, "Yes sir." Following the direction of his young student's eyes, Dr. Naakwa leaned forward and picked up the single sheet. "This," he said, holding it up between thumb and fore-

144

finger as if it were something he had a strong aversion to, "is simply a last minute effort to throw a few sentences together. No time or energy has gone into thinking it through."

"Yes sir." Bhagu had a sudden urge to smile. 'Now why would the exact same words sound so literally different from two people?' he thought, recalling Shali's complimentary comments about his debating prowess. "Have you decided what you wish to do after college?" Dr. Naakwa, fed up with the game of monosyllabic responses, tried to draw Bhagu out with the question. "I don't know sir. I'd like to help others. Perhaps I should become a politician, sir?"

"I think, Shali, Dr. Naakwa was not at all prepared for that rejoinder," Bhagu laughed later. "He almost choked on his creamy cappuccino. Some of the froth flew into his saucer." Shalini laughed with Bhagu too. But she felt a strange disquiet. Bhagu might pretend his rejoinder to Dr. Naakwa had been frivolous but she knew injustice of any kind angered him. He immediately wanted to help, and damn the consequences. Was it some secret, inner longing of his that he'd blurted out? Didn't he know it was a jungle out there? Wasn't it enough that he was active in the Student Union? Doesn't he remember how he's been roughed up once, she thought for the umpteenth time with a slight touch of impatience. She would never understand some things about Bhagu…

Perhaps, she admonished herself, I am weak and selfish; completely lacking in courage. Perhaps I should appreciate his desire to help others; get involved with the union myself, instead of simply sitting around, waiting…, getting bored… There was plenty to do at the Union office. It wasn't Shali's cup of tea but she began helping with the Patrika. It was harmless enough. Besides, it made her feel worthy of Bhagu. Best of all, she was right beside Bhagu all through the week.

And then there were the weekends. They were her greatest problem. Dodging her puzzled mum troubled her conscience, though not enough. "But why take an 'auto' when you can take your own car and chauffeur?" her mystified parent would ask. Shali shuddered at the consequences of such an action. "You keep him mum. Dad might need him if there's an emergency. Besides, I don't like being too different from my friends."

"Don't you think you ought to invite Binny and Lou over too?" - "Umm, yes I guess so."

"Won't you, at least, take a notebook and pen for your extra classes?"

"Oops, almost forgot." The fibs themselves came easily. Shali surprised herself with her inventive abilities. What disturbed her was the fact that she had to deceive her parents at all. They trusted her and did not suspect a thing. And yet she knew with certainty that they would soon put an end to her affair with Bhagu if they even had an inkling. He simply wasn't of the same social standing. It didn't bear thinking.

Her singular lack of enthusiasm for her engagement shopping was a constant source of puzzlement. "What's wrong with this saree, Shali? It would be a lovely addition to your collection." You mean my trousseau, don't you mum, Shali would think resentfully. Then there was the near scene at the jeweller's. Her mum couldn't understand her extreme aversion to the ring they'd chosen for Rajinder. "It caught my eye immediately, Shali. It is outstanding," said her agitated mum, surprised at her vehement dislike. What hope did she have of making her mum understand her loathing for the engagement they were planning? "Oh Bhagu," she blurted, longing to put an end to all the uncertainty, "let's just run away and get married." The moment the words were out, she was shocked. Surely she hadn't said that out aloud! Bhagu hadn't even asked her to marry him yet. Her mouth slackened and fell open as she stared wide eyed at him for his reaction. Tickled by her agonised expression, Bhagu gathered her close. "Am I mistaken or is that a proposal?" he laughed. He buried his face in her hair. "You know I want to, Shali," he said in a tortured voice. "Do you think it is easy knowing about your family's preparations for your engagement with someone else? It doesn't bear thinking about."

"It would be so easy to simply present them with a fait accompli. Then they could never take you away from me. I wouldn't have to live with this constant fear each time you arrive late to meet me, each time you go home, each moment I am without you..." Yet something held him back. He wanted to marry her. He wanted to be able to tell the whole world about their love for each other. Why should he sneak away with her as if he were committing a crime? Besides, he knew his dad would be terribly disappointed. He would like to be present at his only son's wedding. No, there had to be another way. "Call it pride if you will Shali. But if we run away, it will somehow lessen what we share. I will never be able to look your parents or mine squarely in the eye. I am not ashamed of my love for you." Instead of feeling overjoyed with his declaration, Shali felt miserable. They loved each other, they both wanted to marry each other and yet he wouldn't marry her. Couldn't he see there was no other way? Shali was deeply saddened and just a little frustrated. She would be extremely insensitive to keep harping on about what she had already told him indirectly - that Mem would never welcome him as the prospective grandson-in-law. An outsider for her grand daughter – someone who didn't belong to their own sect and one that did not even have a job! To Mem, that was nothing short of sacrilege. She would not be denied a 'somebody' for Shali's groom. She had pinned her hopes on making her eldest granddaughter's wedding an affair to remember. It called for a bridegroom of some importance. Oh why didn't Bhagu understand? If Shali's family had the faintest inkling about her love for him, it would be as good as sounding the death knell on their affair. One thing she knew he did understand, unlike Binny and Lou, was why her parents simply fell in with Mem's plans. Deferring to an elder's wish was a mark of respect in their community and ingrained too deeply to deny.

It left the two lovers confused. Neither Shali nor Bhagu knew where it ended and where disregarding their own dearest wishes to accommodate their elders' began.

- Mood Swings -

At home, Shalini's nerves, as also her parents', were frayed thin. Any mention of the word marriage, her trousseau, the Rais, started her off. She threw tantrums, yelling she definitely wasn't marrying Rajinder. And she often ran from the room, locking herself in her own bedroom. And as the days passed, her behaviour grew more unpredictable.

Her agitated parents discussed the matter amongst themselves. This difficult mood of Shalini's hardly augured well for an invitation to visit. They'd wanted to extend one to the Rais ever since they'd returned after Holi. Shali had so enjoyed the parents' attention in Jaipur. "Maybe," said her mum nervously, "she is simply frightened. It's a new situation. Yes, that's it," she concluded, "she is young and frightened about the big change about to be wrought in her life. Who wouldn't be? I am having pre-engagement nerves myself," she added with a shaky attempt at humour. "I'm sure she'll be fine. She'll settle down," she reassured her husband, or was it herself she tried to reassure? Shalini's dad wasn't so convinced. "Maybe she'll change her mind after meeting Rajinder," he agreed with more hope than conviction. There were days when the sparkle was, very noticeably, back in Shalini's eyes. "She seems happy again," poor Mrs. Dayal said on one such occasion, "I knew she simply needed time to get used to the whole idea of marriage."

"Hmmm," her husband replied, hoping his wife was right. To add to their woes, there were those other unrelenting pressures -sometimes subtle, like the ones from Rajinder's parents, who wanted progression from the 'understanding' to something more tangible like a commitment, or the long overdue invitation to visit - and sometimes not, like the hammer blows from Mem about once every week. Mr. Dayal supposed he ought to consider it merciful that Mem hated wasting money or they would have received more than one relentless, long distance call per day. That night they tentatively broached the subject at dinner. It was one of those conversations where they both talked at each other and tried to gauge Shalini's reaction. "Have you read your emails yet?" asked Mrs. Dayal of her husband. "No," he said. "Why? Has someone written to me?" he queried. "To both of us," she said adding, "The Rais."

"What do they say?" asked Mr. Dayal, glancing quickly at his daughter.

As if you don't know, thought Shalini, her expression distinctly spiteful. She could tell they both felt anxious and it made her feel responsible, guilty and miserable. But unable to help herself she felt the, by now, all too familiar set lines of her face - half way between stubborn and sullen. "They'd like to come to Bombay for a visit," said Mrs. Dayal, beginning to look anxious. "That would be nice," said Mr. Dayal slowly, his words aimed at Shalini in a kind of question. The question dropped into a chasm of silence. Shalini sat there feeling helpless and angry. What a poor, naive attempt at staging a conversation for her benefit! She couldn't wait to escape the dinner table.

A few days later a very quiet trio sat at the breakfast table. The Dayals, deciding they had to make a commitment of some sort, had renewed their invitation to the Rais the night before. Shalini had heard the complete, one sided telephone conversation. Sitting there, pretending to be lost in a magazine article, her rigid stance suggesting otherwise, Shalini had listened with a sinking heart. No date had been fixed as it depended on when Rajinder could get leave. In a way she felt sorry for her parents. She understood their dilemma. Her emotions were so over-wrought they weren't sure how she would behave with their guests. At the same time, they knew the Rais were anxious to wrap things up. They had to extend that invitation or the Rais would begin to wonder whether the Dayals were trifling with them and if it was time to look elsewhere.

Mr. Dayal, for the first time, was beginning to feel impatient. The Rais wouldn't wait forever. Such nice inlaws… And of course, the boy was highly qualified; he had everything going for him; his future was assured. … and, Mr. Dayal thought, he could well slip out of our hands. He decided it was time to force Shali's hand.

When he repeated the tentative arrangements between himself and the Rais, his voice, although quiet, sounded frayed at the edges. Shalini recognised the telltale signs of impatience. "We haven't fixed a date yet. But we have suggested it should be within the month. They will call to let us know when Rajinder can get a few days off."

"He's coming too, is he?" she burst out, her voice nasty, almost a sneer. With jerky movements as if she were unable to control herself, she pushed her plate away. Her father lost his cool. "Yes," he said softly, "he's coming too. And I'd like to remind you, young lady, when he does, you will have to be better behaved than you have been lately. What has gotten into you anyway?" he asked, his voice trembling with barely controlled anger. Mrs. Dayal caught his eye and cautioned him to calm down. It must have had the desired effect because he looked down at his plate in an effort to control himself. Looking up finally, he continued with an effort, "We've had visitors from Jaipur before and we've never seen you behave so unwelcoming. If anything, you have always looked forward to their visits. When the Rais come, would it be so difficult to do the same? After all, it is only for a few days." Shalini pushed her chair back and ran out of the room, but not before delivering a last parting shot. "Yes," she yelled, "and if you have your way, I'll be stuck with them for the rest of my life." As soon as the car stopped at the college gates, she got out and ran all the way to the union office. She was so agitated she wanted to get it all off her chest. It was just as well Bhagu was in the middle of listening attentively to an aggrieved student who was complaining in a loud voice. At first Shalini felt sore at having to wait. He gives too much time to others and their problems, she fumed silently. But it gave her time to calm down. The bell rang. With an apologetic smile, Bhagu approached her. Sighing, she felt the moment was lost. It was hardly a good time to dump her problem on him while they hurried to class. Slipping her arm into his, she gave him a brilliant smile.

It wasn't until the short break an hour and a half later that she had a chance to tell him about the latest developments. But the whole thing seemed to have lost its urgency. She decided to make light of the whole affair. She asked him playfully what he would do if Rajinder were to come visiting. It was such an unexpected question that it left Bhagu feeling secretly shaken. To date, the other man had been a vague, shadowy figure and all of a sudden it loomed large. It even had a name. Rajinder. Such a nice name too, dammit.

Then another thought struck him. For a moment his mind clouded over. After that tender-sweet moment when she'd asked him to marry her, they had begun arguing with distressing regularity about the course of action they should take. He wanted an introduction to her parents and she wanted a runaway registered marriage. Was this conversation leading up the same path again, he thought warily. Was Shali trying to browbeat him into submission? He immediately pushed the thought away. Shali never schemed. It was unworthy of him to entertain such thoughts about her. But worthy or not, it persisted and he reacted to Shali's playful question without comment and with an enigmatic smile. Unaware of what was going through his mind she told him about her mini rebellion that morning. "I did not say a word. Just sat there, stony faced till papa felt compelled to insist that I should be more polite to the Rais – especially Rajinder - when they came." With relish she recounted the entire episode, verbatim. 'After all,' papa said, 'he will be our guest for just a few days.' We were having breakfast at the time. So Bhagu, I jumped up and said to them 'Yes, and if you have your way, I'll be stuck with him for the rest of my life.' Then I walked out of the room. I think that really showed them," she smiled triumphantly, looking up at him for acknowledgement of her smart retort.

But then, her smile vanishing, and with something akin to despair in her voice, she said, "If he comes, I really won't know what to do. Please Bhagu," she said, convinced he would finally see reason, "let's run away and have a registered marriage."

Bhagu sighed. There it was! Didn't she get it? Grabbing her by her shoulders, he spoke urgently, "Now is the time to tell them about us, Shali, before –uh – Rajinder," he choked on that name slightly, "and his parents come to Bombay."

Shalini laughed incredulously. She was frustrated beyond belief. Was Bhagu being deliberately obtuse? There simply was no way of making him understand that 'now' was perhaps the worst time to tell them about him. His desire to be accepted or to do the decent thing, she wasn't quite sure which, was blinding him to the reality of the situation. But whatever it was, Shalini was sure of one thing, to tell her parents was neither prudent nor practical. It was the surest way to end their affair. "I know they'll like me once they get to know me," Bhagu continued, but his voice lost its conviction and his hands slipped off her shoulders as he tried to ignore the fact that he was stung by her incredulous laughter. "Oh Bhagu," she said, despair and exasperation driving her on, "can't you get it? We CAN'T. They have found me a 'perfect' match. Someone who is from our community, has a good job and can give me a decent life. They've given their approval already. To Rajinder."

"Time is running out Bhagu," she said shakily, "and unless I present them with a fait accompli, I know that events will somehow overtake me. Overtake us..." Stung by her words, he went stony with silence. Finally Shalini lost her head. "Do you, or don't you want to marry me?" she demanded. As she looked into his face, she felt she already knew his answer. Bhagu's pinched look of hurt was replaced by blazing anger. "Why don't you tell your parents?" he shouted. "Are you ashamed of me?" he voiced the suspicion which had been eating away at him for the past few weeks. Genuinely upset and without waiting for a reply he marched off, his limp more pronounced than ever.

How could he even think I was ashamed of him, she fumed silently as she sat with Binny and Lou. Would I beg him to marry me if I were? Even thinking about it made her head spin. She let out an angry sigh. Bhagu wouldn't understand, her parents wouldn't understand, Mem wouldn't understand... She wished there was someone who would. For a moment she stared, tempted and big eyed, at Binny and Lou. Then she sighed once more. It wouldn't really help. She knew they'd side with Bhagu. Besides, it was her problem and Bhagu's. They had to sort it out themselves. And sitting there with her old friends, all she really wanted was to be with him again.

The short separation was perhaps the best thing that happened to Bhagu and Shalini. It gave them time to cool off. As soon as they returned to class, something almost tangible seemed to pass between the two. Shalini, feeling the world take on a distinctive rosy hue, turned to him, eyes huge and slightly moist, a tremulous smile on her lips. Bhagu, his heart full, almost faltered for a second as he walked towards her. Feeling much less abandoned for having spent the short break with her, Binny and Lou watched silently. As he reached their desk he turned to them with a soft, slow smile. He greeted them both but once more, his eyes were drawn to Shalini. The genuine warmth in his smile as he'd turned to them did not escape the two friends. After Shalini and Bhagu, deciding to skip the next lecture, went off together, the two looked at each other, not knowing what to say. Finally Binny raised an eyebrow. "That's a lover's tiff?" she queried, shaking her head. Lou shrugged philosophically, grinning. They were both in a happier frame of mind. Things – like inseparable threesomes at college - seemed to change or evolve over time. Nothing remained constant. But with Shali seeking them out for a few precious moments at the canteen, it wasn't such a hard lesson for them to come to terms with…

For the two lovers though, it had been an unbearably long parting. Their first quarrel. They were happy to be together again and amidst protestations of never getting angry with each other, *ever*, they made up. This time, when they talked, each was willing to listen to the other - even try to understand. Shalini couldn't help reproaching him. "Bhagu," she said softly, "how could you even think I was ashamed of you?"

Bhagu chose his words carefully. "I have often wondered what a beautiful girl like you sees in me Shali – why would you want to marry me when you could have almost anybody. I have a limp and a crooked nose and I feel even I wouldn't introduce me to your parents." Losing all power of speech, she could only stare, her heart aching unbearably. She understood how on that fateful day, almost a year ago, it was more than his physical self that had taken a battering. She crept up to him like some wounded animal and put her arms around him. They stayed like that, her head resting on his chest, for a long while. Her voice heavy with unshed tears, she spoke into his shirt, "I still see the same loving, patient, kind, ...giving..."

He could tell she was emotional and in an effort to cheer her up, said light-heartedly, "Not to mention smart, witty, bright, intelligent...". It made her smile. "Why you arrogant, big headed, conceited...," she started to say when he cut in, "....whatever happened to the loving, patient..."

Had Binny and Lou overheard this tender little exchange, it would have made them shudder. But it put the two lovers in a much happier frame of mind. Later, much later, feeling soothed and healed, Shali felt tempted to attempt, once more, to explain the mind set of her family. But wisdom prevailed and she decided to hold her peace. "I hate it when we quarrel," she declared passionately, "and I hate it even more that we have to part every evening," she murmured, unable to help noticing how supple his skin felt against her mouth. He was very fit. Senses heightened, she felt a pure shaft of pleasure go through her as, with a gentle ripple of muscles, he put his arms around her, drawing her close.

– Doosri Aazadi –

Shalini and Bhagu had both made up but she was still afraid. She was unable to express her fears for they were vague and ill defined. She had made it clear she wouldn't marry Rajinder. Still, her family was going ahead with the invitation for a visit. They hoped that meeting him would dispel most of her fears. To be fair to them, they didn't know what was happening in her life. And, they were being very patient with her.

On the other hand, she had made it clear to Bhagu she wasn't marrying Rajinder. But he wasn't marrying her either. To be fair to him, he wanted to marry her but with her parents' approval. To tell the truth, she thought, I wish I didn't understand everyone's point of view quite so readily.

She decided that the best course she could take, for a while at least, was to do nothing. Something would turn up and she'd know what to do.

That 'something' turned up sooner than she expected. It was quite unlike anything she had imagined.

The days went by with them meeting for at least a half hour after college every day and as often as possible over weekends. One night, after retiring to her bed-room, Shali gave in to an urge to speak with him over the phone. Ramu came on the line. Recognising her voice he volunteered the information, "Teen ghante pehle bahar gaye hai"

'What has kept him out for three whole hours?' she wondered, feeling uneasy. Bhagu always told her everything. Or did he? She decided there was only one thing to do. Ask him.

When she confronted him the next day, Bhagu hesitated. It wasn't because he wanted to hide anything from her. But he had been thrilled about the whole experience and somehow his instinct told him she wouldn't share in his excitement. But wasn't she his Shali? Wasn't he supposed to share everything with her? He felt both guilt and slight remorse at his hesitation and plunged in. "Have you heard of 'Doosri Aazadi.'?" She nodded. "Their leader is in town and I attended one of their rallies. Shali," he continued, awe in his voice, "the way he talked about why we needed a doosri aazadi, a second independence, was truly.... inspirational."

The tight band around Shali's heart melted away. A political rally? That was her vague, ill defined rival! How unnecessary the niggling, unhappy, worrying doubts at the back of her mind had been. They simply fizzled out and unable to stop herself, she began smiling as she listened to Bhagu. "You should have heard him," he said, his voice brimming with enthusiasm. "He spoke of the corruption in government."

Shali quickly looked down. But not before Bhagu saw the sceptical look in her eyes. "I know," he said, addressing that look, "....which politician doesn't!"

"But Shali," he continued, "I cannot describe why, his speech didn't sound like heavy rhetoric. It somehow didn't sound ....glib. I am as politician weary and sceptical as the next person. But when that man talked, we listened. His obvious oratory powers had that added dimension – a ring of sincerity. He was full of ideas to improve on ...," Bhagus voice grew a notch louder on that last word as if to counter Shali's silent look of amusement. Shali, who couldn't resist thinking of Bhagu's own words - which politician doesn't... - hastily screened her eyes with her lashes once more. She was unable to prevent a downward turn to one side of her lips as another cynical thought quickly followed the first one - I'll bet he had ideas –all of them crooked...,

Immediately contrite, her eyes flew open. She didn't wish to dampen his enthusiasm. Bhagu saw the change in her face and touched her on the arm, as if to say it was alright. Snuggling closer to him happily she decided she would give him her full, undivided, non-judgmental attention as he continued softly, "You see, Shali, one didn't get the feeling, as with some politicians, that he would argue the other side of the case with as much brilliance if he wanted to. One simply knew he wouldn't. Everything about him seemed somehow above board. He told us exactly how he would implement his ideas which told us they weren't just ideas but well thought out plans. He was interested in infrastructure so that all of India, down to the smallest tehsil would be connected and he identified five major sectors of development...."

Bhagu couldn't stop talking. And Shali was happy to listen. There had been so much dissension between them of late that this was rather a nice change. His prediction was that Doosri Aazaadi's time had come; the moment was ripe. His theory was that most Indians, up until this moment, had bemoaned the state of affairs privately but knew how dangerous it was to take on the might of the money, power, corruption and the underworld; everyone knew that all four were linked to politics. But not with this man. Thanks to him, hope had flared in many an Indian heart. The last time that had happened was in the eighties with the then Prime and Finance ministers opening up the economy.

As Shali stood there listening to the admiration in Bhagu's voice, she realised what was happening. Bhagu wanted to change the world. He had always been unafraid to say what he believed in. He had never hesitated to put his life on the line. He had been waiting for just such a party, just such a leader. Doosri Aazadi seemed perfect for him. The time was right, not only for Doosri Aazadi but for Bhagu as well.

"They do not have the funds to take their campaign to the media," he said, enthused. "…just a lot of professional and hardworking people who are joining in droves. And such is the charisma of the leader that the proverbial mountain - the media, has started following him around. There were T.V. cameras and reporters. And crowds of people. Mark my words. Shali. This man and his party are going places. There wasn't any need to swell the numbers with his own henchmen and 'yes' men. The people simply came. And listened. I was one of them and without exception, we all came away with hope in our hearts."

This, Shalini soon realised, was true. Before another week was up, even her own mum and dad had started looking for news of Doosri Aazaadi in the papers. All of India had started hoping again while at the same time, fearing for the safety of the man who headed the party. The very fact that he was becoming so popular, that people had started pinning their hopes on him, meant that he was a sitting target for the hit men from other parties. The public knew this was the reality of politics in India today. 'Sanctity of Life' was just a phrase in a weary document known as the Indian Constitution. As were other phrases like 'the right to justice'. Words like decency, honour, respect for others and integrity were just that - mere words, never to be underestimated as rhetoric but utterly useless in the murky reality that was life in India today. Words like arrogance, contempt for others, total disregard for the law, survival of the wiliest, protection money, money under the table, Swiss accounts and from time to time, total anarchy, were the reality most Indians lived with. And politics was where one saw this reality at its starkest. But this man alone had given them such an upsurge of hope that people from all walks of life were joining the party ranks. Amongst them were a highly trained team of security men whose sole job was to protect him.

As Bhagu eulogised, it wasn't too difficult to see the writing on the wall. It was inevitable that, ere long, Bhagu presented himself as the newest recruit for Doosri Aazadi. He was proud of his party and their work. He gave his time unstintingly. It soon became the most time consuming thing in his life.

Shali was left wondering where she fit in. The more he was absorbed into it all, the less time he seemed to have for her.

- A Final Appeal -

One day, when Bhagu was unavailable again, on an impulse, she ordered her chauffeur to drive her to his house. She waited there till he got back. The chauffeur and Ramu had a long conversation while they waited. Ramu, innocently believing the chauffeur was in on the secret – after all, he'd driven Shali here - said more than he ought.

Slightly shocked, the chauffeur realised that this affair had progressed way beyond what he'd imagined. He doubted very much if Shali's parents or Rajubai knew. He was in a dilemma as he'd been with the family since Shali was a baby. Should he tell her parents or shouldn't he?

When Bhagu reached home, he was startled to see Shali's car parked downstairs. He hastened upstairs and found her sitting in the hall. She forced him to face her and asked him quietly, "What's to become of us, Bhagu? I feel I am losing you." He hastily reassured her, saying she shouldn't worry simply because he was busy with Doosri Aazadi. His heart was set on seeing his party come to power and that meant giving unstintingly of his time.

She knew his mind was elsewhere but she persisted. "We have only one more term at the college. After that, it will be almost impossible to meet under the same circumstances. Even right now, I can tell you are uneasy about my being here …jumpy because your dad might return from work and see me here." Even as Bhagu shook his head to deny that, Shali turned away, rejecting his denial. "Besides," she said, "I cannot keep Rajinder's family waiting forever. They eventually want much more than a visit. If I knew where you and I were headed, I could simply say 'No'. But you won't marry me…" This was the third time she'd asked him to marry her. As soon as the words were out, she regretted them. 'Have I no pride,' she thought, feeling wretched, 'Even I am getting tired of my own repeated pleas,' and she peered out at him, upset and embarrassed, from under her lashes. She expected his usual gentle, but firm reply about wanting both their parents at their wedding.

But Bhagu didn't say anything for a long moment. He watched her thoughtfully, almost as if he were seeing something in her he'd never seen before. He was finally convinced that Shalini was never going to introduce him to her parents unless they eloped. And he was convinced it wasn't only because he wasn't 'good enough' in their eyes. He wasn't good enough in hers. Her eyes flew to his face but the look was gone in an instant, leaving her feeling inexplicably afraid. "Shali," he said gently, "you shouldn't worry." He hesitated, as if choosing what he had to say with care. "No date has been fixed for Rajinder's visit, has it?"

"No..." she whispered, then "no," she said again, watching him, wondering why she found his answer vaguely disturbing. "Besides," said Bhagu, "it isn't as if your parents want any commitment from you. They just want you to meet him. Who knows, he might have changed." More confused than ever she let it go. On her way back, disturbed, stung and confused, she grappled with Bhagu's unexpected words. And then it came to her. The words themselves had hurt unbearably but more than that, it was the detached manner in which they had been uttered. He seemed, somehow, to have distanced himself from his emotions. He hadn't repeated his desire to be introduced to her parents. 'Doesn't he care?' she asked herself, deeply unhappy, "Is it all over between us?"

So lost in her own misery was she that Shalini didn't realise the chauffeur was deep in thought too. His eyes looking thoughtful, he kept glancing at her through the rear view mirror. Shalini suddenly became aware of his thoughtful glance. Oh, no, she thought in dismay, feeling a flush creep up her cheeks. He knows. I shouldn't have come in the car. She quickly averted her eyes as she sensed another glance.

Over the next few days Shali was acutely aware of the chauffeur's almost certain knowledge. Her overriding emotion, besides her misery, was one of deep anxiety. Would he tell someone? Maybe Rajubai? Or her mum? Whenever the chauffeur had reason to come to the side entrance, as he did from time to time, after having run an errand, bought some groceries or even to have a cup of tea and a roti with Rajubai, she was jumpy. Afterwards, she anxiously watched both Rajubai and her mum for any telltale signs that her secret was out. Her mum, with a sinking heart realised that her daughter's mood was in a down swing. She saw her daughter barely eat, looking unhappy and unnecessarily nervous.

But after a few days, it dawned on Shali that her chauffeur had decided to hold his peace. It was a relief. Still, she knew he knew and the knowledge that she unwittingly shared a secret with the chauffeur made Shali very uncomfortable. She rarely ventured out in the car by herself, except when unavoidable. Once, on one such unavoidable occasion, he ventured the information that he often met Ramu (Bhagu's manservant) at the bazaar and that Ramu always sent his salaams. Shali didn't quite know how to respond to that and simply nodded. Feeling a little resentful, she wondered how much the two servants had gossiped about her. She looked out of the window, her face closed and distant. And then a thought struck her. Perhaps it was Ramu who had something to do with the chauffeur not divulging her secret. On thinking about it for a while she felt fairly certain she was right. After all, Ramu had never spoken to Bhagu's dad about it and he must have cautioned her chauffeur too. Grateful to Ramu, she started breathing easy, at least in that quarter.

The irony was that it didn't matter any more. Bhagu hadn't been in touch since the last fortnight. Every night, she wondered if she should 'phone him. But some terrible knowledge which she couldn't quite put her finger on, made her hold back. It was one thing liking a man, knowing he reciprocated. But she didn't know how or why, this time it felt like it had all become terribly one-sided.

- A Confession -

Shalini had never felt more wretched in her life. There was only one bit of good news to brighten up that week. Rajinder and family had postponed their visit. One weekend, on an impulse, Shali called up her two friends. She was casual about it all saying Bhagu was busy and she was free if they wanted to do something that evening. As always, they were absolutely delighted but within minutes of meeting her, they realised she was miserable.

"So, how's Bhagu?" asked Lou, watching her closely.

"Fine," said Shali in a bright voice.

"...a bit too over bright if you ask me," said Lou caustically to Binny that night as they hooked up over the phone.

"So...?" said Binny, thinking Lou was making too big a deal of it, "they've had another lover's quarrel. So what? At least we got to see Shali over the weekend. I'll bet they've made up already. We probably won't see her again any time soon."

But Binny was mistaken. The very next day Shali called again. This time there was no pretence in her voice. It sounded raw and hurt. They immediately decided to meet at Binny's. They wanted Shali to be able to talk freely. They could go to Binny and Roshni's bedroom or, they could go for a long walk within the grounds and sit on one of the benches under a shady tree. They opted for the latter.

Shali, soothed beyond belief at being with her friends, breathed in deeply. Lou turned to her casually, "...So, how's Bhagu...busy with studies?" Binny grimaced. Her friend might think this was delicate probing but it sounded like hammer bludgeoning glass. But Shali didn't seem to mind. It was as if she were waiting for an opening. "No," she said, the rawness back in her voice, "not with studies..."

"...the Students' Union?" queried Binny softly, looking anxiously at her friend.

"Not even that," said Shali. "He's found a new passion..." she said brightly.

"What?" said Binny and Lou unable to hide the shocked disbelief from their faces.

"Oh, er... not that," said Shali. She looked with sightless eyes at the antics of a nearby squirrel. "It's Doosri Aazaadi..." she said, her eyes suddenly full of unshed tears. Her voice trailed away on a hurt whisper.

"Wow," said Lou, something akin to awe in her voice, "you don't mean the Doosri Aazaadi?" Shali looked at her sadly. The admiration in her friend's voice was unmistakable, a poignant reminder of Bhagu's own admiration. Her voice gruff as she struggled valiantly with the deep pain in her heart, she said, "Yes, the very one. It's his raison d'etre now…"

Lou and Binny were silent, their eyes on the squirrel. It hastily skittered up a tree, out of the way of a group of little kids as they ran past. It was twittering excitably, either in fear or indignation, they couldn't decide which, well after they were gone. Its bushy tail twitched in fright and its delicate little claws clutched at the branch. Its head, normally upright, was almost on its paws, peering down from the safety of its perch in nervous little darting movements. It was quite oblivious to the sparrows it had displaced from their perch who flapped wildly through the leaves for a moment before settling down a bit higher.

Binny and Lou, seemingly absorbed at the antics of the squirrel, exchanged a quick smile. They were secretly relieved it wasn't over between Shali and Bhagu. She was simply feeling neglected because of Bhagu's new-found interest. For some reason, it seemed to make their normally exuberant friend extremely wretched. Neither had any genuine words to console her. Wordlessly, Binny turned to Shali and put her arms around her.

That night, over the 'phone, both exclaimed at the effort Shali had made to hold back the tears. "I've never seen her this unhappy," claimed Lou. "It's almost as if she feels Doosri Aazadi is some kind of a rival," she laughed incredulously.

"Binny," said her mum, "we've been waiting dinner for ages now. Can't you get off that 'phone?"

"Got to go, Lou," said Binny hastily. "Bye."

Over the next few months, it slowly dawned on them how complete Bhagu's devotion to the party really was. Shali spent more and more time with them.

The two girls discussed how completely Doosri Aazaadi seemed to have displaced Shali in Bhagu's emotions. They ran into him often and even to them he sounded cool and distant.

"Whatever has gotten into him?" asked Lou, into the receiver. Whatever it was, this time they felt a huge barrier between them. As far as Shali was concerned, the subject was closed too. It saddened them to see how gaunt she looked.

- Binny and Lou on another Mission-

It was two months into the last term. Binny and Lou desperately wanted to cheer Shali up. But they were confused. This time they felt incapable of intruding on her privacy. They knew she suffered. She had horrible dark circles under her eyes and they had never seen her so serious. It wasn't easy watching Bhagu either. He seemed happy on one plane and did seem rather busy. But whenever he looked at Shali, a shadow seemed to cross his face. It was such a shame. It wasn't that Bhagu and Shali didn't speak to each other. They did. But the connection was lacking. There was no sizzle underlying their words. They behaved like polite strangers.

Was there no chance of reviving the romance? Was it totally over? It couldn't be. It mustn't be. It was so unbelievably impossible but it seemed to be true...

And so, they cooked up another one of their plans. They'd take Shali shopping. It might cheer her up, at least for a day.

The very next day, sitting at their favourite table at the canteen, looking out at the milieu of students on the field, Binny reminded her friend about the outfit she'd always wanted. "Why don't we go shopping during

168

lunch hour? You could show us some decent shops you know," she suggested.

Shalini had no stomach for it. She knew they were trying to cheer her up but she didn't really wish to be cheered. It was better to be miserable at the college than to be physically removed from his presence. 'Not that it matters to him,' she thought unhappily. Bhagu seemed to spend all his time at the Union office. He seemed busy and his face, whenever she did dare to dart a quick look at him, seemed calm and collected ...totally unaffected by the rift in their relationship. He isn't bothered, thought Shali. He couldn't care less for the pain he's causing me. She simply wished she could hide away somewhere to nurse her misery.

She realised with a start of guilt that Binny and Lou were waiting for her answer. I'll show him two can play at that game, she thought defiantly.

"Well," she said, turning brightly to face her friends, "there's this little boutique I know … my absolute fav…." Shali's voice trailed away for Lou was looking at her queerly.

Lou slowly repeated what Shali had said, "…there's this little boutique I know… A boutique?" she repeated in absolute wonderment.

"Ye-es," said Shali, smiling slightly. 'If I know her well, she's having me on,' she thought, watching Lou warily.

"She did say …'boutique'?" Lou turned to confirm with Binny who nodded solemnly. "Correct," she said wondering mildly what Lou was up to but quite willing to play her game. It was good to see the slight smile in Shali's eyes.

"…as in a tiny shop that sells expensive clothes?

Binny nodded, "Mmm …very expensive…"

"Hmmmm," said Lou, looking into the far distance with exaggerated wonder. Finally, she turned to look at her friend pityingly. "There is a real need to point certain facts out to you, young lady."

"Ye-es?" said Shali, still wary but smiling in spite of herself. "Not everyone," said Lou in tones one reserves for the really dumb, "has that essential and crucial commodity, that undeniable something one needs to be able to shop at boutiques ......" Shali, although still wary, was unable to prevent her smile from widening as Lou paused dramatically. "...your parents' bank balance." The soliloquy ended with such abrupt bluntness that Binny laughed outright. Shali, although slightly embarrassed, couldn't help smiling. Much to Lou and Binny's delight she emitted her first genuine little chuckle. She'd forgotten how good it was to be with her friends.

Soon, the three were merrily making plans. They certainly didn't wish to miss the computer class – the accounting software package they were studying was incredibly interesting. But it would be o.k. to miss the next class. "We'll photocopy someone's notes and read them later" said Lou

The three were so busy enjoying each others' company, they failed to notice a young man standing quietly on a far away balcony, watching. Bhagu could distinctly hear the laughter as it travelled on the still air. He turned away with a wan smile and hurried off to the union office. Who could deny the special bond between those three?

He pushed aside the momentary feeling of hurt that escaped the solid prison wall he'd built around it. It was effective and impenetrable most of the time. Besides, he was much too busy. It was a struggle juggling his time between his union activities and Doosri Aazaadi. Anyway, he didn't bear Shali any ill-will at all. In fact, it was better this way. All along, although he understood she didn't realise it herself, Shali had kept running away from the knowledge that he and his father were probably ill mannered bachelors who had lived without the graceful influence of a woman for too long. She knew he wouldn't fit. Wouldn't belong. Who could blame her for not wanting to introduce him to her parents, for not being able to make that final commitment to their relationship? Not that it mattered any more. Anyway, he thought nobly, in the long run, it might be better for her to marry her own kind. As he approached the union office he squared his shoulders. Not for him the moping and the looking back. He had finally found somewhere he could, and did, belong. He'd gained a lot of insight and valuable experience from working at Doosri Aazaadi and it was helping his work at the union.

The three friends, oblivious of Bhagu's thoughts, continued making their plans. They decided they would, after all, go to Shali's favourite boutique. It would give Binny an idea about the latest fashions. After having a good look at all the couture outfits, they would pretend they didn't quite find what they were looking for and walk out the shop. Then, off to buy material and a good, affordable darji[37]. It all sounded easy enough. Their spirits lifted in anticipation. It would be just the three of them .....just like it used to be. They went back to class. As soon as the bell went, the three girls walked to the gates to hail a rickshaw. They only had an hour. Binny was pleased. "Oh it's been such a long time," she said,

---

[37] Darji - tailor

"...us three, out together again." Immediately the words were out, she felt guilty. 'What a selfish, insensitive thing to say,' she chided herself.

"I'm looking forward to it too" said Shali, understanding the hasty, guilt-ridden, worried look Binny darted at her. She smiled at Binny and linked an arm with her. The worry, immediately wiped off her friend's face, was replaced by a look of pure happiness. "This is going to be such fun," said Binny. But seconds later, doubts started assailing her. She'd never seen the inside of a boutique before - only the extravagantly dressed mannequins from the outside. "I think it will be fun," she said uncertainly, her step faltering. "I hope it will," she added, her look of extreme doubt belying that hope. She felt intimidated at the thought of entering "Aarohi's" and turning to her friends for reassurance, she asked in a small voice, "Will it?

They laughed, and, with an air of extreme confidence, told her to leave everything to them, which sounded kind of ominous. She hated leaving things to others. It made her feel like a puppet and did nothing to reassure her. Shali gave directions to the rickshawalla. Soon they were outside the boutique. Binny peered out. Lordy, it looks posh, she thought. The chrome and aluminium etched glass windows displayed elaborate salwaar-kameezes and ghagras – the latter being decidedly filmy clothes as far as she was concerned. She couldn't help being amused for they were draped on very western looking mannequins weighed down by tons of Indian jewellery. "Reeks of money," she said, nervously turning to her friends. "Of course," said Lou a little dryly.

"It's all artificial," said Shali scornfully. Shali's unconscious airs amused the other two and they exchanged a smile. But, in her present state of mind, Binny could not stay amused for long. Almost on the verge of panic, she looked blindly at the mannequins unable to take in or appreciate the detail. Then she turned to her friends – 'friends!' she thought on the verge of panic - and said, "You actually propose I make the owner, who, I'm sure is more haughty than her mannequins, bring out all those outfits and display them for me? And I, in my faded jeans, inspect them and pretend I don't like them?" Binny's voice ended on a very high note. She breathed in shakily. Shali and Lou, worried she might bolt, did not even bother to reply. Instead, hastily positioning themselves on either side, they almost shoved her in through the door. Almost immediately, Binny noticed the difference in temperature. Unconsciously lifting her face to the air-conditioned coolness, she felt slightly soothed. She looked pointedly at Lou and Shali's tightly grasping hands till they dropped them apologetically to their sides. The three stood uncertainly, just inside the door. Then Binny's nerves gave a little lurch for she saw a lady, looking very elegant in a Rajasthani lengha, walking towards them. Her feet tread the plush carpet softly. Her payals (anklets) made wondrous music as she walked. The only thing that marred the entire exquisite effect was the single frown line furrowing her beautiful forehead. To Binny her expression was reminiscent of the proverbial lady who wondered what the cat had brought in. Turning swiftly Shalini whispered to the two girls that the lady was Aarohi - the owner herself. Turning back to the lady with a smile Shali said, "Hello Aarohi. How are you? I'd like you to meet Louella and this is Binaifer. They are friends from college. Binny would like to buy an outfit - for a job interview." Poor Binny. That was the first she'd heard of a job interview. What if the lady asked her, 'what job?' Her brain ceased functioning. The crevice on Aarohi's forehead disappeared immediately she recognised Shalini. This wasn't any old bunch of shabby college kids come in for a bit of a lark. She had been all set to crush their silly little game and send them packing. This was Shalini and friends. She had amassed a small fortune off the Dayals before Holi. And Shalini's marriage, she did believe, wasn't too far away... She joined her hands in a beautiful, if slightly exaggerated, namaste and smiled. Lou, startled by the arc those hands made before coming together, almost subconsciously, imitated the gesture, her hands making a little arc too. She returned Aarohi's perfect smile with one of her own, conscious of the others watching. She was already beginning to feel slightly less intimidated. Aarohi made polite noises about the interview which made Binny blush. Shali obviously invented that so it would really seem like I, in my faded old jeans and comfortable T-shirt, meant business, she thought. Poor Binny. If anything, it served to confirm what she already knew. That her wanting to buy one of Aarohi's creations was such an unlikely tale, even Shali had problems crediting it.

Aarohi had already moved on to the business of selling her clothes. "What kind of a job are you applying for?" she asked. "That," she continued without noticing Binny's eyes darting wildly from Lou to Shali, "would decide the 'look' you ought to have - business-like, feminine, modern, traditional..."

"Do you have something that's modern and feminine?" Binny blurted out, relieved she didn't have to answer her earlier question. "Maybe a kurti...?" she ventured,

slightly bolder, only to blush again as Aarohi darted a
quick, amused look at Shalini that clearly suggested
Binny was exhibiting her ignorance. Shali, not about to
let anyone mock her friend and get away with it, didn't
quite meet Aarohi's eyes. Aarohi, getting the message,
hastily let her amused expression slide away, replacing
it with a slightly more circumspect one. "Fashions have
changed dramatically," she pronounced kindly, "and
everyone does wear kurtis now, but they are playful –
more for youngsters who want an evening out" she said,
making Binny feel like a dimwit. "What you need is
something that makes you look responsible. You are
tall. Why don't you go in for something flowy, like this,
"she said brightly to Shali's ignorant friend, holding up
a dramatic salwaar kameez swathed in a large chunni[38]
of contrasting colours. Lou, deciding she didn't quite
like the tone Aarohi had adopted, said emphatically,
"Well fitting clothes suit her much better. I think for the
interview, she should wear something that blends the
traditional with the contemporary. And nothing that is
too fussy..." and her eyes seemed to drift towards and
linger ever so slightly on the outfit Aarohi was holding
up.

For want of something to do Binny quickly hid her face
in the rack of outfits behind her. Aarohi, ever professional and deciding to concentrate on Binny and Shali
and ignoring their rude friend, brought out a few more
outfits for Binny's inspection. Growing more uncomfortable by the minute for having to reject those outfits
Binny blindly picked one out and held it against herself.
Her hands came across what she thought was a loose

---

38 Chunni, scarf

thread on the garment. She was surprised to find what looked like a tiny price tag attached to the end. She hastily turned it over and stole a quick look. Her eyes went wide at the impossible figure mentioned on the tag. Surely, she thought, no one would pay that much for one outfit. But it was beautiful...

The long kurta was plain and fitting. It had just that touch of bold colour along a fairly modest slit on one side. The short, three-quarter sleeved jacket in the same bright, bold colours was its piece de resistance. It was lined and looked tailored in front but around the back, it draped itself in surprisingly soft, folds right down to the top of her legs. The effect was a business like front until she turned.

She could picture herself smartly shaking hands with a panel of job interviewers, then turning and walking out, all fluid grace and feminine dignity. She was quite taken with the idea. The other women could see it plainly in her wistful expression. Aarohi put aside the other outfits and held it up for Binny to gaze on. "Would you like to try it on?" she asked. Binny hesitated. It was best to end it here. "It is lovely, Aarohi, but I...I..."

"Wait," interjected Lou hastily. "At least put the jacket on Binny." They'd come this far. Why waste the opportunity? Binny really didn't care for the idea and stood there feeling helpless. Aarohi held it open and she slipped her arms in. Then Arohi slowly turned Binny to face the mirror. Binny, a robot until then, clearly liked what she saw in the mirror. She stared at herself for a bit. Unexpectedly, she gave a wide smile of delight to the three women and gave a little twirl. The jacket swirled out gently at the back. Unfortunately for Binny, so did the price tag. Discreetly hidden until then, it floated past her vision. She faltered, looking dazed. 'What am I doing?' she thought. 'Before I know it I will have agreed to buy the damn thing.'

Abruptly stopping in mid turn, she stood looking awkwardly from one to the other. "I...I...," she said, unable to articulate anything more coherent.

Shalini interjected smoothly, "Aarohi, Binny needs to think about it before making a decision." She took the outfit from Binny's nerveless fingers and handed it back to Aarohi saying, "Thanks for showing us your gorgeous outfits."

Aarohi took it surprisingly well... and then again it wasn't all that surprising. Shalini was a very valued customer.

With awkward goodbyes, the three finally made a hasty getaway. As they went out the door, Binny saw that Lou and Shali had the grace to look slightly red in the face too.

Once the girls were completely out of sight, they looked at each other soberly. They felt as though they were out of a messy, sticky and uncomfortable situation. Lou tried to laugh it off. "We have a right not to buy something we don't like," she said with unconvincing bluster. "..except that I loved the darned thing,' said Binny with uncharacteristic tartness. Then, sheer agony in her voice she said, "Never again, Shali, don't make me do this ever again. And Lou, I thought I had escape within my grasp till you butted in ..." Her hands went up to her hot, tormented face. The anguish in her voice made Lou and Shali emit their first genuine chuckle.

Coming out of the air-conditioned comfort of the elegant shop had made them hot. They stopped at a roadside sugar-cane juice stall. Sitting on a rickety bench, they relished the delicious, sweet, ganna with loads of crushed ice and just that perfect twist of lemon. Wiping off a moustache of froth from her upper lip with deep satisfaction Binny held her thick, cheap and empty glass to the light, "I could buy a glass a day for ten whole years and it still wouldn't pay for that outfit," she said. Bit by bit, as they re-lived the entire episode, Shali and Lou's spontaneous bursts of laughter coaxed Binny's jangled nerves back to normal. It had been one crazy idea going into that impossibly posh boutique together but now that the ordeal was over she had to admit it had been fun.

The gannajuice-walla, watching them, couldn't help grinning at their high spirits. Life seemed to be all fun and games for these college students!

– Friendship –

It was imperceptible, but once again things were different. They met each other everyday and knew each other well. But there were occasions when they appreciated their friendship with each other as never before. This was one such occasion. They returned to Gyan Shakti looking slightly flushed and happy. Bhagu looked wistfully at Shali for a moment. Lou, conscious of a feeling of déjà vu, caught him looking. This time, unlike the very first time outside the college gates, the wistfulness was gone in an instant. Instead, with perfect self-control and without looking away, he replaced it with a bright smile, careful to include all three in that polite, almost indifferent smile before turning away. The three girls, also adept at playing games, smiled back, with only Binny looking as unhappy as she really felt. She was unable to hide her feelings but the others were getting to be really good at it. That evening, for the very first time, neither Binny nor Lou called each other to discuss the young couple. Finally, grudgingly, they accepted the facts. It was over. And perhaps it was for the best. Bhagu and Shali wanted different things from life. Even if the lovers decided to patch up their differences, Lou and Binny didn't feel part of the game plan any more. They had to let go although Binny still kept praying fervently for a miracle. The night of their outing, as they lay awake in bed thinking about their lunch hour together, each knew the other two were special. The bond between them was never stronger. Theirs was a once in a lifetime friendship. It allowed them to be foolish, vulnerable, young, happy or unhappy without any fear of criticism from the others. In the precincts of their college, Gyan Shakti, it had been easy to bridge the cultural gap.

The next day, hurrying to class, the three came across Dr. Naakwa. They smiled respectfully at him and he gave them a smiling nod. For a moment his thoughts turned from the intricacies of supply and demand to the three of them. "They came to the college as young girls," he thought, remembering them as he'd seen them on that first day, "...but seem to have done some growing up since," he marvelled. "Such bright young ladies! Tremendous potential!" he thought with some satisfaction. With a slight pause in his step he turned. "I wonder what they'll make of their lives," he mused, glancing at the three receding figures, one in a salwaar kameez, another in a midi, and the third in faded jeans. Then turning, he too hurried on and disappeared through a door.

- CHAPTER III –

- An Unlikely Go-Between –

At the start of the holidays, Bhagu got in touch. Shali was confused. She was just beginning to believe she might heal. There were times during the day when, to her surprise, she almost forgot to think about him. Nights were another matter. She lay awake for hours, nursing a broken heart, longing to hear his voice, feel his touch, lost in endless yearning. Every morning she woke from a fitful sleep, reluctant to put him from her mind and get out of bed. Her heart felt heavy with misery but her mind chalked up a victory for having resisted the temptation to call him.

Bhagu's message to her was through a most unlikely channel – her chauffeur - although upon thinking about it, Shali realised it was the obvious one. Ramu would have mentioned to Bhagu he met the chauffeur often at the bazaar and Bhagu would have decided to use that obvious, yet discreet route to get his message across. Shali would never forget the moment her chauffeur spoke up. It was heady and awkward at the same time. To hear from Bhagu after almost giving up was undeniable bliss but to hear the words through her chauffeur detracted from her pleasure. The man had hardly ever spoken to her except to ask where she wanted to go and now, he was being forced to share a guilty secret with her. He looked just as uncomfortable, even slightly diffident as he told her he had a message from "Bhagu sa'ab". He said he was in the vegetable market when Ramu had asked him to pass on an urgent message -

180

that sa'ab, sir, wanted her to meet her at the college at 7 pm that evening. He had something important to tell her. Shali lowered her eyes for she didn't want the chauffeur to see her expression as she took in the message. Her heart thudding, she felt her misery drop from her like a cloak. She realised she had never recovered but simply learned to live with and manage her deep hurt. Barely able to contain her excitement, she managed a polite 'thank-you' with averted eyes as she got out of the car and headed for the lift. All the way up she could only think that Bhagu still loved her. He wanted to see her again. He had missed her as much as she had missed him. Hugging the knowledge to herself, she ran to her room. Hands on both cheeks, she looked at the bright eyed girl who stared back at her happily. She was amazed at how, in a matter of moments, her despondency, her miserable companion of the last couple of weeks, had fallen off. I am well rid of it, she thought, her lips curving into a slight smile as she imagined a little amoeba-like creature jumping off her and slinking away on two little protrusions. Be off you miserable creature, she ordered happily, be gone forever. She watched the sad little thing till it was a tiny spot in the distance. Then it was swallowed up by the brilliance of the evening sun reflected in the mirror.

From the urgency of the message, it seemed like he might have had a change of heart. He couldn't let her meet with Rajinder after all. He must have come up with a plan. Full of hope, she slid open her wardrobe door. It was packed with clothes but she felt she had absolutely nothing that was perfect for the occasion. She laughed softly, knowing what Binny and Lou would have to say about that. But they wouldn't understand.

She could well be eloping. By day's end, she could be married. Now don't get carried away, she admonished herself. But a part of her believed he might be making a last ditch desperate effort to snag her before Rajinder could get his hands on her. She wanted to look her stunning best for Bhagu. He had to see her in her best clothes. Yet, they shouldn't be her flashy best. She knew he hated flashy. Besides, she didn't wish to arouse her parents' suspicion by dressing up to the hilt. Which reminded her, she had to cook up an excuse. Without even thinking about it much, she pretended to dial Lou so that her mum would hear it on the extension phones in the lounge or master bedroom. Then, glowing, she went into the lounge, gave her mum a warm hug and told her Lou was throwing a party for friends that evening – the first one at the start of the holidays. And that she and Binny were invited to stay overnight. Shali didn't even blink as she dished out the lies. Bless her heart, thought her mum, she looks happy again. The two chatted together for a while, with Shali aware of how dramatically she might turn her own and her parents' lives upside down in a matter of hours. But, she thought, I know they want my happiness. And once my marriage to Bhagu is a fait accompli, I know they will grow to love him as much as I love him.

That evening, she got into the car and with a shy smile, asked the chauffeur to drive her to the back gates of the college. She knew they shared a guilty secret and it made her blush. She had never looked prettier. On her instruction, the chauffeur brought the car to a halt at what looked like the impenetrable trunk of a mango tree. Excusing herself, she was about to get out of the car when the chauffeur, puzzled, asked if m'emsa'ab

didn't want to be driven a bit further down to the back
gates. Shali was hard put not to laugh. Did he think
she'd climb over the gates and into the college? With a
little shake of her head, she went towards the tree at the
wall and disappeared. She kept a wary look-out for
Chacha. He was the last person she wanted to run into.
He might appear malleable to the others but they hadn't
seen the malevolent look he had given Bhagu. Shali
headed straight for the banyan tree. She wondered what
Bhagu's plan was. It had to be something loving. She
felt it in her bones. And the banyan tree did hold a lot of
tender memories for them both. It was the perfect place
for him to share whatever his big surprise was, especially if it was a proposal of marriage. She felt tears rush
to her eyes. Bhagu had always been a romantic. By the
time she reached the Banyan tree, every other thought
was expelled from her mind. She felt she was floating
on air. Every cell in her body cried out to be with him
again.

She reached the banyan tree almost at a run. She
couldn't see Bhagu anywhere. Her heart drumming
wildly, she wondered where he was. Was he playing
one of those silly games of his? "Bhagu," she called out
in an urgent whisper, "Bhagu, where are you?" She
looked around anxiously. Perhaps he was a bit late. She
turned to look at the gap beside the mango tree and saw
the tail end of a white uniform quickly disappear behind another tree. Her dulled mind wondered what her
chauffeur was doing inside. Hadn't she asked him to
wait in the car? And why was he ducking behind trees?
Confused, she sat down on one of the thick over-ground
roots. Her mind was unable to make sense of anything
at all. Where was Bhagu? Why wasn't he here. Her sub-

conscious mind was beginning to grasp that something wasn't quite right. Why had Bhagu asked her to meet him at the college? After the two had discussed Chacha's look of pure hatred, they had both kept away from the banyan tree. It was much too close to the canteen. Didn't he remember that? Had he forgotten they didn't even go much to the canteen unless it was to join either the union members or Lou, Binny and Partha's crowd? With ever growing conviction, Shali was beginning to feel that the last place Bhagu would ask to meet her was the deserted college. Could her chauffeur have got the meeting place wrong? Was Bhagu waiting for her somewhere else? Or is he not coming at all, she thought, feeling almost physically ill at having to face up to the painful probability. Utter hopelessness threatened to engulf her. She had built her hopes up for nothing. Her voice escaped on a sob. She'd been a perfect fool. In her eagerness to believe what she wanted so desperately to, she hadn't stopped to think. Why would he use her chauffeur as the messenger? Could it not have been Binny or Lou? And if he didn't wish to bring them into the picture, he would most likely have called himself, talking only if Shali answered the 'phone. Or, he would have called her on her mobile. Which registry[39] is open at this time? she asked herself as if talking to someone really dumb. Yet, her dulled mind was unable to grasp what the far reaches of her consciousness were trying to tell her.

Slowly, a horrible suspicion began piercing the fog in her mind. Why had the chauffeur lied to her? She stood up in slight panic. Some knowledge of danger began to alert her. Her abject misery gave way to a growing sense

---

39 registered marriage office

of fear. She started breathing in short, sharp gulps. She had been a fool to believe the chauffeur's story. And yet, he had been with them since she was a little girl. It was impossible to do otherwise. Besides, she had wanted to with all her heart. But that was earlier this evening. She knew now, without any doubts, that she was in grave danger. Every sense alerted, her mind started thinking fast. She desperately looked around for somewhere to hide. She realised she couldn't make a run for it to the mango tree. He would be keeping a close watch. She wouldn't stand a chance sprinting across the field and trying to clamber the back gate. He was the faster and the stronger of the two. Besides, thanks to the care the college took to discourage vendors or squatters there, the back ally was one of the few completely deserted roads in Bombay. Even if she reached the outside, she would have to run the length of the road before she was completely out of danger.

She realised she had to hide as he would be upon her in a matter of seconds. She dropped her chunni, knowing it might fly out behind her and be seen. Even as she ran towards the back of the canteen, her mind tried to work out a plan. She knew the college better than he. In fact she knew every inch of it well. She would make her way through a complicated, roundabout route through the college corridors to the front gate. Yes, that was quite the best thing to do. He wouldn't expect that. He'd be keeping watch to ensure she didn't run back to the mango tree or the gates, not in the opposite direction and into the college. That would catch him by surprise and give her a few precious moments to get away. Even as the plan formed at the back of her mind, she worked out the route she must take. She could clearly see it in her mind's eye. She began to hope. Feverishly opening the outer pocket of her handbag to extricate her mobile before dropping the bag behind the canteen, she worked her way quickly and silently to the clump of gulmohrs. When the chauffeur reached the banyan tree where, she was sure, he had seen her go, she would wait till he headed for the back of the canteen where he would obviously conclude she had run to hide. it would give her a precious thirty second headstart while he searched, to quickly run from behind the trees to the main building. If she were lucky she would make it inside the building before he came round again. Even if he did see her disappear inside, he would probably get lost in the corridors. She felt the front gate was her only chance. She didn't need to clamber over. Just rattle it and scream. There were people there.

She waited a few seconds till she felt he must be behind the canteen. Then she rushed straight for the building. But that was her miscalculation. The chauffeur hadn't moved from behind the banyan tree. He was fingering his young mistress' dupatta. It proved she had spotted him. He cursed silently. The game was up. He paused to plan. The vaguely instinctive thought at the back of his mind was to kill her after he'd raped her.

A sudden flurry of movement caught his eye. He saw Shalini emerge out of the clump of gulmohrs and make a dash for the college. He immediately understood her intentions. Cursing profusely, he sprinted after her. There was no pretence from either of them any more. Panting, Shalini entered the courtyard of the building. Without hesitation she dashed into one of the corridors, knowing it split into four which would help confuse the chauffeur. Her skin crawled with fear and her senses were alert to every sound. She forced herself to stop the sobbing sounds that escaped on every breath. Moving silently, she unhesitatingly took the twists and turns that would lead her to the front gates. And then her 'phone rang. For a heart stopping moment she stared blankly at it. Then, realising the need for silence was gone, she made a wild dash for the exit. But the chauffeur was upon her. He clamped his hand on her mouth knowing they were too close to where there might be people and dragged her back through the corridor to the back of the building. Even though her mind had accepted what his intentions were, the moment he grabbed her paralysed her with shock, fear and revulsion – each vying for precedence over the other. She felt like a hunted animal, caught in the death grip of a terrifying hunter. She struggled feebly. She wasn't aware of the sounds emanating from the depth of her being – sobbing sounds of sheer terror. The chauffeur felt a heady rush of power as he realised how utterly futile her struggles were. She realised it too and the fight went out of her. She slumped for a second. But nausea threatening to engulf her, she realised, even as he propelled her along, that he had begun pawing her. On another sobbing breath she began hitting out harder, kicking and clawing. Her fear gave way to hatred and such utter loathing she fought viciously to regain control. The man was taken aback at the unexpected assault. She let out an ear splitting scream. It echoed through the building. He cursed and clamped her mouth hard again. He decided he would take the prisoner – she was no more a person to him; just a hunted and captured animal whose spirit he was going to break at all costs – almost to the back of the building where there weren't so many echoing corridors. His clamp like a vice, he once again dragged, pushed and half carried her back to where they had entered the building.

The look on his face was almost maniacal with lust. All vestige of respect was gone from his eyes. With his free hand he made a grab for all her private parts. His grip on her mouth loosened for an instant and she let out another scream. This time, to his satisfaction, he realised her voice barely carried at all. Confident they were both far enough away from the edges of the college, he yelled at her to shut up or he'd kill her. Then he started screaming abuses at her. "You slut. It always puzzled me how you came out through locked gates in the evenings. Now I know. You lose woman. Pretending you were at the college studying while F-ing around all the time. God knows what you two have been up to. You whore. I'll teach you a lesson. Women like you deserve nothing better."

She was horrified to hear the filth pouring from his mouth. Gone was the respectful veneer. She felt his rough hands close around her wrist and knew there was no escape. Unceremoniously he threw her on the floor and fell on her with ferocious energy. "You are going to get what you deserve," he said. His face close to hers, she saw the raw, naked lust. As he came closer, she could smell his breath. Nauseated, she turned her face away. She thought she would throw up and gave another scream. Even as she struggled to free herself she realised how pitiful and puny her ebbing strength was, compared to his. She became semi conscious, floating between reality and another plane. She saw a whirlwind hurtling through her mind. And suddenly, as if by magic, the weight was lifted off her.

Chacha and Chachi walked in just in time to hear her scream. After her household chores were done, Chachi often left the kids with his uncle's widow and accompanied Chacha to the canteen to clean up or nurture the herbs they grew to avoid paying for them in the market. It was easier to use the tree entrance even though they had a key to the back gate.

Chacha immediately saw the man and the almost inert body of the woman under him. His dirty paws were all over her. He saw the last remnants of her struggle to resist and realised what was happening. The chauffeur was about to overpower her. Without even thinking Chacha charged like a raging bull. For a moment it was his little girl who was being raped. He was back in the field in his village. He had a second chance. He would save his daughter from both, the rape and the murder that was to follow.

There was a fierce battle between Chacha and the chauffeur. Chacha fought to save his daughter's life and the chauffeur, to save his own. Neither had any compunction about hurting the other. And hurt each other they did. Chachi joined in, pelting the man with stones and still keeping a wary distance. Not for nothing had she watched hundreds of Bollywood movies with the villain fighting the hero suddenly making a grab for the heroine to hold her hostage.

The chauffeur soon realised he had no chance. It was two against one. He put his arms over his face in self defence and lay there, beaten and covering with fright. Chacha wasn't satisfied. He wanted blood. Chachi begged him to reconsider. What brought him to his senses was her saying it wouldn't bring back their daughter. That the police might punish him didn't bother him in the least. With one last hard kick aimed at where it hurt most, Chacha finally stopped. Shalini knew she should get up and run but her limbs had given up on her. She simply sat there, huddled and in a complete state of shock, unable to move. Chachi tore up bits of her sari and together, she and Chacha tied the chauffeur's limbs and mouth so securely, he grimaced in pain. But he didn't dare protest.

Finally Chachi was with her. She knew it was over. At least for her. She pointed silently to the mobile phone which Chachi brought for her. With hands that shook she dialled her dad. He would take charge. He would know what to do. After a moment his voice came on line. "Yes, Shali," he said sounding perfectly normal. Shali simply sat there, breathing hard, watching the receiver end from where the warm voice with its familiar thread of affection flowed. She felt choked, unable to talk. "Papa," she kept saying, "papa…" Chachi took the phone gently from her unresisting hands and started talking into it excitedly in her native tongue. Quickly realising she wasn't getting far with the person at the other end, she switched to broken Hindi, managing to convey what had happened.

Dr. Dayal understood enough of what she said to know there was no time to waste. His heart started racing but so did his mind. He needed to get to his little girl as soon as possible. He managed to warn Chachi not to phone anyone else, especially not the police then asked to speak to his daughter. He spoke to her very gently. Shali could only keep crying and staring at the 'phone. He instructed her to stay put. He and mum would be with her soon. He repeated his earlier instructions, warning her not to call another soul.

While Shali was talking, Chachi left her to tend to Chacha. Shali watched, as if from a great distance. Chacha sat there, slumped. She could tell he was hurt. Not that he noticed. For the first time in years, where he had built a stone wall around his heart after having lost his little girl, he was weeping uncontrollably. Even from such a mental distance, watching him, Shali forgot herself for a moment. She knew he was slightly injured but somehow, the wracking sobs seemed not to be for any physical pain he felt. Forgetting her own ordeal she watched, her heart wrung tight as she witnessed his pain. She did not even notice her own tears falling soundlessly from huge, unblinking eyes. The tears were for him. Then they were for herself. Even Chachi, standing by helplessly where earlier, she had fought so valiantly, hurling those rocky missiles to protect her man from harm, cried silently. She had been able to grieve for their little girl. But not he. He had become overprotective of his womenfolk, to the point of being a mini tyrant. Today was the first time he was venting his grief. Her heart wrung with pity, she stood by helplessly, watching him, wiping her reddened eyes with the ends of her sari.

Soon Shalini's parents arrived. They'd been instructed to walk into the deserted street behind the college. They came as quietly as possible and walked in through the little gate at the side entrance which Chachi had left open for them.

Shali's dad immediately took charge. Ever since the 'phone call, he had forced his emotions to take secondary place. His mind took on the same sharp edge it did before a complicated operation, seeing things with clarity in his mind, planning ahead to the next stage while his heightened senses paid full attention to the present. His wife, anxious to get to her daughter, did not flinch while he paused to open the safe in his steel cupboard and grab a little box with five hundred wads of 100 rupee notes. He knew what he was doing. He cautioned her not to look agitated as they went out the door. He informed Rajubai they were going to Lands End for a drive as they often did before or after their evening meal.

He understood one thing with dead certainty. Even the whiff of a whisper about his daughter being the unfortunate victim of a would-be rape, would ruin her reputation. From being one of the most eligible young ladies in her community, she would suddenly become a pariah, an untouchable. No respectable Indian family would want a bahu who had been pawed by a chauffeur. She simply wouldn't be pure and pristine in their eyes any more. She would be second hand goods, sullied forever. He was determined to protect her from that while the matter was still within his hands. By the time they reached the college he had come up with the vague outline of a plan. But first, he had to speak with the man who had saved his daughter. He took Chacha aside and the two had a hurried conversation. By the end of it, for the second time that evening Mr. Dayal was in shock. He was unable to get the picture that Chacha had drawn so vividly, of the disgusting creature who was now abject in fear and defeat, but who, only a few minutes earlier, had tried to defile and probably kill his young daughter out of his mind. Regrettably, there were other, more urgent matters he had to attend to and this would have to wait. He shared his plan with Chacha and they shared it with the rest so their story to the police would be consistent.

Safe in the arms of her mother, Shalini was ready to be led away when Chachi handed her the handbag and chunni. Her eyes thanked her although she had lost the power of her tongue. Tears began to prick her eyes as she turned them to Chacha, unable to say much but her eyes said it all. She did not know why but finally she realised he was a person – a human being – and not quite the villain she'd thought him to be. Her mum led her away and sat her in the car. Softly running to the other car which was parked nearby, she collected Shali's little overnight duffle bag from the boot and ran back to the car she and Mr. Dayal had come in and where her daughter waited, abject shame and misery in her face. There the two women waited with the mum talking softly and soothingly to her daughter, ready to drive away as fast as possible as soon as Mr. Dayal got in.

Mr. Dayal tended to Chacha, checked him for broken bones and satisfied that none were, turned to the most hateful task he would ever perform. Fighting his desire to squeeze the life out of the man, he cursorily tended to the chauffeur, who lay there, still and defeated, where earlier he had been writhing in pain. At first Mr. Dayal wondered if he might be dead but knew that wasn't the case. From a slight distance Chacha sheepishly explained where he had aimed his last kick and the two men couldn't help exchanging a quick look of grim vindication. Unable to help being slightly rough on the lowlife, Mr. Dayal, more to ensure Chacha wouldn't end up being punished if the sub human ingrate lost his life, than out of any humane or noble intent, tended to him enough to reassure himself he wouldn't die before the police got there. As he told his wife later, it was one of the hardest things he had been called upon to do. That unfortunately, although slightly hurt, he would survive. As Mr. Dayal hurried away, Chacha limped to the canteen and hid the box full of money which Mr. Dayal had discreetly handed him before dialling the police. When he returned, Chachi had already let Mr. Dayal out and shut the gate. Mr. Dayal ran to his wife's car and they drove away leaving Chacha, Chachi and the chauffeur behind.

On the way home Mr. Dayal spelt out his second plan. The idea, he said, was to have a water tight story as to why the parents and daughter went out separately in two cars but came home together in one. Mrs. Dayal gently straightened out Shali's dishevelled appearance, combing her hair and making her put on her shoes.

They were quite certain Rajubai hadn't known Shali's tale about the party at Lou's. She had been out market shopping for the next day's meal when Shali had left the flat. Shali on a shopping spree would be a much better idea. It would preclude having to bring Lou and a whole gang of friends into the picture.

They would pretend that husband and wife, deciding to enjoy the cool evening sea breeze like hundreds of other Bandraites, were sitting at the parapet at Land's End when they'd received a 'phone call from their daughter. This would explain the phone call she had made on her mobile to her dad if the police decided to check that story out for some reason.

Shali would pretend that after shopping she'd been waiting ages for the car and chauffeur. Had he, for some reason, forgotten to pick her up? The parents would say they didn't know as they weren't home themselves.

Shali would then say she'd take a taxi home but since they weren't too far away from the shops the parents had offered to pick her up.

After they got home Mr. Dayal asked Rajubai if she'd heard from the chauffeur. She hadn't. In a tight voice he said he hoped there would be some explanation as to where the man had disappeared leaving Shali stranded at the shops.

Around midnight Mr. Dayal was summoned to the police station. There they informed him that his chauffeur had broken into the college through a gap in the wall, probably to defile Chachi. To his bad luck the chauffeur hadn't known that Chacha wasn't too far away. Chachi saw the stranger and screamed and before he knew it, Chacha was upon him. A hatha-hathi, hand-to-hand, followed. Both were hurt. But Chacha being the stronger of the two and having Chachi to help, had overcome the chauffeur very quickly. They told him the husband had almost beaten the man to a pulp. Then the couple had bound and gagged the man so tight, he'd almost choked. It had left red weals on his wrists and ankles. The police didn't bother to conceal their smirks. In shocked tones Mr. Dayal said the man had been with his family for a long time and that they would never feel safe unless he was locked away. The police told him not to worry. The man was an imbecile to even lay a finger on Chacha's wife.

With both Chacha's and Mr. Dayal's stories corroborating and the chauffeur being left in no doubt as to what Chacha and his entire slum would do to him if he ever contradicted the story, the case was closed. The overworked police didn't need to pursue the matter further. They informed Mr. Dayal his chauffeur would be a guest at their prison for a long time and that he had best look for another.

Uncomfortably aware that he was in the same seat his daughter's would-be rapist had sat in, Mr. Dayal drove his second car home from the police station. A very worried Mrs. Dayal and Rajubai met him at the door. He told them the chauffeur was locked up in jail because he had attempted to rape someone. "O my Budha," said Rajubai, looking shocked. This was the man she had invited into her kitchen for a roti and a tea, often when nobody was at home. Hands on cheeks and unable to hold herself up, she sat down on her haunches.

Much later, in the privacy of their bedroom, Mr. and Mrs. Dayal finally had time to talk about their daughter. Mr. Dayal told her what Chacha had told him about the chauffeur's desperate attempts to justify his rape. He said it was because Shali was a loose woman. Mrs. Dayal, looking contemptuous and angry, turned to her husband, a cutting remark at the tip of her tongue. "How dare he…" she started saying when, taken aback by something in her husband's sober expression, she stared at him in astonishment, angry retort completely forgotten. Instinctively she knew her husband was about to reveal something significant about their daughter. Realising his wife was waiting impatiently, he hastily took up where he'd left off. "He said she was loose," he hesitated, "because Shali was friendly with a boy from college."

"Chacha had often seen the two together," he continued, as if to lend credence to the chauffeur's story. The chauffeur was capable of saying anything to validate his own actions, but Chacha, the hero who had saved their daughter from harm, couldn't possibly have any reason to lie. "According to Chacha the two had been together since the past three years although recently they seemed to have grown apart." Mrs. Dayal was in a state of mild shock. It was an astonishing revelation. Why hadn't she guessed before? Did life really get that busy that she didn't know what was happening in her daughter's life? Why did Shali not tell her? Didn't her young daughter confide in her any more? Then she remembered her attempts at matchmaking. But that is how it has always been done, she beseeched her daughter mentally. How was I to know you had grown to like someone else? Why didn't you tell us? Don't you trust us anymore? Mrs Dayal's thoughts were confused but she finally understood why Shali had hated the thought of Rajinder so much. It wasn't because she wasn't ready to take such a giant leap into the unknown. She was more than ready. Only, it was with someone else. And if she had seemed to enjoy the company of Rajinder's parents in Jaipur, it was because Rajinder wasn't there and they were likeable enough for themselves. Besides, it was alien for Shali to be rude to her elders.

Through the night the parents kept puzzling over many things – why did Shali and the chauffeur end up at the deserted college at all? Was there really an overnight party at Lou's? Well, she sighed, putting away all the questions for now. Being from the medical profession Mrs. Dayal decided there were things that had to be done first. Tomorrow she'd get in touch with a very good friend, a psychiatrist. She knew Shali would need all the help she could to recover.

As they lay awake in bed, disturbed, puzzled and making plans for their daughter's future well being, Shali lay in bed, semi conscious, waiting for the injection her mum had given her to help her sleep, take effect. As she looked up at the bright, starlit night sky, she knew she had had the luckiest of escapes. Apart from a few bruises, there was no physical evidence of what she had been through. She lay there for a long time, half drugged but battling sleep. She felt nauseated at the thought of the ugliness that had almost tainted her life. Strangely, a part of her recalled the incident with the autorickshawalla outside the movie theatre. Had they not been in a crowded place, she was certain he would have done more than just leer at them. She shuddered.

She shuddered again. She wished her mind wouldn't keep churning up these thoughts. She didn't want to think about anybody or anything. She was …so …tired. Within a few minutes, overcome by exhaustion, she fell into a deep, fitful sleep.

The next day at the police station Mr. Dayal, pretending to meet Chacha for the very first time, listened as the head police officer disclosed the fate of the chauffeur. He would be locked away for a very long time. That is what the man deserved. Dr. Dayal offered Chacha free medical treatment and gave him a small sum of money at the police chowki, station, as a token of his gratitude. The story barely made the bottom of the middle pages – an unsuccessful rape by a chauffeur was hardly headline news. Those still belonged to the leader of Doosri Aazaadi and terrorists.

Chacha and Chachi never breathed the truth about that day to anyone. In some strange way, they both knew that Chacha had finally put his own little girl's ghost to rest.

Since the incident had taken place at the college, the police informed Dr. Naakwaa and the trustees. Over the holidays the gap in the wall was permanently sealed.

- The Parents -

Shali knew her parents would have many questions. Her story about the chauffeur having forced her through the gap in the wall was possible but not probable. She couldn't bring herself to come clean about Bhagu. She didn't see the point. It was best to let it remain a secret. It wasn't worth revealing now that it was over.

As for her parents, it sufficed them to know she had almost been a rape victim and had been saved by Chacha in the nick of time. They decided they wouldn't evoke the spectre of Bhagu as, according to Chacha, the affair seemed to have ended.

They knew it would take time but were determined she would have a second chance at happiness. At the moment, Shali was gratefully aware of two things. Thanks to her dad's intervention, the secret was safe. She didn't have to deal with pitying looks from others nor ostracism from the Dayal clan. The offers for her hand in marriage were still coming in hard and fast. But her parents shielded her from all that. All they wanted was for her to heal, not only through time, not only through their patience and understanding but through all possible practical and medical help available in Mumbai and elsewhere. She knew how hard they tried. She found heaps of books and even internet sites they visited to make use of the research and expertise they knew they'd find there.

More than anyone else, Shalini was passionately grateful to her therapist. From finding herself completely repugnant, from blaming herself and even feeling slightly suicidal, she began seeing things in a completely new light.[40]

She explained how after the attempted rape she had strangely remembered the autowallah. Her therapist helped her see the connection. She finally understood how such people needed to convince themselves the female was at fault. That seemed to give them the justification to do what they really wanted, which is, to foist their unwanted attention on the opposite sex, to satisfy their baser instincts uncaring of the other person's wishes and well being. The therapist also went on to explain what Shali already knew - that there were the others, the decent and caring ones.

Like the ones in my world - my dad, my uncles. ....and Bhagu, thought Shali. She knew how much he had loved and wanted her. They had been away from society's eyes on so many occasions. And she was hardly a 'victim'. She had wanted him as much as he'd wanted her. Yet he had let her decide how far they would progress in their physical relationship. She had set the boundaries and he had respected them. She remembered the passion they had shared but quickly pushed

---

[40] Psychiatry is a misunderstood profession in India. Some Indians associate help from a psychiatrist as an acknowledgement of 'madness' They would rather live with whatever ails them emotionally than let the world think they are mad. And since their own family members subscribe to that view, they aid and abet the victim in either not seeking that help or, keeping the knowledge under tight wraps. Some members of the junta – common man in Indian parlance – have often been heard to declare with great scorn that psychiatry is best left to others who have money to spare; they have much better use for their own hard-earned cash, thank-you very much.

that memory away. The thought of anything even re-motely physical still seemed to make her want to retch. The other ugly memory – too fresh in her mind - came crowding back. That is when her therapist's explana-tions of exactly what she was going through and why, came in handy. She knew she wasn't to blame. She had to keep reminding herself she was the victim and the one way she could fight back was by not punishing her-self for what had happened.

She had been reassured, and had started hoping it was true that over time, this episode would be a far and dis-tant bad memory, one that wouldn't disturb her any more. Shali longed for that day. In the mean time, she had to take each day as it came. Some were good and some, not so good. Her next challenge was to face the college again after the holidays. She was grimly deter-mined she would overcome her fear and revulsion and get back as much of her old life as possible. There was to be no backing out of college. She owed it to herself, her parents, her future.

- Last Term –

It was the last term of college. There was an air of hushed expectancy. Professors, who had come in half an hour before students, savoured their final moments of peace. Dr. Naakwa had forgotten what loud laughter sounded like; he recoiled at the thought of his first en-counter with it after an absence of three blissful weeks. He really looked forward without much hope, to the day that fad would pass.

He stood admiring the clean lines of the back section. Every weed had been dug out of the grassy field and it looked soft and new. The atmosphere was still mopping up the early morning dew. One or two droplets caught the sun in sudden sharp glints. The trees, rejuvenated after the receding December rains, showed off an abundance of leaves. As he watched, the cool, January breeze sucked the leaves in like a giant vacuum, pulling them all in one direction. Then, suddenly, it decided to blow on them instead, making them flutter in wild confusion. Bombay winters lasted till the middle of February. Temperatures plummeted to around twenty degrees celcius. Unused to the early morning cold, some Mumbaikars wore cardigans and shawls smelling faintly of mothballs. Others, knowing it would get warmer as the day wore on, preferred to shiver the early morning hours away and not be saddled with bulky baggage later.

There had been a lot of excitement at the college during the holidays. Chacha, with Chachi's help, had saved the college from a would-be robber, the story Dr. Naakwa preferred to put out. What had amazed Dr. Naakwaa was the change it had wrought in Chacha. He was a new man. Dr. Naakwaa had known for a while about Chacha's young, twelve year old daughter's rape and murder in the fields of his village. The dossier had explained a lot to him. The daughter's rapists were caught and were languishing in jail. But Chacha had been unable to vent his grief for a long time. He had become hard, almost dictatorial with his wife and his sister-in-law. When his young uncle in Bombay had offered him the job, the family had urged him to accept. After an initial struggle, he seemed to have found his niche. The residents of the slum where he lived were slightly in awe of the man. After the other Chacha's tragic death, he had assumed the mantle of leadership easily. No one could deny his ability to get things done – he had managed to get them a tap with running water and a urinal just a little distance from the slum.

He wasn't quite the complete hero. Being human, there was another side to him. The power he enjoyed at the slum had gone to his head. He was unable to accept a young pup like Bhagu questioning him when adults showed him deference and respect. He was unable to come to terms with the freedom enjoyed by women in his adopted city. He thought the female students he saw at the college were the worst of the lot. He hadn't been scrupulously honest at the canteen. His salary, though generous, hadn't been enough. Watching the profits the canteen raked in, he thought he deserved a bigger cut. In his desire to make a hasty buck he had started going down the wrong path, adulterating food and drink, not registering sales and pretending to the world that he remained lofty in his ideals. He had been stopped in the nick of time. The student body policed him and the college introduced, much to Jayaram, the clerk's chagrin, a system of coupons. Still, Dr. Naakwa was thankful the man didn't dabble in drugs or that he wasn't linked with gangs.

After the latest incident Chacha had finally laid the ghosts that tormented him to rest. It was as if some immense strength within him, borne out of anger and grief, had drained away. It left him feeling soft and relaxed. In the strangest of ways, he was the happier for it. The college instated two night-watchmen from a security agency. The gap in the wall was sealed.

- Changes –

Shouts of overjoyed greetings told Dr. Naakwa the students had started walking in. Before long, the corridors, the common rooms, the library and classrooms were all filled to overflowing.

Binny, Lou, Partha and their crowd headed for the canteen. One or two students had heard of Chacha's heroic rescue. Rumours were rife. Everyone eyed Chacha, chattering excitedly. He scowled back, standing there, very much in command. Two smiling young women bustled about with vigour in the kitchen. Chacha, who had let the Chachis work in his canteen while he was nursing his bruised body back to health realised he rather enjoyed their help. He continued delegating "some" of his work to the Chachis. At first he ensured they were relegated to the kitchen and didn't come out much. Over time, they were all over the place, cooking, serving, gardening, washing...

The students were fascinated. They had met one of the Chachis when she was the first Chacha's wife. They had always felt a lot of affection for her. Rumour had it that the other Chachi had shown a villain the stuff women were made of and in spite of Chacha's discouraging scowls which they ignored, they couldn't help smiling at her too. The Chachis smiled back happily.

And sala![41] Did they know their stuff! Everyone wanted to try the new paper dosas. At a reasonable price and with coffee thrown in for half price, they were a steal. As they waited, the busy little canteen boys scurried between tables, holding aloft plates bearing those culinary works of art. Each was like a fat, hollow scroll fried

---

41 Sala – mild expletive, "Oh Boy!" closest in translation

to a pale perfect brown. Each was much too big for the plate it was in and was accompanied by little bowls of saambhar and fresh coconut chutney.

Partha's group eyed a dosa with hungry anticipation as it was cruelly whisked past and set in front of a smug young person at the next table. Finally it was their turn. Before putting the dosas down, the canteen boys gave their table an extra wipe with a flourish. There seemed to be a new energy to their step. With the wet, stinky rags slung over their shoulders, the kids ran off to serve the others. The crowd at their table stoically bore the slight stink emanating off the table not knowing if they were amused or disgusted.

Partha turned to Lou. "Perhaps this could be Bhagu's next project..." he said, an eyebrow shooting up to meet his hairline, making the others laugh.

Dr. Nakwa, desirous of seeing for himself how the two Chachis were coping, was half way to the canteen when a host of wild screeches carrying clearly on the cool morning air made him hurry all the way back to the sanctuary of his office.

– One Step at a Time –

It was almost time for the bell. The students, replete, declared the dosas had been the best they'd eaten in a long while. Binny turned to Lou, anxious eyebrows raised in slight enquiry. "Why isn't Shali here yet?" she said in a quiet aside. "Perhaps she is already in class," whispered Lou. And then they saw her. She looked lovely and frail. They both jumped up chattering on about the best dosas in town and making her smile. Had they observed more closely, they would have seen the discreet smile one of the Chachis gave Shali from the kitchen. Under strict instructions to pretend she didn't know Shali, she still couldn't resist the slight interchange. Shali felt grateful. She was surrounded by people who cared for her. Besides, Binny, Lou and the entire group looked so normal. None of them knew what had happened to her and perhaps it was best this way...

Walking through the corridor of the college she had almost lost her nerve. But she knew if she wanted to give herself a chance at happiness, she would have to go through with this, the hardest test of all. The message had been re-enforced by her therapist. She had her mobile phone on. It was her lifeline. She listened more than talked. Her parents and her therapist sat in the car, just a little distance away, outside the gates. They knew she was at the spot where it had all happened. Her therapist did all the talking.

Shali stood for a heart stopping second and stared, almost hypnotised, at the dreaded place. Her memory of that night came crowding back. As if from a long distance, the voice on her mobile penetrated her mind. "He was scum – unsuccessful scum who is now locked away. You are free to enjoy the beautiful day. Feel the breeze on your face. Isn't it cool? Look around. Look at the faces of the happy youngsters surrounding you. This is real. It is what's happening. This is now."

Shali did as she was told. She forced the dark image imprinted on her memory to recede, looking at the smiling students surrounding her. They chattered excitedly, they waved and yelled out to friends they hadn't seen in a fortnight. One or two gave her a smiling nod. With a rush of warmth she responded. A group of young girls and boys walked all over the very spot with utmost unconcern. Shali almost squirmed when she saw that. But their indifference was a blessing. It made her realise what had happened – almost happened, she corrected herself – was, indeed, in the past. Her mind, almost unconsciously echoed her therapist's voice - this was real; this was now. No one suspected a thing. There, that seemed to help.

She spotted her friends at the canteen. They were laughing their heads off. A slightly harried looking Dr. Naakwaa walked past, then turned and smiled at her serious face. "Good morning sir," she said quietly. He nodded pleasantly and hurried away. Shali felt the dread dissolve. These were familiar sights - sights she had lived with for the past three years. They made her feel safe. Speaking into the mobile she told her parents she was fine and that they could go home now. Were they imagining it or was her voice sounding slightly happier? Her therapist felt it too. Smiling, she congratulated Shali. "One step at a time," she reminded her, "Well done."

Shali slowly walked towards the canteen. Tomorrow, she knew it would be easier. Walking back with Binny and Lou, she gave her two friends a brilliant smile. They looked back at her, slightly anxious as they were on a completely different thread of thought. She would be meeting Bhagu for the first time after the break.

Shali knew what was on their minds. Bhagu and her past life seemed a million years away. If he had no desire to be with her anymore, she knew her desire to be with him was a hundred times less. She wanted nothing to do with men at all. She didn't even pretend to look out for him in the classroom. Bhagu reacted by getting more involved with the student union and Doosri Aazadi. He worked like someone driven. It was almost as if he simply transferred whatever he felt for her to Doosri Aazadi. He accepted there simply was no way of dragging out and prolonging an intimacy that neither felt any more. Her destiny lay with her own kind. Rajinder...

In due course, the Dayals received an invitation for Rajinder's marriage. His family, sensing the Dayals' about face, had arranged his marriage with an even more accomplished and beautiful girl from their community – a distant relation of the Dayals. Shali realised with relief that she had lost one of the biggest catches of her community.

- CHAPTER IV -

Life moved on. The four graduated from college. Neither of them opted for higher studies. Binny, realising she had made the wrong choice in economics, was bored senseless with her job in a chartered accountancy firm. She was happiest in her garden. Having completed her degree and being in a 'good' job the pressures from parent and peers were off. In that happy situation she was left in peace to nurture and grow plants in her free time – a hobby that, over time, grew into a fledgling business. Bhagu had only ever wanted a career in politics but was persuaded by his dad to help run the family business. Lou became a reporter for a prestigious newspaper.

TWO YEARS LATER

Even the tone of the telephone seemed loud and insistent. Mrs. Dayal winced. Peeping out from the kitchen, she frowned at her husband. Mr. Dayal, hopes dashed she or someone else would leave him in peace to read the Sunday paper, smiled guiltily as he hastily dumped it on the sofa, regretting it was in such disarray when only moments ago, he'd enjoyed watching a ripple go through the smooth, uncrumpled, neatly folded pages. He hastened to stop the dull and insistent ringing.

Mem's voice came over the line immediately. She said in Hindi, "Why doesn't your wife answer the phone promptly. Do you have to do all the work in this household?"

"Namaste ma," he said, the dry and slightly resigned expression on his face not evident in the respectful tone of voice. "Jeetey raho, betey," she said in a softer voice, "Long life." Her calls had become a daily affair. Ever since Rajinder had been lost to another girl, she only had one topic of conversation… Shali's marriage.

"We are looking at a list of possibles, mum," Mr. Dayal said, hoping to deflect her questions by infusing his voice with the confidence of someone who had things well under control. Mem, not to be deflected so easily, asked for specifics. "Who is on the list? Mujhey to batao…" (do tell me) Mr. Dayal, stumped, handed the conversation over to his wife and went back to his papers with obvious relief. Mrs. Dayal, looking daggers at her husband, faced the conversation with her mother-in-law. The elder lady lambasted her over the phone. The younger one, after disconnecting, lambasted her husband for playing dirty with her. Next time, he was not to hand the phone over to her. The onus was squarely on him to answer Mem's uncomfortable questions.

Mr. Dayal didn't have long to wait. Within a few days Mem called. He awaited the dreaded inquisition anxiously while pleasantries were exchanged. Surprisingly it never came. 'Perhaps she has taken the hint,' he thought, hopefully. Another part of his brain told him that was quite impossible.

"….. coming to Bombay next week…."

"Yes ma," he said mechanically without taking in what she was saying, except that her voice didn't sound sharp. "My daughter-in-law," she continued, "and sorry to have to face the fact," she added grimly, "my son as well, are unable to fulfil my grand daughter's destiny." Ah there it is, thought her son, the sharpness is back. "Yes, m……" he said, thinking, I'm in for another telling off.

"I realise I will have to take matters in my own hands." She sounded exasperated as she rudely cut her son short. "I won't shirk my responsibility any more."

"Yes, ma," said Mr. Dayal automatically. "Rajinder was an absolute nothing – of no importance at all – compared to this young man," she was saying, exultation creeping into her voice.

"Wha…," said Mr. Dayal eloquently. "Haven't you paid attention to anything I've said?" she curtly cut in, "I have found a perfect match for Shali." Mem's voice was a study in triumph. She almost crowed as she continued, "I've met with his mother a couple of times. It has had to be very discreet because she is very famous." Mem sounded slightly awed. Mem awed? Mr. Dayal shook his head, overcome with awe himself and extremely nervous at the sudden twist this conversation had taken. Mem continued excitedly, "I have spoken to the boy a few times. I must say he is respectful. What a wonderfully well mannered boy. I have arranged the meeting. I'm coming to Bombay." Mem could hardly keep the triumph out of her voice. Mr. Dayal had gone quite pale. He looked around desperately, as if for some support. After a long silence he said, "That's good news, ma." When he finally disconnected, even Shali realised something significant had happened. Mute, she and her mum looked up at him expectantly. He remained motionless for a good minute, staring at the phone. Then he slowly turned to them both. "Mem is coming for a visit next week," he said, his face going from a distinct nervous to an artificial bright. Even as he spoke he realised he was planning on taking the easy way out. He wouldn't tell Shali the purpose of her visit. He'd leave it in the hands of his capable wife with whom he exchanged a meaningful look. She understood he didn't want an inquisition from her in front of their daughter – they'd talk later.

"And?" said Shali, looking clearly suspicious.

"And?" he repeated as if surprised, "That's great news, isn't it?" Shali looked doubtful but didn't say anything. Normally, she would have been overjoyed, immediately drawing up a list of things she wanted from Jaipur, not least her favourite foods – mirchiwada, maawaa – there were some things the Bombay mithaiwallahs, sweet vendors, simply didn't know how to make like their Jaipur counterparts. Today, she remained silent. Excusing herself, she went to bed.

Mr. & Mrs.Dayal had a long discussion. Mrs. Dayal sat there, a worried look on her face. But mingled with the worry was hope. "That ...that incident happened almost a year ago," she said, "I must admit Mem has been extremely patient after losing Rajinder."

"On the other hand," said Mr. Dayal anxiously, "we don't want Shali's recovery to be jeopardised in any way." They decided it was time to call another meeting with the therapist. Shali trusted her implicitly and they would leave it in her capable hands to break the real reason for Mem's trip. When Mrs. Saroj broached the subject, Shali was consumed with anxiety. But the therapist reminded her that the plan had always been one step at a time and the time had come for her to take the next logical step. She would meet the boy. That's all she had to promise. No more. She didn't have to agree to marry him, she reassured Shali, "Just see him and treat the whole incident as part of the healing process. We'll have another session the next day." With the words, "You owe it to yourself," ringing in her ears, a thoughtful Shali saw Mrs. Saroj off.

There was so much to think through that she didn't know where to begin. She knew she eventually did want marriage and the whole package. She understood she would have to work more than others at leading a normal, happy, fulfilled life. Why bemoan her fate? Instead, she'd simply get on with it. One step at a time. She knew she would never have taken the first step without her therapist. She would have hidden herself away and felt suicidal for the rest of her life. But with Mrs. Saroj's gentle encouragement and strong support, she had gone back to college and completed her degree. Anything after that had to be easy. As for her family, she knew how impossible it was to deflect Mem once she had made up her mind. Her poor parents probably had nothing to do with Mem's plans. And yet, she sensed how eager they were for her to say yes to simply seeing the boy. All things considered, she realised Mrs. Saroj was right. She told her parents she would see the boy and warned them she didn't have to say "yes". That it would most probably be a 'No'. Her parents were overjoyed.

Excited and full of hope her parents talked well into the night. If Mem were to succeed, and they hoped she would, she had to bring all her skills and charm to bear with Shali. Not wage war. The two kept their fingers crossed. Only Mem knew how to turn on the charm if she so decided. She would tease and indulge, she would adore and scold and she would pretend everything was fine even if she sensed Shali was nervous. "That is what Shali needs right now," said Mrs. Dayal happily, "...a good dose of Mem. "

"I'll start preparing the guest bedroom," she said with a fond look at her husband.

Shali had mixed feelings about Mem's visit. She knew the memory of that incident with the chauffeur didn't haunt her anymore. If anything, it made her angry to think he even dared foist his unwanted attentions on her. She felt repulsed. The major difference between now and when it first happened was that her disgust was well and truly for him. Not for herself any more. Yet she couldn't help feeling a slight sense of panic at the thought of the 'meeting'.

- The Meeting –

Shali sat in the bedroom, aware of a sense of unreality about her. The buzz in the other rooms contrasted sharply with her apathy. Rajubai had been cooking since morning, her daughter was on hand to help with the sweeping, swabbing, dusting, polishing; Shali's dad was sent on innumerable errands, happy to oblige and more than happy to get out of the bustling household where he seemed to be in everyone's way; her mum ran around in circles around Mem, trying to satisfy all her demands, one or two of them whims, couched in the word 'tradition' to give them legitimacy.

Trupti, truly happy after having spoken long distance to her beau from the privacy of Shali's room, turned all her attention to Shali. She complimented her on her choice of clothes. They couldn't help exchanging amused smiles at that as earlier, Mem had said the exact opposite, hoping to get Shali to wear something of her choice. "What you've laid out is not appropriate for the occasion, betae (child)," Mem had infused her voice with kindly authority which suggested Shali might be her adored grand daughter but when it came to dress protocol she was really a silly goose who would have to put her trust in Mem's greater experience and better judgement. She was slightly taken aback when Shali, with a sudden show of spirit had replied, "What you want me to wear is more for a wedding, not a first meeting." She might have given in about seeing this boy but she had no intentions of letting Mem dictate what she would or wouldn't wear, especially since her ideas were totally old fashioned. Stuck in time.

"You don't know how important this family is, betae." Shali waited expectantly, a tiny niggle of curiosity stirring inside. Mem wouldn't say more. Her moment of triumph was a matter of hours away. Oh what a coup! She wisely decided she'd let Shali win this battle. "I would have preferred a 'heavier' sari but this one is simple, but quality," she said.

The whole clan had wanted to come to Bombay but Mem had been instructed to keep it low key. She had decided she would take only her second grand daughter. Not only was it a very indirect peace offering to her second son for choosing that clerk for her, but with the catch she was planning for Shali, she felt magnanimous. She knew Trupti would be good for Shali. The cousins were really close and barring her two secrets – one, about Bhagu because she knew it would have been the end of the affair if Trupti innocently let it out, and the other, about the incident with the chauffeur which was best forgotten - Shali had always shared everything with her. Trupti was on hand to help her dress, Shali having firmly locked the elders out. Arranging the pleats of Shali's sari so they would fall with graceful precision, Trupti whispered that everything was pretty hush-hush. "Only the family knows why we are in Bombay ... - a direct request from the groom's family. They must be pretty important," she said. "to have Mem listen to them." The more Trupti prattled on, the more nervous it made Shali. What if she didn't like this man? It wouldn't be as easy to shake him off as she'd thought. Deciding it was too late to change her mind now, she thought she would go through the motions for now and put everything else from her mind for later. One step at a time. As she leaned forward to put on her bindi, her eye fell on the silver rod. "Didi, you're smiling..." Trupti's voice pierced through the haze of memory. Shali told her about the incident with Binny, about how she'd warily eyed this very rod, half believing Shali would lunge for and lance her nose. The sound of their giggles could be heard in the lounge. The parents exchanged smiles.

The soft chimes of the doorbell announced the arrival of the guests. Shali's heart missed a beat. It was one thing deciding she would meet the boy and say "No", it was quite another having to come face to face with him and his family. She sat there conscious of the dread creeping into her heart. Trupti's eyes went round with excitement as her eyes met Shali's sober ones in the mirror. Shali would make her entrance a little later, after everyone was settled, a tray of something sweet in her hands. Trupti would stay hidden in the kitchen with Rajubai, completely out of the picture.

'Well,' thought Shali, 'let's get it over with.' She decided she wouldn't say much at all, aware that whatever she did or didn't do, she would still be the focus of everyone's attention. She got up and turned to face the door. This was supposed to be a girl's most exciting moment.

But the thud of her heart had nothing to do with excitement.

Trupti fussed over a last minute detail, adjusting the silk to frame Shali's face before they silently headed for the kitchen. As they passed the lounge, Trupti shamelessly peered in, carrying out a whispered commentary about the occupants – His mum is sitting with Mem on the three seater; he and his dad are standing by the window with Taoji[42]. I can't see him clearly. His back is to us. The disappointment in Trupti's voice half made Shali smile. She continued walking towards the kitchen, aware of a total lack of curiosity about someone she was planning to refuse. Raajubai gave her a beaming look of approval. Picking up the tray that was ready for her, she quietly walked into the lounge. As she approached, conversation tapered off. A sudden hush descended on the room. Every face turned towards the door. She had her eyes downcast. But as she approached, the young man, who she instinctively knew was sitting on the single seater, suddenly stood up. Startled, she looked up and met his eyes. "Bhagu," she whispered, her hands beginning to shake. She almost dropped her tray. Darting a quick look around the room, Shali looked terribly agitated. Nothing made sense to her. What was Bhagu doing here? Surely he wasn't the groom. But he must be. Earlier Trupti had told her he was there with his parents. But Bhagu didn't have a mum. Perhaps this was all a cruel joke. Perhaps he was only accompanying the groom. But there couldn't be two eligible young males there. As the thoughts chased each other in rapid suc-

---

42 Taoji: Dad's elder brother; Shali's dad for Trupti

cession through her mind, confused, she stood there, the tray of sweets forgotten in her hand.

She darted quick looks at the other male sitting with her dad. He was obviously Bhagu's father. There was such an unmistakable resemblance. The lady was none other than the woman touted to be the future first lady of India. Shali went into total shock. Her photos were splattered all over the newspapers too regularly for her to be mistaken. Why, Shali had a photo of the future Prime Minister and first lady too. If one looked carefully, one could clearly see Bhagu in the background. As she stared, the lady gave her a smile. She had wondered if the girl loved her young ward as much as he seemed to love her. She wondered no more. Shali responded to that smile as a candle would to a light. Perhaps it wasn't a joke after all. A small glimmer of hope began to kindle itself in her fast beating heart. Her eyes fluttered. She managed to give a faint smile to the first lady before lowering her eyes. The warmth in her heart started to spread, suffusing her entire being.

Bhagu stood there, the tight knot of dread dissolving from his heart. There had been that off chance she might think him an unwelcome ghost from the past – a chance he knew he had to take. But Shali, thank God, was still his. She would always be his. A slow smile began to spread itself through his heart and into his eyes, till he too became aware of the others. He realised this had been a most unusual proposal. He sat down, making a tremendous effort to play by the rules as he tore his eyes away from her beautiful, beloved face.

Not even daring to breathe, Mr. and Mrs. Dayal looked on, unwilling to intrude, aware that whatever they said or did would spoil this exquisite moment. They couldn't have thought of anything to say if they had tried. Of only one thing they were sure - the young man seemed quite bowled over by Shali. That much was obvious, although he tried hard to conceal it. But more than him, they were struck by Shali's reaction. Her apathy of the past year had all but flown. They watched their daughter, fascinated.

Mem saw it too. She had been secretly worried by her grand daughter's utter listlessness. It had made her vaguely uneasy. But now she was exultant. She motioned for Shali to come and sit between her and the future first lady, "Come, my child," she said, patting the seat next to her, aware of the moment in her own way and the role she was destined to play in it. She was triumphant. Kusumji – the future first lady, no less - had approached her for her grand daughter's hand. She'd surpassed her own expectations.

It was many days later, when all the fanfare had died down, that Shali and Bhagu were completely able to fill each other in on the events of the past year. Bhagu had been shown many girls by his relations, fobbing them off with excuses they were beginning to challenge. The truth was simple. He was unable to get Shali out of his mind. He would never be happy unless she was his wife. He also knew that wasn't going to happen. She was probably married to that fellow, Rajinder, by now. He threw himself into his work in a desperate bid to forget her. After work he didn't dare stop. Every moment he was free, Shali's ghost troubled, tortured and haunted him. It refused to stay buried in the deep recesses of his mind. His evenings were completely taken over by Doosri Aazaadi. He attended their rallies and did any and everything he possibly could for them. It was a punishing routine but the alternative was worse. Doosri Aazaadi soon recognised his loyalty and later, discovering his talent for words, they promoted him to the inner caucus. Being so close to his leader, his admiration for the man grew. He was as happy as possible except in the few and far-between moments when he found himself free.

"But Bhagu, what if I were already married?" Shali scolded him, her face flushed with happiness as she held her hand out to admire the diamond and gold ring on a slender, beautifully manicured finger for the umpteenth time. She shot him a quick, teasing look from under thick eyelashes. "Since the past six months I knew you weren't. I knew you had refused that chap, what's his name, Rajinder or something," – the name still stuck in his throat. "How did you know that?" she asked in wonderment. "Did you keep tabs on me through detectives or something?"

"I knew because your dad told me," he said softly. "My dad!" she exclaimed in disbelief. "I thought my parents met you for the first time when you came over that night."

Bhagu shook his head. "Your dad got in touch almost seven months ago." Shali sat up. It was unbelievable. "It was over a year after we finished college and I had decided it was all irrevocably over between you and me. That it was best to let you get on with your life. Perhaps marry that fellow…."

"…I know," said Shali with a smile, "what's his name…"

"But after your dad told me you'd refused him-whose-name-I-prefer-to-forget," Bhagu grinned, acknowledging the fact, "hope rekindled in me. But back to the beginning…"

"Your mum and dad first heard about our college romance through Chacha on the day he and Chachi rescued you from your chauffeur."

Shali went pale. "That means," she said in a bare whisper, "that...that..."

"Yes, I know about that incident. I have known since the past two to three months. Your parents had to be sure I could live with the knowledge. They checked me out for four whole months before daring to divulge the secret. As if I ever could be put off you because of what that bastard tried to do, Shali. You live in every cell in my body; you course through my veins." His voice shook with passion. Keeping a tight rein on his feelings he held her close with gentle tenderness. It was too soon after the awful experience she had been through and he didn't want to frighten her off. Shali couldn't help thinking that the chauffeur's vile attacks were so completely at variance with Bhagu's finer sensibilities there was no comparison. She felt desirable and secure. Letting her head rest on his shoulder, she pressed a light kiss of gratitude in the hollow of his neck. The pulse throbbing just under his skin seemed to fascinate her. Loathe to break contact, her lips lingered, delighting in the drugged, sensual pleasure the touch aroused deep within her. Her lids came down partially on eyes heavily laden with ardour. Bhagu inhaled shakily. Her physical proximity attacked his senses. "Shali...," he said urgently. She tightened her arms around him, holding him close before letting go, shaken by the strength of her feelings and unable to meet his eyes. Her actions held out the promise of a passion that would reign unchecked whenever she was ready. He sensed he wouldn't have too long to wait... Forcing himself to concentrate he took up the tale again. "I wanted to run to you as soon as your dad told me. But he said it would have to be carefully planned. There was Mem to win over and after that, the biggest test – we had to see how you would react to me after that incident and after such a long absence. I realised he was right, of course. My heart was full of dread and happiness at the same time. Happiness because your dad and I warmed towards each other on that day.

"But how did you meet him?"

"It seems that he and Chacha sat in his car one evening during our last term and Chacha pointed me out to him. Your dad followed me to the bus stop and all the way home. He knew my name, looked it up on the board downstairs and the rest was easy."

"As easy as looking up the 'phone book…" murmured Shali, remembering her first call to Bhagu.

He smiled back, happy to see the light shining from her beautiful brown eyes. "That's right," he said, "for our foundry address is just below our residential address. He came over to the foundry. I didn't know who he was. Some old business crony of my dad's, I thought and didn't give him a second glance. But he kept looking towards me through my dad's office glass pane. So I finally went across. I knew who he was as soon as my dad mentioned his name. He casually handed me his card. On the back he'd penned in the words, "Please call me." I got in touch the very next day. We met at his clinic. He asked me many questions and I decided to come clean. I told him everything about us. I also told him I knew about Rajinder and that he had nothing to worry about from me. I told him why we'd broken up thinking it would reassure him to know I'd refused to run away with you. I said I wanted you to be happy. What I didn't tell him was that I was fighting feelings of insane jealousy for another man. All my old insecurities rose to the fore as I realised Rajinder would probably be a much better match for you than myself. Up to that point, your dad didn't say much. He listened rather than talked. For the first time, he volunteered the information that you weren't engaged nor married to Rajinder. And that nothing was planned between you two. I think he must have seen the blessed relief on my face for he smiled for the first time. I asked him why he had come looking for me. He answered that with a question of his own. He wanted to know if there was anyone else in my life. My heart full of hope I told him there was no one. We ended the meeting on that note. We kept meeting regularly after that. I wondered when or if he'd propose I meet you. But he never did. On thinking back about it, I sensed there was something bothering him but it was elusive. He never mentioned what you had gone through on that day. He wasn't sure if I loved you enough to live with that knowledge. So here we were, two people trying to gauge each other out. I kept meeting him, hoping something would come of it. He kept meeting me, trying to decide if my love for you could withstand the terrible knowledge. Four months after our first meeting I concluded he thought I wasn't good enough for you. Yet on another plane, I could swear he enjoyed my company. By now, I was already driving myself hard at work and at Doosri Aazadi. But it was hopeless. I felt I was losing my ability to concentrate. One day, unable to bear it any longer, I told your dad he had never answered my question about why he had come looking for me. Four months

223

down the road I was still wondering. I didn't bother to
hide the torture I felt when I baldly asked him how you
were and if you were engaged or married to anyone
else. Your dad went silent for a long time. Finally he
said you weren't. And that it wasn't due to a lack of offers but that there was a reason. I think I went pale because I started jumping to all kinds of conclusions. My
incoherent thought was that you had been physically
injured in some way. I stammered out the question, my
heart full of dread. He smiled slightly as he shook his
head. Finally he confided in me about that night. To say
the least I was shocked. I couldn't believe what you had
gone through. "Nobody guessed," said Shali. "Everyone
at the college simply put my sober expression down to
our broken romance."

'I suppose so," said Bhagu. "I, for one, never guessed.
But when your dad told me after four months of knowing me, I was angry that he hadn't shared it with me
earlier. I declared I wanted to go to you immediately. I
wanted to comfort you. I couldn't bear being away from
you. But your dad cautioned me, slowed me down. He
said you and I had been together a very long time ago,
as far as you were concerned. That stopped me in my
tracks. But I was much happier when we ended that
meeting for I was full of hope."

A small part of her brain couldn't help thinking with
admiration, I have to hand it to him. He said he would
marry me only if he had both our parents' blessings.
And he not only has that, he's even managed to get
Mem to arrange the entire proposal. How on earth did
he manage that, she wondered, turning her attention
back to Bhagu's story. "At my place my dad jocularly
mentioned the string of far away relatives who kept

popping up out of nowhere, showing keen interest in me for their daughters. He said he was but a mere male and didn't quite know how to handle it all. It was too hopelessly bewildering and had begun to interfere with the even tenor of his life. He wished my mum were alive. He said that he might have to write to his sister to organise things. That is when I hit upon a plan. I would enlist the help of the future first lady. She had become a close family friend and had often teased me about my bachelor status.

The next time she brought up the topic about finding me a nice girl, I was ready. I think I shocked her speechless for a moment by quietly but clearly stating, "As long as her name is Shalini." Shalini couldn't help the bubble of laughter that welled up inside at the thought of Bhagu stumping the first lady speechless. "She recovered very quickly and teased me for being such a dark horse," he smiled back. "She wanted to know all about you. Needless to say I was happy to oblige." Bhagu smiled again. Shali, overcome, flung her arms around his neck, showering him with kisses as the two fell back on the mattress. After a while, he continued, "I also told Bua, aunt, the story of our college romance - about us breaking up because of your wanting to elope and my wanting an introduction to your parents. She wondered if it wouldn't be better for me to move on. I told her it wasn't; that I'd "accidentally" met your dad recently and would she please ask him on my behalf. She said she would like an introduction for starters." Then things started moving. Your dad introduced me to your mum. We were the only three who knew everything and decided to keep it that way. The very next day I invited your parents to meet my dad. Buaji was also there. The

225

evening was a big success. We all had a lovely time together. I was happy. As far as I was concerned, it was
only a matter of time before you and I would meet. But
although your dad responded positively to Buaji's gentle prodding about a match between his daughter and
her "adopted son", he kept hesitating to physically
bring you into the picture. He wasn't sure if your recovery was complete. He didn't want a relapse. But now, I
was impatient. I wanted to meet you again. I couldn't
sleep nights because my arms and heart ached with
emptiness. I understood, of course, that your parents
hesitated only because they loved you. I toyed with the
idea of 'phoning you or even running into you by
"chance". I was so desperate, I would have done anything. One day, I was with your parents when your
mum murmured with a little smile, that Mem would
know best how to handle you. She would demand in-
dulgence for her seniority; coax and bully at the same
time and where everything and everyone else might fail,
madam Mem might just be able to carry the whole thing
off. That is when I hit upon, even if I say so myself, a
brilliant idea. The next time I met Buaji I told her your
parents had one last request before bringing you into
the picture. Would she ask Mem - without letting her
know her own son and daughter-in-law were in on the
secret - for your hand? Buaji was reluctant again but
agreed when I told her that had been one of your major
fears in college – that Mem would disapprove. If that
fear were laid to rest, it would improve my chances.
She, bless her heart, threw herself into the role. Campaigning for our Prime Minister incumbent was hard
work and I think she enjoyed taking some time off to
devote to me. She asked her friend the Maharani

(Queen) of Jaisselmer to invite Mem for one of her profile raising functions. During the function she managed to have a private meeting with Mem. You know the rest"

"She's never stopped talking about it. It flattered the life out of her," said Shali, smiling as she remembered Mem's account of what had happened. She had received an invitation to dine at the Maharani's palace. The dinner was in honour of Shrimati Joshi who was in Jaipur, campaigning for her husband. An invitation from the Maharani! A summons, no less. Not that the thought of refusing had ever occurred to her. Everyone, including the Dayals in Bombay had heard about it. In hindsight, Shali thought she'd imagined her mum and dad exchange a private smile. It was during the huge glittering affair that Shrimati Joshi had managed to have a word with her for five whole minutes. By the time Mem returned home, she was on first name terms – "Shrimati Joshi" was now "Kusumji". She couldn't believe her luck. If she was reading this right, the future first lady wanted to discuss a possible alliance between her (Kusumji's) protégé and Mem's grand daughter. She'd never heard of this protégé but if the future first lady was speaking on his behalf, even she, Mem, couldn't hope for credentials to better, or even match, those. There had been one, very hard to fulfil, condition. The whole thing had to be done with utmost tact and discretion, else, the 'deal' would be off. Absolutely no one could be told as Kusumji's very safety depended on complete secrecy. It had been unbearably hard. Mem was torn between her desire to boast and jeopardise the entire deal, not to mention compromise Kusumji's safety, or, keep it secret and have it succeed. She had reluctantly decided on prudence, aware that she would have her moment of glory later if all went well. Setting her aversion for Bombay aside, Mem had gone to the city personally, to conduct the 'introductions'.

Once the engagement was announced, Mem had come into her own. She never tired of recounting how she'd played an instrumental role in the whole affair. And she couldn't exalt Bhagu enough. He was handsome, influential – the future PMs closest confidant; he was an extremely wealthy businessman – no harm in exaggerating a bit; he and Shali had attended the same college and he had been taken with Shali since the first moment he'd laid eyes on her; Kusumji was like a mother to him, his own mother having passed away when he was very young. She boasted about his oratory powers, his integrity and Gandhian simplicity, which, if she paused to think, completely confounded her. But who was pausing. She was on the roller-coaster ride of her life. She wasn't complaining. It was enough that these very qualities in Shali's groom had given her access to someone who everyone knew was destined to be the future first lady. Nowadays, Mem only had to vaguely mention her connections and her will prevailed more than ever. It was heady stuff. Shali laughed. Bhagu couldn't help laughing with her, aware that she was rapidly getting back to being her old self again. Instinctively she knew what he was thinking and with a sigh of contentment moved her head so she could bury her face a tiny bit more into the hollow of his neck. She loved the faint smell of his after-shave and planted little kisses wherever her lips touched his skin. Oh, the bliss of being able to do that again. She hadn't realised how starved she'd been for him, how much she had craved to feel his voice resonating against her, the touch of his skin against hers. Her need for him, after being denied for almost a whole year, was often so great, even a little space separating them felt like a chasm. She was so consumed with passion, nothing else mattered. Shali knew she had every chance to lay her ghosts permanently to rest.

- Traditions –

In Jaipur the groom's party would have gone all the way on foot behind the groom on his steed but in Mumbai there were adaptations. The wedding procession was in cars. That is, until they arrived at a pre designated spot about a kilometre from the Willingdon Club where the reception was being held. After a mad scramble to park, they'd gathered behind the groom who'd clambered onto the waiting horse. With a liveried band leading the entire procession, the groom's party danced all the way to the grounds, starting off almost diffidently and dancing themselves to a frenzy as they approached the venue. They were keen to show off their best footwork to the 'bride's' side. The younger ones far outdid the elders with complicated steps they'd learnt at the highly lucrative dance classes.

Binny and Lou, looking very elegant and grown up, were unable to resist a quick, shared moment of secret amusement. Bhagu, who throughout college had preferred dressing down – they'd ragged him enough about his inverted snobbery – was astride a horse in full regalia. They took in the creamy gold achkan, a long Nehru jacket, and all but stared at the magnificent rust orange safaa on his head. The head dress resembled, to a degree, a Sikh's turban. But while both were long pieces of cloth pleated with knife-edged precision around the male head, there the similarity ended. The two ends of the Sikh turban were tucked discreetly out of sight while Bhagu's saafaa had one end fanning upwards in a proud tuft of pleats and the other descending in a wave of free, flowing lines from under the turban, staining the muted tones of his achkan with colour as it meandered down. To hold the pleats in place Bhagu wore a monstrously huge brooch of pure gold filigree, a gift from Mem. Lou and Binny relished the thought of getting him on his own. Through his curtain of white mogra he spotted them, noticing the wicked look they exchanged. He smiled ruefully. He knew he was in for some merciless teasing. Shali didn't miss it either, the suspicion of a smile lighting up her solemnly beautiful face, eyes downcast modestly as she awaited her groom. The music came to a crescendo and then suddenly stopped. The grinning dancers, looking slightly flushed, the adrenaline coursing through their veins, stopped too. The groom, desperately looking for cues from under the cover of his veil of flowers, alighted from his horse. Bhagu was simply not used to the fanfare with him as centre of attention. But he accepted this wasn't just his and Shali's day. It belonged to the entire Bhaguseth and Dayal clans, especially the women, and he had to play his part.

Mem, looking magnificent in a traditional Rajesthani lengha, a long skirt heavily embroidered with spun gold thread, awaited him with a silver tray of tiny diyas, lit oil lamps. Someone lifted off his head gear and the curtain of flowers. Relieved, a slight breeze cooling his face and gently teasing his mop of fine, straight hair, he waited patiently as his clan fussed over him, straightening out his achkan and draping a long rust coloured

scarf over his shoulders. Then he turned to face Mem.
She blessed him, aware she looked grand as befitting
the head of the bride's household, rotating the tray of
diyas in a slow clockwise motion in front of him. She
did so nine times and then almost reluctantly handed
the tray to Shali's elegant mum who repeated the action
looking as solemn as her daughter, yet quietly happy.
She felt secure in the knowledge that the young man
before her would look after her daughter. She was followed by Shali's four aunts, each smiling benignly. That
was the moment Bhagu began relaxing, for he was already on teasing terms with the four of them. "Where
are my uncles?" he asked them. "Getting to know
Johnny Walker in the back room," they replied, making
him laugh. Mem shook her head at the hopelessness of
the male species but not before they saw her lips twitch
in a slight smile. "My sons have finally decided to show
their faces," she said dryly, spotting them standing not
too far away. On hearing the band heralding the arrival
of the groom and his party they had hastily downed
their glasses and rushed out. Their sheepish smiles told
the unconcerned Chachis they had overheard the entire
exchange.

Bhagu gave himself up to the enjoyment of all ceremonies until he was led to a vacant red and gold chair on
the stage next to another identical one on which his
beautiful bride sat. It was an emotional moment for him.
"Hi," he said softly his heart full. Whispering back a
barely audible "hi", she buried her face even deeper into
the heavy but wonderfully fragrant garland that
weighed her down. Her palms open slightly, she studied the intricately beautiful pattern of mehndi on them.
Early that morning the mehndi lady had stabilised the

colour with lemon juice and mustard oil before allowing her to wash off the dried green paste which had already begun cracking and caking off. Everyone wanted to see the mehndi for themselves. It had left a deep orange stain on her feet and hands. They exclaimed on the rich colour and the minute detail. Shali hadn't had a moment to have a good look herself, there were so many ceremonies to go through. Right now, when family traditions played an important role and she felt it would be indelicate to look directly at Bhagu, seemed a good moment to study the mehndi on her palms.

Much of the rest was a blur except the moment when the first lady and her husband put in an appearance. It was brief for security reasons but Shali could see it meant a lot to Bhagu. They had specially flown in from Delhi where they now resided at Number 10, Janpath. Mem was once again in her element, welcoming them, smiling, gracious, aware of the flash of cameras going off in the background.

The arresting trio walked towards the stage where the new bride and groom sat. For once eyes were turned away from Bhagu and Shali. "Happy?" he asked softly. "Yes," she nodded, overcome, her brown eyes moist. For a brief moment they broke with tradition and turned to look at each other. He saw her tremulous smile give way to one of incredible happiness. Then the majestic trio were on stage, walking towards them, smiling. Who could deny they wished the young couple well.

The End

About the Author

Through her insights into the human condition and human spirit, K.Mathur, author of Never Mind Yaar affirms the ordinary, mainstream, middle-class, urban Indians. Hers is a bold and refreshing new voice in the literary world.

Born and brought up in Mumbai, she currently lives with her husband and pets. When not writing, she spends much of her time at home reading or on the net.

For more information about the author, why she gave the book its title, why she thinks secular Indians should organise and where they can learn to organise effectively, visit her website www.nevermindyaar.com

Your comments and queries to: km@nevermindyaar.com

A Very Special Dedication:

To "India Redefined" – a movement of, and for, ordinary Indians who donate a very valuable resource - their time, for a clean, green, healthy, prosperous and happy India. Join the movement – visit http://www.indiaredefined-a4c.org to find out more.